Out of the Park

A Romance

Anne Trowbridge

Out of the Park

A ROMANCE

Anne Trowbridge

AUTHOR OF CURVEBALL

ISBN: 979-8-9865072-1-7

*For my husband Wilson, who has spent the last
25 years making me feel loved and cherished every single day.*

I adore you right back!

Other Books by Anne Trowbridge

The Curveball Incident Series

Curveball: A Love Story

Curveball: A Wedding Novella
(coming soon for newsletter subscribers)

Out of the Park: A Romance

Standalone Titles

The Honeymoon: A Second-Chance Romance
(coming in 2023)

The Bridesmaid
(coming in 2023)

Prologue

THERE HE WAS in the flesh: Zach Hiller. Standing on the pitcher's mound like he owned it, along with the whole city it was built upon. *In a way*, Tommy thought, *he does sort of own it.* Hiller had been racking up twenty-win seasons and Cy Young Awards before Tommy was even out of Single A ball. The man was basically a legend.

"Strike!" the umpire called.

Crap....

That fastball blazed right by him while his thoughts were wandering. He needed to get his head in the game, and fast. No guy in the privileged position of standing up at a major league home plate could afford to take his mind or his eyes off that ball. Those balls turned into missiles when fired from the fingertips of a pitching ace like Hiller. If Tommy knew nothing else, he knew that.

Daydreaming at the plate was a costly mistake, and it was one typically learned the hard way. Tommy definitely had learned this particular lesson in spectacular fashion. He'd seen "the hard way" and walked right past it until he successfully located the *hardest* possible way. He was the poster boy.

"Ball one!" came the ump's second call.

*There...*that was better. It was time to face down this particular pitching ace...and personal nemesis, of sorts. The whole world, he knew, was watching to see if he'd fail again.

He stubbornly shook off these negative thoughts. He'd messed up in this spot before. But not this time.

He stepped back out of the batter's box and chanced a longing look up into the crowds as he adjusted his batting gloves. As much as he wanted to hit Hiller's fastball into next week—and prove what he was made of to himself, his family, the fans, Hiller….really, to the entire world—there was something else he wanted even more.

He glanced around again before stepping back into the box.

Unfortunately for him, he knew deep down it was pointless. He wasn't going to spot what he was looking for in this crowd. He was doomed to keep wandering a lonely path of regrets, even after all this time. Yet another lesson he was learning the hard way. And far too slowly.

This was one battle he likely wasn't going to win, he realized, as he set his gaze toward the mound where Hiller stood.

No matter how this duel with the pitcher played out, he was pretty sure he'd already lost.

Chapter 1

"I can hear you, you know," Tommy growled softly, his patience with his family getting thinner by the moment. "I didn't lose all my senses. I have a concussion, that's it. Everyone stop talking about me like I'm not here or like I'm dying."

An awkward quiet descended over the room before being swatted away by the green-eyed brunette—and the bane of his existence—who was currently standing closest to him in the assembled crowd.

"Shh, the adults are talking now," Tommy's sister Jenna said as she patted his leg. A patronizing smile—the kind that could only be pulled off by a taunting younger sibling—mischievously crawled across her face before she turned her attention back to the conversation swirling around the hospital bed.

"The bottom line," the doctor continued saying as though he hadn't been interrupted, "is that his brain needs time to recover from a concussion this severe. Tommy can't take any chances, and the process can't be rushed. You know the advancements that have occurred in this field in recent years. You've seen the news reports about the cumulative effects of concussions and the long-term problems associated with them. He's done playing now, period. I'm shutting

"

him down this season, if not longer."

"*NO!*" Tommy yelled as stabbing shards of pain jackhammered through his skull, his punishment for speaking so loudly. "No....," he tried again, this time much more quietly, as he squeezed his eyes shut. Nausea rocked through him in waves, battling the pain as his dominant tormentor.

He knew he wasn't doing a good job of convincing anyone that the doctor was off-base as he willed the nausea and thundering pain to subside. He took a deep breath and tried to exhale gradually through his mouth. The urge to throw up lessened a little, and he took the opportunity to open his eyes again.

Expressions from pity to concern to exasperation were reflecting across the faces in the room. Desperate worry emanated off his mom and dad. Jenna, despite her earlier teasing, looked scared for him, too. His agent, manager, a couple of suits from team management, and a few of his teammates were covering the other emotions in the room. He knew the exasperation wasn't directed at him, exactly, but rather at the situation. He certainly could understand the sentiment. He was exasperated and frustrated too.

Years of dedicated hard work and single-minded drive had landed him in baseball's Major Leagues. As a rookie with the Orioles, he'd been lighting it up and was already being mentioned as a leading contender for American League Rookie of the Year, if not MVP. But if his doctor was shutting him down for the rest of the season and maybe longer…well, none of those things had the slightest chance of being his.

Even worse, though, he might just lose his shot at being in the Majors at all. Nothing, he knew, was a guarantee in this game. If you went down and couldn't cover your spot in the lineup, hundreds of eager, hungry guys were out there clamoring for their chance to replace you.

"I don't want this," he tried again, struggling not to give evidence of the sloshing nausea and relentless pain cascading through him. "A couple weeks, a month, I can beat this. I can! I'll…." He trailed off as an angry bolt of pain scattered his thoughts and terminated their journey toward speech. He closed his eyes again, a grimace making him clench his teeth tightly together.

"Tom," his manager, Jack Hooper, said after another awkward silence fell over the room, "it's done. The whole team wants you back, you know we do. You owe it to yourself, to the fans, and to every man in our locker room to do whatever's necessary to return to playing form. And what your doctor is telling you is that you need to *take time*. So take that time, Tommy. Don't put your energy into fighting the decision, put it into fighting for your recovery."

"And we need to get started on that healing," the doctor interjected, "by clearing this room out. I appreciate that we have a lot of people with a stake in how the big guy here is faring, but for right now what he needs most is quiet and rest."

Tommy watched helplessly as the room began to empty, with everyone whispering good wishes and solemn goodbyes. His parents each grabbed a hand and squeezed tightly. No one in this room knew more than they did how devastating it was for him to be torn away from the game he loved. These were the people who had watched every single game from tee ball to the Majors. The ones who drove him to every practice and conditioning workout and travel game. He could see his own suffering mirrored in their faces, and his mom eventually lost her battle against the emotions as a few tears slipped off her lashes and began to wind their way down her cheeks.

"It's okay, you guys," Tommy forced out for their benefit. "I'm going to be fine. Go on and get some sleep."

He watched as they nodded, released his hands, and walked solemnly toward the door. "Love you, son," his dad said before going out.

Tommy closed his eyes in defeat, willing the last few minutes to have been only a dream. But, of course, it wasn't—it was pure, harsh reality.

The door opened again a moment later, but Tommy didn't react. Didn't matter who was there, he was still stuck in this nightmare. Though his eyes were still closed, he could hear the progression of footsteps as his unknown visitor crossed the room, and then the crinkling sound of someone sitting down in the chair next to his bed.

"Son?" Jack said, causing Tommy to force his eyes open again to meet his manager's steely gaze. "You're a fighter, and you're going to be okay."

Tommy looked into the eyes of the man who'd been there for him since he'd received that life-changing call from the Orioles, the one saying that the team was pulling him up for his big chance. Jack had been a mentor, coach, father, and friend to him since that day. The least Tommy could do now was speak honestly to him. He took a deep breath and finally gave voice to his thoughts and fears.

"I messed up, Coach. I didn't move out of the path of that curveball fast enough, and now my career might be over before it ever really gets started." Tommy was whispering again and actively fighting back tears.

"You didn't get hit by any old curveball. That curveball was off the fingertips of Zach Hiller. That guy's a beast. He has a rocket for an arm. No one thinks you messed up. *Anyone* could have gotten tricked by that pitch. It was coming in wild and fast. Accidents happen, you know, even in the Majors."

"Yeah," Tommy said, still unconvinced. Why hadn't he made the switch to the batting helmets with the face guards? Why hadn't he seen that the ball was so close sooner? Why hadn't he jumped back or hit the dirt? *Why did I just stand there?!*

A part of Tommy wanted to roll his eyes, but he was afraid the action might taunt the jackhammer still working away at his brain.

"I heard Zach came here to see you. Wants you to know he wasn't head-hunting with that pitch," Jack added.

"Yeah, my family talked to him. I was kind of fading in and out at the time."

"You blame him?"

Tommy went to shake his head no, and then remembered how much that movement would likely hurt. "No," he finally choked out. "Who goes head-hunting on a full count?"

"Right," Jack said. "It couldn't have been on purpose. He's not known for that kind of thing anyway."

"No, I fully blame myself for not moving fast enough."

"Kid, I'm serious, shit happens. Even as a rookie, you know that's true."

"I know, Coach. It's just…this was it, you know? My big break. Finally out of the minors. Finally making the league minimum. Flying instead of riding buses.

Living the life. And now…I don't want to get Wally Pipped, you know?"

He couldn't help but make the comparison because Wally Pipp's case—a master class in how to lose your job in spectacular fashion—was one that always fascinated him. In 1925, Pipp was a first baseman and frequent roommate of Babe Ruth. One day, just before a game, he decided to bench himself simply because he had a headache. A young and very eager Lou Gehrig stepped in to fill his spot. Gehrig turned out to be a superstar, and Pipp famously never got his job back.

"Listen kid, you can't worry about that. Your only job right now—are you listening to me?—your *only* concern is getting better. This is about more than the game or your place in it. It's about your whole life. You want these headaches sticking around until you're an old man like me? Right now, you're so miserable you can't even keep your eyes open. Shut it down, son, and do it now. If you don't take this seriously, you'll have a whole bunch of problems. Being Pipped is the least of them, you got me?"

"Yeah, I got you," Tommy whispered begrudgingly, still not wanting to accept Jack's words as truth.

"Okay, well, I'm heading out. I've got a series to prep for and a right fielder to replace…at least temporarily." As Jack turned toward to go, he added, "And keep in touch about how you're doing."

"I will."

The click of the door echoed in the room and around Tommy's pounding head. He focused on breathing evenly and steadily as his battered brain tossed around his coach's words. Jack was certainly right about one thing: There was no way he could live with this pain for the rest of his life. He was obviously going to have to take getting better seriously. Play baseball? In his current condition, he couldn't even talk above a whisper without feeling like he might pass out.

Self-pity intermingled with the pain in his mind until, finally and mercifully, he succumbed and fell asleep.

Chapter 2

"LUCY, CONGRATULATIONS!" Stanley said, abruptly thrusting his arm forward, the gift jerking its way into her personal space. "Here, these are from all of us!"

"Oh, uh, thank you so much!" Lucy stammered, awkwardly accepting the bouquet of white and pink roses from Stanley's hands. "They're…beautiful. Really, I, uh, thank you."

"We're just so pleased that you finished your degree! And we hope, of course, that after you pass the bar, you'll come back here and be a permanent member of our team!" Stanley said this sort of absentmindedly as he worked to straighten his red power tie—which, as far as Lucy could see, was already about as straight as it was ever going to get.

"Does this firm pay for the price of the bar, by any chance?" Lucy blurted out as she watched. It was a sad, desperate sort of question, she knew. But then it was only fitting. She was, after all, in a sad-and-desperate kind of situation. She needed all the help she could get, even if she had to grovel to this jerk.

"Hah!" Stanley burst out, causing her to almost drop the bouquet she was still clutching like a beauty pageant queen about to gush out her acceptance speech. "What's the registration fee now? A few hundred dollars? A thousand? We might be in the position to reimburse it. After you *pass* it, of course.

You do understand? We're not running a charity after all."

"I…yes, thank you. I do understand. The thing is…." Lucy started, but trailed off as she froze in indecision, debating just exactly how much of her current personal crisis to divulge. This was *Stanley,* after all, who, as near as she could tell, had no soul.

How could she have gotten to this place, she thought with a feeling of irony mixed with severe regret, where her very survival and path out of misery depended on a guy like this? He was the personification of what everyone generalized all lawyers to be, the flowers notwithstanding. Stanley Morton was a shark, the type who would bill even the most impoverished client an hour just for taking a moment to remember the client existed. *If he thought about it too long, he'd probably send me the bill for these flowers*, she thought, *and charge an hour for the time he spent handing them to me.*

"Yes?" he urged, beginning to shuffle the papers on his desk in an officious manner. It was probably meant to stress for her just exactly how important he was and how little time he had for lowly, jobless law students who hadn't yet passed the bar.

And it was kind of working.

"Well, yes, sorry," she began again. "It's just that…well, you know I'm in a bit of a bind in my personal life. You do remember my father died earlier this year?"

"Oh, yes, of course. We sent flowers!" Stanley said proudly, as though those flowers had been a grief sponge, soaking away her feelings and problems.

Lucy battled the sudden urge to whisk the current bouquet around his desk and mess up those stupid papers he was still organizing furiously.

"Right, yes. You sent flowers. Thank you. Again...," she bumbled on as she decided to lay her cards on the table. "Until my dad died suddenly, I didn't know just exactly how bad my mom's dementia had progressed. My dad, I now realize, was essentially her full-time caretaker. Now the disease has gotten to the point that she can't be left alone anymore. At all."

"I'm terribly sorry. That must be quite a burden on your whole family," Stanley said, looking uncomfortable now. He was probably wishing he could hand her some more flowers and make her, and her sniveling problems, get out of his office.

"That's just it. I don't have any more family. It's just me and my mom now. Me, my mom, and my mountain of student loan debt," Lucy said ruefully. "If I can't get a job as a lawyer, I can't earn enough to start making the payments on it. And I can't selfishly use the rest of the money my parents set aside for my education, because my mom is going to need it for her care."

"I see," Stanley said. "Well, certainly the offer stands to reimburse your bar exam once you pass. That should help ease your burden. Get across this last hurdle and begin your new life as an attorney, Lucy. That's all you need to do. Don't let some student loan debt stop you."

What was I even expecting him to say or do? she thought in frustration. She honestly didn't know, exactly, but she'd come this far. She may as well give him the whole story.

"It's not just the hundreds of dollars for the exam, though, it's the hundreds of dollars for the study materials as well. Plus, there's the time that's required for studying. That's time I'm either going to have to use to get a job so I can pay bills or care for my mother. I can't afford around-the-clock health aides so I can go sit in a Starbucks and study." Lucy's words were rolling now angrily off her tongue, and she knew she had to be careful. It wasn't Stanley's fault or even his problem. But finally being able to confide in someone was liberating, even if that someone was clearly neither terribly moved by her words nor seemingly interested in them.

"You'll figure it out, Lucy, you will. I have complete faith in you," Stanley said as he picked up his phone. "Now, really, I have a call I need to make. My offer stands. Let us know once you receive word you've passed. Have a good day."

That was it. He was dismissing her. It was over. She gave him a half-hearted wave and made her way out of his office and down the impersonally carpeted hall toward the elevators.

Lucy felt thoroughly deflated now. Withered. Beaten. She'd been reeling in grief since her father died, knocked further and further into despair as the blows kept coming. First came the realization that her mom was much, much worse than her father had ever let on. Then she'd discovered, once she assumed her new role as executor of her father's estate, that the biggest chunk of their money was the funding her father had earmarked for her law degree.

Take the loans for now, Luce, he'd assured her. *We've currently got the funds to cover them in an investment. They're tied up for another couple years, but they'll mature right in time for you to graduate! You'll be able to start your new life debt- and worry-free. It's important to us, honey. Let us do this. Let us take care of you. Please. You're still our little girl. You always will be.*

His speech had touched her deeply, but nevertheless she'd resisted over and over. Her parents were loving and generous to even suggest such a wonderful gift, but she was an adult now. Fully able to pay her own way, despite the astronomical costs associated with the three years of tuition, books, fees, room, and board that went hand-in-hand with pursuing her dream of getting a juris doctorate, passing the bar, and using her degree to help those less fortunate.

Her ultimate goal had been to work with a group of attorneys who would support her yearning desire to take on some pro bono cases. She'd love to be in a position to help, for example, families struggling to battle their way through the tangled red tape associated with the immigration laws. She couldn't donate all of her time, of course, but she could find a way to donate a portion of it at least and make some sort of positive difference in the world.

These hopes and aspirations fueled her rocky climb through the miserable slog that only a fellow law student could fully understand. The long hours, the seemingly pointless study and memorization, the self-important law professors, the back-stabbing classmates. She'd plowed her way through all of it by keeping her eyes directly on that magical finish line. And she'd done it! The degree finally—*finally*—was hers.

That degree, however, turned out to be the joke that the legal profession played on you. You worked yourself into an aching, throbbing, miserable state to claw your way to the graduation stage, but it was all a painful mirage. The degree wasn't *actually* the finish line. It wasn't actually anything other than a water break and rest stop on the race to the *real* goal: passing the bar.

That elusive treasure was a miserable journey all its

own. You didn't just sit down and take the bar like you were taking the finals at the end of a semester of algebra or English lit. No, first you had to buy the incredibly expensive preparatory materials. Then you had to put your life on hold and do absolutely nothing else except eat, sleep, and study. And, frankly, taking the time for eating and sleeping during those long months was ill-advised. Getting ready for the bar was a full-time job in itself. You had to devote your whole self to it, heart and soul—about eight hours a day, at least five or six days a week, for *months*, if you had any real chance of passing.

Not preparing enough and not passing it would be a terrible, critical disaster. It meant you wasted all that time and likely hundreds if not thousands of dollars. Plus, it was a setback in landing a job that would pay enough to help you even hope to make minimum payments on the mountains of student debt you almost certainly racked up during the journey.

Failing the bar would mean starting over with the studying and paying once again hundreds of dollars for the "privilege" of trying a second time. And once again, you might not pass. Not passing meant you had a degree and more debt than some small countries, but absolutely nothing to show for it and no way out.

So, yes, in the end she'd agreed to accept—to happily accept—her parents' kind offer. She jumped into her studies and her immense debt with complete abandon. Go big or go home.

And just as she was nearing the end of her studies, her father's surprise heart attack had toppled her Jenga Tower of a life. Next thing she knew, he was gone before any of her plans, or his promise to help them come true, could become reality. All she had then was an ocean of grief.

Yes, there was newly freed-up money...but her mother's situation had become highly critical. She was doing things now like putting a pot on the stove, turning on the burner, and then wandering off and falling asleep. She'd burn the whole house down or injure herself—or worse—if she was left alone. No, those funds had to go to her mother's care. Her debt was solely *her* burden now.

The dream of finding a solution to her troubles with the firm where she'd been interning as a research assistant had just morphed into a nightmare. Stanley and his fellow sharks would not be swooping in to rescue her like a prince or a fairy godmother in a fairytale. Sure, the offer to reimburse was nice. But the hundreds of dollars needed to cover the exam registration were only the tip of the financial iceberg. How would she pay for the prep materials? Where would she find the hours to devote to full-time study when her mom needed to be watched constantly? She'd have to take out more loans and start dipping into her mother's limited funds to hire health aides.

Financial law wasn't going to be her specialty or life's focus, but even she knew that the way out of crippling debt didn't involve accruing more debt.

The ding of the elevator startled her as the doors opened. Numbly she followed the crowd spilling into the lobby and out onto the busy downtown street. She braced against the cold as she sullenly made her way to a nearby diner. She'd noticed the HELP WANTED sign in their window earlier, and it was as good a place to start as any. Step one: get any old job. Step two: ....survive?

That's as specific as her battered mind would allow

her to get with her plan. Just get a job. Any job. That's it. Just do it now and forget about the law. Pay the bills, find a way to pay the taxes and keep the house, make sure mom was safe, file for a loan extension...she'd do it. She'd manage. Somehow, she'd find a way.

Lucy leaned into the wind and continued her journey into an uncertain future.

Chapter 3

"AAAAAHHHHH!!!"

Frustration crawled through Tommy's chest and ripped its way out of his throat in a demented war cry.

"Son of a…!"

His string of curses and angry incoherency were punctuated by the staccato drumbeat he created while bashing a branch furiously against a tree.

As therapy went, it wasn't a very sophisticated or particularly wise method of releasing pent-up anger and worry. It also wasn't very smart since it was merely serving to compound the headache already threading its way through his skull. Like always.

It was, though, kind of helping release the almost crippling rage and frustration that were his constant companions since the accident months ago.

He just wanted to feel better.

Thwack!

He wanted these blasted headaches to go away.

Thwack!

He needed to clear concussion protocols.

Thwack!

He wanted to rejoin his team.

Thwack!

He wanted to play baseball again!

Crack!

The stick he'd been mercilessly beating against the tree finally had enough—the long and jagged tip flew off into the bushes like the end of a broken bat shattered on a fastball. In a final fit of frustration, he flung the other half of it out of his clenched fist. He could hear it fall with a thud in the distance, taking the last bit of his energy with it.

He bent over, hands braced on his knees, and gasped for air. He was completely worn out from hitting that tree with a stick. It was all beyond pathetic. He was so far away from being in game shape. In fact, he'd need binoculars and a map to find "game shape" again. He'd never before been this weak and exhausted. It struck another spear of horror into his heart. Was he *ever* going to be ready to play again?

Roughly, jerkily, he stood up straight, moving his hands off his knees and instead bracing his aching head. A sudden urge to cry—or maybe to make his head the next thing he was going to bash into a tree— brought an ironic chuckle out of his mouth and into the quiet that had settled in the park now that his aggressive run-in with the defenseless tree was finished.

I'm such a mess, he told himself. It was frightening how quickly and easily his life had managed to fall apart. Terrifying, really. One moment, he had absolutely everything he'd ever dreamed of—a spot on a Major League team and all that went with it: money, women, the adoring and supportive Orioles fans proudly wearing his name and jersey number on their backs.

LAYTON, 67.

Then, in a split-second, one fastball to the temple took it all away and replaced his dream life with nothing but worry and pain. He didn't want to sink into a pit of depression and self-pitying despair, yet here he was, standing in a secluded section of a park, wailing away on a tree like a deranged psychopath.

Secluded...

Oh no....

He better *hope* this spot was secluded enough, he thought suddenly as a spike of nervous energy worked a path through his weary body. The last thing he needed was someone to see him, recognize him, and post a video on social media. A media hailstorm would be the icing on his pathetic cake.

With visions of *Orioles Rookie Gains Concussion, Loses Mind* headlines swirling through his still-throbbing head, he slowly spun a jerky circle as he scanned the trees around him.

Searching...no one there...turn....

Searching...no one there...turn....

Searching...no one th—wait, no...someone....

He froze.

"Aww, hell," he muttered, as his gaze landed on the face of a woman seated on a park bench, barely visible through the thick trees that he'd thought were completely surrounding him. Then he realized her wide eyes were securely locked with his, her mouth hanging open in shock.

So...not quite so secluded after all....

The drumbeat in his head got louder. He closed his eyes and took a deep, leveling breath while he pondered his choices. Run? Well, that might not be necessary. She was pretty far away, after all. Maybe she hadn't seen anything.

No.... She was staring pretty intently in his direction. She almost had to have seen some part of the show he'd just put on.

Great. People whipped out their phones and hit record for even the smallest of events these days. A maniac freaking out in a public park would almost certainly warrant such a reaction. Especially a professional athlete, even if he was just a lowly rookie.

Tommy blew out another deep breath of frustration. Headache or no headache, he couldn't just walk away without knowing how bad this was going to get for him. How much, if anything, had she seen of the meltdown? Did she take any pictures or video? Had she recognized him? Did she call the cops? How much was it going to cost to buy her silence?

The list of questions kept hammering their way through his pounding skull as he braced himself.

Enough wondering, he finally decided with a sigh. He may as well go talk to her and face up to this latest in his long string of problems. He slowly began making his way through the trees in the direction of the unwanted spectator.

How can I ever hope to catch a baseball again when I can't even catch a break?

The unanswered question swirled around his aching mind as he moved closer and closer to the woman seated on the bench in the distance.

Chapter 4

"AW, HELL," Lucy muttered. *Seriously, can I ever catch a break?*

One hour. That was it. She had precisely one hour to herself every day. One lousy hour. Normally she spent it eating her sack lunch on this secluded park bench. She almost never saw other people this far out. The crowds typically thronged around the walking loop that circled the lake or in the swings and slides of the playground.

She'd often wondered what had compelled the city—or maybe the county?—to install this remote bench so far out in the trees, removed from the popular public spaces and restrooms and concessions.

Whoever had done it, though, must have understood the magical, healing powers of solitude, because that's exactly what this bench had offered to her each day since she'd stumbled across it months ago. It was everything she didn't otherwise have in her life: peace, serenity, calm....

Here, it didn't matter that she was working a lousy job serving lousy food to sometimes lousy people. Here it didn't matter that her mother was getting progressively worse to the point that she almost never recognized Lucy anymore. The park bench didn't know that, even with her mom's Medicare, Lucy was barely able to pay for the health aide who came each day to feed her mother, bathe her, and manage her medications while Lucy worked. The bench also didn't know that Lucy was using her parents' limited funds to pay the bills and taxes while her own crippling debt sat waiting in silence to devour her.

Nope, none of those things could touch her, not here on this simple bench, lovingly crafted from wood and wrought iron and left to stand alone among the tall trees.

But now her peaceful sanctuary was offering her something else, something she definitely didn't want. No, she had no desire to have her blissful solitude upended by an angry, tree-hating manbaby. And yet, here she was, bracing herself as Angry Manbaby sheepishly made his way over to her.

She sighed, shoved the remnants of her lunch back into her bag, and braced herself to deal with her intruder as she watched him approach.

As he drew closer, she realized just how tall and muscle-bound he was. Well over six feet, she guessed as he came within a few feet of her. Then he halted, a nervous and pained look now evident on his shockingly handsome face. Blue eyes—*or maybe green?*—quietly assessed her, looking as uncomfortable as she felt.

"Brown, curly hair. Well over six feet tall. No visible tattoos," Lucy said after a few awkward moments, breaking their silence as she examined him more closely now.

Her visitor may have anger issues, but he was stunningly beautiful. His chiseled jaw would be right at home in any modeling agency. She pictured him as one of those broody male models, striking disinterested poses while wearing designer jeans and angstily clasping scarves. The vision in her mind made her fight back a surprising urge to smile. Despite his handsome face, the image in her head really didn't fit him, making it somehow funnier. He looked strong, rugged, tanned, and physical. The kind of guy who worked outdoors with his hands. Beating trees, apparently.

She suddenly realized the smile she'd been fighting had reached her face. When was the last time she'd felt like smiling? She honestly couldn't remember.

She'd definitely surprised *him*, she thought with some satisfaction, as she watched him try to process her words and puzzle through their meaning.

"What?" he finally replied, the impossibly perfect face now marked with confusion.

"Just practicing what I'll tell the police sketch artist," Lucy said. "Are you planning to do to me what you just did to that tree?"

She didn't actually think she was in any real danger—helpless frustration seemed to be radiating off her visitor, not murderous rage. Still, they were secluded enough that she felt the need to be cautious.

"I...what?...no!" her visitor stammered as he ran his hands through his hair. Then he stopped abruptly with a wince. His arms dropped back down to his sides like he wasn't quite sure what to do with them. "No, I'm not going to beat you with a stick in a public park."

"Good to know. Now might be the right time to tell you, though, that I think you might have missed some classes in lumberjack school. That's not actually how you cut down a tree."

"Wha...? No, I'm not...." He once again ran his fingers through his hair roughly, only to stop with another pained wince. "I'm not a lumberjack. Or a psycho. And I'm not a former park employee bent on revenge, either. I'm...." He trailed off here, looking like he was debating how much to tell her.

As amusing as it was to tease him, she needed to cut this off. She didn't actually want to know his story. Obviously, something was bothering him, something bad enough to make him want to hit something and release his rage. She knew that kind of pain. She didn't need anyone else's. Her plate was full.

"Great. I'm so glad," Lucy said. "It's been terrific meeting you, though, really. Really, really just …so…terrific. I'll often look back on this moment fondly and think about this time we shared." Why was she babbling sarcastically at him? More importantly, why wasn't he getting the hint and going away? If anything, he looked even more determined to explain himself to her.

"I…," he started, but then she cut him off with, "No…." Then *she* stopped, uncertain what she was going to say. All she knew was that she wanted—no needed—him to stop talking. She didn't want to know what was so awful that trees needed to pay for it.

"Bye," she finally added lamely.

She wasn't usually this terse or sarcastic with strangers. But then again, she didn't normally witness tremendous fits of psychosis in the park. Seriously, she had enough problems of her own right now. She could sell off hundreds of problems and still have a whole warehouse full of them to spare. She didn't need a curly headed, fantastically handsome stranger's burdens, too. That poor tree already knew that the stranger most definitely had problems of his own cascading off him like a waterfall.

He's still not leaving, though, she realized. He was just sort of staring at her in confusion. *Honestly, what's this guy's problem?*

"Look," he said finally, clearly undeterred by her

icy greeting. "I'm sorry you had to witness…that." He gestured in the general direction of the victim-tree. "I promise I don't normally beat trees—or anything else, I swear—with sticks. Or with anything…really…."

"Okay," Lucy said. "It's fine. *Really.* I'm sure there's a perfectly terrific reason for your explosion of rage, but that can stay between you and the tree. So, you can go. Honestly, we're good. I'm not going to tell anyone. Or laugh at you. Much."

"Really?" he asked, looking a little skeptical. "You didn't happen to, say, take a video or post pictures online or anything, did you?"

"No, Manbaby, I didn't," Lucy said, getting annoyed now. "Believe it or not, your angsty burst of emo is not actually the most important thing happening in my life right now. I've got stuff of my own to deal with. Making the effort to post 'hashtag anger issues, amiright?' just doesn't even crack my top-ten list of things I could be doing with my free time right now."

To her surprise, instead of getting mad, pouting, or stomping off like a deranged yeti, the stranger instead burst out laughing, a sound that seemed to surprise him as much as it did her as it echoed through the trees. It also erased his worry lines, making him seem younger than she'd previously guessed.

She couldn't help it and soon found herself smiling up at him yet again. The yeti's amusement was infectious.

"Can I sit down?" he finally asked after his laughter slowed. He was searching her face again, the amusement, as well as the wariness, still evident in his eyes.

"Whatever," Lucy finally said, scooting over. Clearly, she wasn't going to get rid of him, so he may as well sit. She still didn't want to know his story, however. "But there are ground rules."

"Ground rules?" he asked, still towering above her. Her neck was going to be stiff tomorrow if he didn't either go away or sit down.

"Yes, ground rules," Lucy said, her thoughts whirring ahead as a legally binding contract wrote itself in her mind. *Hey, at least that law degree is finally paying off,* she thought as a wave of bitter irony flowed through her.

"Okay, hit me," he said as he sat at last. "Well, you know, not literally. What do I have to do to keep this seat?"

"No names, no back stories, no explanations," she ticked off quickly, watching the surprise cross his face on each point. "I don't want or need to know what that tree did to you. Just…either sit here quietly and anonymously with me and enjoy the peaceful, healing powers of this bench or leave. Okay?"

She could see the myriad emotions he was feeling. Shock. Then confusion again. Then doubt. Finally came defiance. *Uh oh….*

"Oh, come on," he said stubbornly. "At least let me explain myself. I don't want you to think I'm completely deranged. And what would it hurt to exchange *first* names?"

Lucy sighed as she listened to him. He was right, in a way. Really, what was the harm in letting him unburden himself with whatever had brought him to that tree today?

On the other hand, this park bench was her oasis. Her calm. Her therapy. She didn't even want to think about her own problems here; why would she want to take on someone else's? *No, not here. Not now.* She only had one hour each day. She didn't want to spend it acting as a stranger's therapist, even if that stranger was blindingly handsome.

And if they exchanged names and stories, then she might start to care about him or his problems. She might even end up liking him. She certainly was attracted to him already. And maybe it would be mutual, and he'd want to be friends or to see her again, too. That just wasn't something she had to offer. New friendships? Relationships? She didn't even have time for her old ones. Her life had nothing to do with what she wanted or needed right now. All of the energy she had was focused on one thing: taking care of her mom. Anything else was just impossible.

Anything, that is, except for this. One hour on this bench each day.

"Those are my terms, Manbaby. Take it or leave it," she said, looking straight ahead and avoiding his perplexed gaze.

He was quiet for a moment, pondering her words, probably trying to decide if he believed her claim that she hadn't been livestreaming his breakdown.

Eventually, though, he leaned back and turned his head away from her face. So, he must have decided to accept her words as truth, she thought as she watched him in her periphery. He had mirrored her pose and was now looking out in the distance, too. The quiet sounds of the birds and squirrels and rustling leaves surrounded them as they sat together in comfortable silence for several long minutes until he broke the quiet again.

"Okay, have it your way," he finally said. "But it's 'Mr. Manbaby' to you."

Lucy turned and gave him a small, rueful smile before standing. Her hour was over, or it would be soon enough. Time to get back to her real life.

"It's time for me to go, though, so I guess you earned yourself an empty park bench," she said, gathering her things.

The stranger watched all this quietly, just as she had requested, with a sort of amused puzzlement on his face.

A feeling of regret and sadness worked its way through her as she picked up her bag and slung it over her shoulder. She shoved her lunch into it with a sigh. At any other time in her life, she probably would have wanted to get to know this man.

"Thanks," she finally said, her eyes meeting his as they shared a quiet smile one last time before she turned to go.

And she was surprised—maybe even a little disappointed, if she was being completely honest with herself—when he let her walk away.

Chapter 5

WHAT THE HELL had just happened?

Tommy shook his head in disbelief as the mysterious and captivating woman walked away from him through the trees and toward the path.

Soon she disappeared from his view. He battled back an urge to chase after her and beg her to at least give him her name.

Crazy....

Yeah, this is just crazy, he thought in frustration. Twenty minutes ago, he'd been circling the emotional drain, as low as he'd ever felt in his life. But now? Things were somehow different.

Now he felt...how? He didn't even know. Words escaped him. Then again, how could simple words, mere combinations of letters, even begin to capture the absolute astonishment that was currently coursing through his veins? He felt alive in a way he hadn't felt since his accident. If ever.

He felt...well, honestly, he felt like he'd just taken another baseball to the head.

Blown away. Knocked out. Amazed. These descriptions came close, kind of, to explaining how a simple and fairly meaningless conversation with a stranger had just made him feel. What in the world had him so amped up about it, though?

He ran his hand through his hair yet again, then winced at the pain it caused his still-tender injuries up there. When was he going to remember that making certain simple motions really hurt now? He'd run his hands through his hair his whole life. It was a nervous habit, his "tell" if he was playing high-stakes poker. Oddly enough, this little nervous habit didn't even seem to be linked to a particular emotion. Frustrated? Hand reaching for his hair. Mad? Hand reaching for his hair. Sad? Hand reaching for his hair. How about completely off-kilter because of a closed-off, sarcastic bench lady...?

Yeah—hand reaching for his hair.

He froze, hand mid-air, and made himself pull it back down. He needed to get a grip.

Come on, he thought, *nothing actually happened.*

He'd been upset, so he went for a walk in the park. But the longer he walked, the deeper the negative thoughts, worries, and self-doubts had burrowed into his mind until he couldn't breathe under the weight of it all. Before he knew it, he'd stalked off the path, grabbed a fallen branch from the ground, and started releasing his pent-up frustrations through furious blows against the base of an unsuspecting tree.

Had it helped, though? Was the physical release really the reason he felt so different right now? He didn't think so, remembering he'd simply been gasping for air like a blowfish when he was done, not in a state of serenity.

Then he'd spotted his prickly little intruder. *That* was when things got weird.

Well, you know, weirder.

She said she hadn't recorded him. He was pretty sure he believed her. She hadn't seemed to know who he was. That was also good. But she also didn't *care* who he was. That one wasn't so great. He had no idea why it should matter what a stranger thought about him, or what she thought about anything else for that matter. But Tommy couldn't get the brown-eyed beauty out of his mind. She'd been terse. Sarcastic. Dismissive. Funny. Sweet…and sad.

Boom! That was it!

Sad….

His overwhelming depression and anguish had drawn him to this stranger like a magnet. This was a woman who knew what it was like to be drowning in misery. How did he know that, though? he wondered. It wasn't like she'd told him a single thing about herself.

Or had she…?

He closed his eyes and tried to recall their conversation. He focused first on his memory of her face. Delicate features. Long, straight, brown hair. And serious brown eyes studying him from behind blue glasses that gave her that studious, hot-for-teacher look that he loved. He smiled at the thought. Hot. Yeah, his bench lady was a stunner. Not in a stereotypical, Malibu-Barbie kind of way, though. She was more…ethereal. But, like, *smart* and ethereal.

Wow, I really am a wordsmith today, he thought with a bit of frustration…and then once again found himself at a loss for words.

What was wrong with him? Had the baseball knocked some of his vocabulary out of his head? He should download a thesaurus app. *Do they even have thesaurus apps?* he mused. *They have apps for every other ridiculous thing in the world….*

Holy hell—FOCUS….

He stubbornly brought the vision of her into his mind again. Okay, yes, bench lady looked like a…librarian? College professor? Rocket scientist?

Angel?

Yeah, that was it. She was a sweet little angel, sitting here alone in the woods and patiently dealing with the rantings of a crazy person. She'd asked him first if he was going to attack her. She was pretty brave to stay glued to the bench when a suspicious, violent, and likely deranged madman was stalking toward her in the first place.

All right, so the angel's brave, he thought. Yeah, that seemed exactly right. He felt better, like he really had learned something definitive about her. And something else about her made him believe she was also smart. *Was it really just the glasses? And if so, wow, way to follow the stereotypes....* But she definitely proved herself to be brave with the way she fearlessly faced him and made him agree to her terms.

Those terms, he thought with a smile. Wow...what in world was *that* about? Wasn't she even a *little* bit curious to know what had made him pick up that stick? Sheer nosiness would have made most people listen to at least some small part of his explanation before shutting him down once they realized what a self-pitying child he was being.

Manbaby...that's what she called me.

Now he found himself chuckling again. The bench angel was funny.

That was the real miracle, and likely the reason he was still feeling so off-kilter after his short run-in with her. He hadn't laughed, or really even smiled, in months. He'd been too lost in his whirlwind of worries and headaches and general despair. Ten minutes with his park angel, though, and suddenly he was smiling—even laughing out loud!—and finally focusing on something else.

That was it. Mystery solved.

That's why he'd felt so blown away by his encounter with the stranger on a bench. Somehow, for the few precious moments he'd spent in her presence, he'd actually *forgotten*. He hadn't been thinking about his ever-present headache or the unpleasant fact that he didn't seem to be getting any better. He stopped, at least momentarily, worrying about being Pipped and never returning to his spot in the Orioles right field.

Instead, he'd thought about *her*. How captivating and beautiful she was. How shocking it was that she hadn't recorded or live-streamed his angry meltdown. How interesting it was that she didn't want to hear any explanations and excuses for his behavior. How astonishing it had been when she'd scooted over and let an angry stranger share her peaceful space.

Suddenly her words came flooding back to him.

"Either sit here anonymously with me and enjoy the peaceful, healing powers of this bench or leave," she'd said.

The peaceful, *healing* powers of this bench. That was it! Those words were precisely what had helped him identify her as a fellow sufferer. As someone who knew doubts and pain and maybe even depression. Apparently, instead of beating trees with a stick, the beautiful stranger had found therapy and healing by sitting in the woods on a secluded bench.

And now—maybe...possibly...*hopefully*—he'd found his own therapy and healing. Only his wasn't an isolated park bench. No, his road to healing just might lie in the hands of the mysterious stranger who somehow made him laugh and forget his problems.

The park angel.

She'd smiled up at him, too. He didn't think he'd been the only one affected by their unexpected meeting.

Maybe she could help him—and maybe he could help her in return...?

He had to see her again. The sudden and urgent need burned through his chest with certainty. He'd come back to this spot every day for a year if he had to, but he was going to find her.

As he felt the resolve coursing through him, he realized a smile had once again made its way to his face.

Chapter 6

Whatever you called it, Lucy had it in spades: that special ability to shine every cell in her body on the purpose at hand. And she had that skill no matter how trivial her task or how monumental the issues swirling around her.

Sometimes it was a good thing. But other times it was bad. Very, very bad.

Studying for a big test and not getting distracted by friends urging her to party instead? A good thing. Working relentlessly toward finishing her degree despite the long hours and miserably hard work? Also a good thing. But focusing on school and work so hard and so exclusively that she didn't even realize when friends had given up and stopped reaching out to her...?

Not so great.

The very gift that had given her exactly what she needed to go beyond any hurdle or task was precisely the reason she now found herself completely, totally, and utterly alone. She had laser-focused herself right into a sad and isolated existence, and she had absolutely no one but herself to blame.

She'd been so intent on getting through her law degree that she hadn't even noticed how far her mom had slipped into dementia. Yes, her father clearly had been sheltering her from the harshest aspects of that truth. But really, how difficult had she made that for him? A toddler injected with truth serum could have fooled her. Because she hadn't even *tried* to notice almost anything that had been going on around her. Not for years.

Now that her life had switched tracks so abruptly, even *she* could see just how bad things had gotten. Friends from high school and college had fallen away one by one. She had to work pretty hard to even remember when she'd last heard from some of them.

And law-school friends? Hah. No one goes to law school to make friends. The very structure of the institution pitted students against each other. You didn't have to be the fastest or smartest to get through law school, but you had to stay ahead of the rest of the pack. So once again, Lucy had done what she always did best: turn all her attention to the task in front of her and turn off the lights on the rest of the world.

And she was doing it *again*. That was the super crazy part.

When her dad died and she realized how bad her mom really was, she finally received the sharp sense of clarity that she'd needed all along. Specifically, she understood exactly how much of a mess her life really was. And there was no one in that moment of her darkest misery to whom she could turn. No siblings to help share the financial and emotional burdens. No plucky best friend to give her wacky advice and sisterly support over margaritas big enough to drown her problems even temporarily. No sweet but meddling older neighbor to give her sound life hacks while they sipped lemonade on the front porch and yelled at kids to stay off the lawn. No distant, creepy relatives looking for a payday when her mom inevitably would lose her health battles and join her father....

Ugh....

Lucy stopped her mind from continuing down this road and thought back to the moment when she fully realized the degree of her isolation. Had she, in that short moment of pure clarity, tried to reach out for help? To someone from her past? To anyone? Had she seriously considered it even for a moment?

Nope. Instead, she focused in on the problem at hand; that problem, of course, being her mother's care. That's where she'd been putting all her energy, and *not* on her isolation or even on taking steps toward passing the bar. She'd left the law offices where she'd spent her internship and had headed straight for a local diner to apply for a job. Now she was working the breakfast shift at the diner *and* caring for her mom. Head down, laser-focus engaged.

It wasn't until she was walking away from her ridiculous run-in with the yeti on her bench that she realized all this. She'd met a hot guy in the park—to whom she was instantly attracted, and who kind of seemed to be interested in her, or at least in having some sort of conversation with her. But had she done anything about that interest or attraction?

Nope, not her. Instead, she'd actively shut him down and essentially told him to get lost.

No wonder I'm so alone....

On the other hand, it really did seem like he had plenty of his own problems. She honestly didn't have any room in her life for more. That had been her first instinct, and it certainly wasn't a lie or an exaggeration. But normal people could probably do two things at once. They could likely continue to focus on their own issues and simultaneously listen to someone else's. That was probably the literal definition of the word *friendship*.

Right...?

Lucy let out a frustrated sigh.

This couldn't continue. She absolutely could not keep stubbornly worrying about her mother's care to the point where she was basically locking herself in an emotional quarantine. It was nuts. And she was going to need other people to lean on when her mother...well, eventually she really *would* be alone. And then what?

This wasn't the life her mom and dad would have wanted for her, she finally realized. Her dad would have hated it if he knew how she was currently living. Her parents had been her biggest cheerleaders, and they'd made a lot of sacrifices to see their only child achieve her goals and dreams. Getting herself into this hole was basically a slap in their faces, even if it was done out of love for them....

Sitting there now, in the northern New Jersey house where she grew up, Lucy suddenly became startled when she thought she heard a sound. She got up and investigated. She was relieved when she found her mother still tucked in bed, fast asleep. One of the many hazards for dementia patients is that they sometimes get restless at night and wander right out of the house, then become disoriented and lost. Lucy had alarms and locks set up, but it was yet another thing to worry about right now.

Satisfied that her mother was safe—at least for the moment—she crept back to her room and lay down again, allowing memories of the handsome stranger to continue flipping through her mind. His embarrassed desire to explain. His confusion over her refusals. His eventual laughter and smiles.

She found herself smiling back in spite of the dark

room and the difficult situation that forced her to be in it. She wanted to see him again. She couldn't put her finger on why, exactly. She still didn't want to take on his burdens—with her track record, she'd probably laser-focus on them to the exclusion of everything else in her life.

But maybe, just maybe, she could do what she hadn't been able to accomplish successfully before. Maybe she could still be a hundred percent devoted to her mother *and* get to know the yeti, or at least spend a little time with him...just on her park bench and only during her free hour.

What could it hurt?

Of course, there were zero guarantees that he'd be there again. She'd never seen him before, she was pretty sure. And what would make him come back to her after the icy reception she'd given him?

Still....

Once again, the vision of his ruggedly handsome face—with that look of surprise and then amusement as he laughed at her words—floated back into her mind.

She had to see him again.

She rolled onto her side and tried to close her eyes against the sudden rush of hopefulness that was coursing through her. For the first time in a long time, she felt excited about something. She wasn't going to deny herself. Not like so many other times in the past. If her handsome stranger showed up again, she was going to follow that feeling.

She had to.

Chapter 7

TOMMY COULD FEEL the frustration with his little sister bubbling up through his chest. He'd been trying to get out the door of his apartment and over to the park so he could be there at the same time as yesterday. He wanted to find that mystery woman, and he figured looking in the same spot at the same time was his best bet.

"Jenna, I know!" he said forcefully. "*I know* Mom and Dad are worried about me! You're worried about me! Hell, *I'm* worried about me! I know, I get it!"

"Well, if you get it so thoroughly, Mr. I'msowellinformed," Jenna snapped back, "then why aren't you knocking it off? You walk around in a constant cloud of surly depression, and it's getting old, Tommy. Seriously, why don't you go see a therapist? A doctor? A team trainer? Or maybe talk to some of your buddies or your teammates? You're clearly lonely, very obviously depressed and, not gonna lie, super annoying."

Tommy bounced his keys up and down in a show of nervous, noisy irritation as he considered how best to approach getting her to shut up and leave. It was so typical of his luck lately—just as he was grabbing for his wallet and keys, Jenna had picked this day to blindside him by appearing at his door and staging an intervention, or whatever this was.

"You're going to make me late," he said, finally,

making exaggerated "off you go" sweeping gestures with his hands.

"Tommy, you're not going to blow me off about this!" she huffed, ignoring his cues and walking right past him. She ended her display of defiance by flopping onto his couch dramatically. "I'm not going anywhere until you talk to me and tell me why you won't get help!"

"I *am* getting help!" he replied, maintaining his position at the door. "You're trying to make me late, but I was actually on my way to talk to someone right now."

"Really?" Jenna said, looking excited. "Who? A therapist? A doctor? Team trainer? Who?"

Now Tommy felt guilty at the lie. Sure, he *was* technically off to see someone, but chasing down a gorgeous stranger obviously wasn't what Jenna was pushing him to do.

"None of your business, nosy," he fired back. "Now get out of here."

Jenna's green eyes narrowed at him in clear frustration. "Nope, not gonna happen. Who. Are. You. Seeing? If you won't tell me, I'm *NOT*. Going. To. Believe. You." Each word landed forcefully, thudding into the room via her impressively staccato delivery.

"Jen, give it a rest. I appreciate you coming here. I really do. But that doesn't give you the right to take over my life. I heard you; I really did. And I agree that things need to change, okay?" Tommy was trying his best to reel back the impatience in his voice. "Go back home and report to Mom and Dad that I'm up and moving. Look at me! I'm not eating fast food on the couch and sobbing into a beer while watching old game footage on a continuous loop. I'm up! I'm wearing jeans and holding my wallet and keys! Come on, read the social cues!"

Tommy jangled the keys for emphasis, then decided he should try a little harder to lose the cutting annoyance from his tone.

"Tell them I'm doing okay," he said. "And that I agree I need to do better going forward. Then you can add to your detailed report that I'm heading out now to talk to someone."

"Seriously, Tommy, get as annoyed with me as you want. But it's been months of you feeling sorry for yourself because you're not with your team and there's no end in sight. We're all sick of watching you suffer. So, tell me what's going on. Why should I believe that you've suddenly seen the light?" She was really digging in now with no signs of getting up and walking away.

He briefly considered walking out the door and slamming it in his wake, but he figured his bratty little sister would just follow him. No, he had to find a way to shake her first. Should he actually tell her the truth? Somehow, he didn't think that hearing he'd had a meltdown in the park and then actually laughed about it with a stranger was going to douse the fires of her concerns about him.

On the other hand…why the hell not? he mused. It might be useful to get an outsider's opinion about why he was so thunderstruck by the angel on the bench in the first place….

"Okay…," he started, nervously running his hand through his hair and more or less ignoring the pain it caused. "I kind of met someone."

"I know that already," Jenna said quickly. "You're off to meet someone. I get it."

"No, you don't. Yesterday. In the park. I *met*

someone."

"Ohhhhh," Jenna said, and now her eyes lit up with enthusiastic glee.

Uh oh. He didn't like that look at all.

"You mean a woman!" she went on. "Someone you're interested in? Wow, wait until Mom hears this!"

"Oh no you don't," Tommy said, cutting her off. "This stays between you and me, got it? I'm only telling *you* so you'll get the damn hint and leave already."

"Details!" Jenna said with a squeal. "I'll leave, and I'll even keep it secret, but not until I have details."

"Oh, for the love of…," Tommy bit off, giving up and tossing his wallet and keys back on the counter before flopping down in the recliner. "Why can't you just leave me alone?"

"Sorry, it's not in the little sisters' handbook. Now spill it!"

So…he spilled it—the walk, the frustration, the tree branch, all of it.

The one thing he couldn't really find the right words to explain, though, was why the encounter had affected him so deeply. For some mysterious reason, this beautiful woman had reached into his soul and right past the fears and frustrations that had come bursting out of his chest and temporarily turned him into a madman. She reached past all of those things and just…what? Calmed him somehow? Made him feel— for the first time in a long time—like things might be okay? The explosion of physical release from the assault on that defenseless tree hadn't helped at all. But through a crazy connection forged in a seemingly meaningless conversation, *she* had.

"Jen, I can't explain it," he said, glancing at the time on his phone. "I don't know her name. I don't know if I'll ever even see her again. But I've got to try. You know, if my annoying little sister will shut up and let me go."

"Are you sure she's not some baseball groupie?" she asked suspiciously. "Did you check social media to make sure she was telling the truth about not making a video of your little freak out?"

"No, I really don't think she had any idea who I am. I'm not exactly a household name, you know. That's what I was worried about at first, too. But honestly, you'd have to be a pretty hardcore baseball junkie to recognize a rookie Oriole outside of Baltimore. Especially one who's been on the injured list for months."

"Yeah, I guess…," she trailed off, looking at him searchingly. "I just don't want to see you get hurt, you know? I mean, I realize I'm only your annoying little sister, but I've been worried about you. This has gone on for months. And now this? You don't need some psycho park stalker on top of everything else."

"She's not a park stalker! Remember, *I'm* the psycho in the story. Listening comprehension isn't your thing, is it?" He smirked as he stood up again and grabbed his keys. "So, would you please just go away? I'm fine. Everything's fine. Go!"

Jenna made a grand, exaggerated show of sighing as she climbed off his couch and headed to the door.

"Fine. I'm glad you felt a little better. Now I'll do my part by leaving. But please, just let me know if you find, y'know…," she said with a mischievous smile as she preceded him out the door, "…the psycho."

"*She's* not the psycho," he repeated, stopping to lock up before following her down the hall to the elevator. His frustration with his sister quickly evaporated as they entered the elevator together. Tiny wings of excitement and hope started to flutter in his chest as he thought about the gorgeous stranger. Hopefully he would see her again. Hopefully he wasn't too late.

Chapter 8

HE TRIED TO RACE his way to the park, but he got stuck behind every red light and slow driver on the way. By the time he finally got there and circled until he found a parking spot, he had to jog to make it to the wooded section that hid the secluded bench. He was exasperated with his sister again. It was almost one o'clock—the time the angel had left the bench last time. He kept up the pace despite the headache that was working overtime to remind him that jogging wasn't on the list of approved activities during his extended concussion protocols.

As the bench finally came into view, relief and excitement flooded through him when he spotted her. She had been shoving her things into her bag, but his noisy arrival made her glance up anxiously, a look of surprise crossing her face before being replaced by a shy smile.

He smiled in return as his heart hammered in his chest. From the physical exertion, yes…but, if he was being completely honest, also from the joy he felt at seeing her again. He'd *found* her! And she was just as gorgeous as he remembered. Her hair was pulled up on top of her head in a sexy, messy little pile, he noticed. It made his fingers itch with the desire to pull it down again.

"Hey," she finally said, breaking the silence. "I was just leaving."

"No, don't go!" Tommy said. "I just got here."

"My hour's up, unfortunately," she said, shrugging her bag onto her shoulder. "But hey, you've got the bench and the trees all to yourself."

"Wait! Can I…can I have your phone number before you go?" Tommy asked. "And your name?"

"I…no. I really have to go," she told him, looking a little pained. "Bye, Yeti."

"Wait! Come on! Please, just your name? What could it hurt?"

"I'm sorry, I can't do this right now," she said, fidgeting with the long handle on her bag. "I'm sorry."

"Did I scare you? Is that the problem?" Tommy persisted. "I swear I'm not a psycho. Which I know is probably hard to believe, given the circumstances, but…."

"No, no, it's not that," she said, then searched his eyes for a moment. "The thing is…I do want to get to know you, but my life is detonating spectacularly right now, and none of what's causing the explosion is good stuff. I just…well, I got the feeling yesterday that you're going through something, too, and I…I'm sorry, but I can't take it on. I can't…fix you, or whatever."

"Yes, you're right. If things were great with me, I wouldn't have had that meltdown that you witnessed. But honestly, I'm not looking for a therapist." Tommy didn't even know if he was saying the right things here as frustration and confusion swirled through him. "I just…I like you! I'm attracted to you. I felt this crazy connection with you yesterday."

He decided to stop here, and he took a moment to study her face carefully. He couldn't decide if he saw some sign of her resolve beginning to melt or a deep wish for him to leave her alone. He sighed. It was probably the latter.

"Okay, listen," he continued finally, "I'll drop it. I get it. It was one-sided. But I just wanted to let you know that being here with you is the only thing that has felt right to me in months. I thought that maybe we'd connected. But that makes no sense, obviously, because we've barely spoken, and you clearly don't want anything to do with me. I can't even get the first letter of your name out of you, let alone your phone number." Tommy surprised even himself by laughing, then he stepped back from her with a rueful smile. "Sorry to have bothered you, angel."

"You didn't…it's not…," she stuttered, clearly unsure of how to reply. She took a deep breath before adding, "I really do have to go now. But you're not crazy. It wasn't one-sided. I felt it, too."

Then, as she turned to leave, she added, "It's 'L' by the way."

"Wait, what?" Tommy called to her as she began walking away, just like the day before.

"The first letter of my name!" she called out, a hint of laughter carrying her words along the cool afternoon breeze.

Chapter 9

IT WAS ALL still there. The worry. The dread. The debt. All of her problems were still right there, stalking her and waiting to pounce. But for the first time since her dad died, Lucy found herself inexplicably…happy? Excited? *Elated*, even?

Yes, all of those feelings were rushing through her as she made her daily trek to the bench the next day. Instead of seeking peace and quiet and serenity, today she was hoping her refuge was going to offer time with her sexy stranger.

She made her way from work and into the park just as she'd done every other day, weather permitting, since she found the bench. It had been during an otherwise not particularly noteworthy day months ago when she'd first stumbled across it during her precious time between leaving the diner and heading back to relieve the health care aide.

Maybe he'll come again. Hopefully he will. And hopefully he'll get there before I have to leave.

She desperately wanted time with him. Time to…well, time to just soak in that sizzle of chemistry and connection that flowed so effortlessly between them.

And if she believed his words from the day before, she made him feel that way, too.

That was the really crazy and unexpected part. He looked like the kind of guy to whom women flocked constantly. She had been such a studious, serious bookworm throughout high school, college, and her law studies that she'd never had much of a social life. Sure, she'd gone on dates and even had a few boyfriends here and there. But never with the type of guy who was captain of the football team or president of the fraternity or whatever. Mostly she'd just been out with other bookish types she met in her classes or the library.

Certainly no one as physical and muscular and, well, as sexy as her park stranger.

She recalled the way his face lit up with laughter as she smiled to herself. Luck hadn't exactly been on her side lately, but she would cheerfully view it as a gift from the gods if he appeared again today.

Happy excitement fueled her path through the trees, and a burst of giddy anticipation blasted through her as her bench—and her stranger—suddenly came into view. He was already there!

He stood as she made her way toward him, another brilliant smile lighting his face.

She beamed back at him as she approached, but then stopped short, astonished with herself. She'd almost jumped right into his arms for a hug, which would have been pretty crazy considering the circumstances.

Really, what was it about this guy, to whom she'd barely spoken just twice, that made her feel so welcomed, so comforted, so...at home? Was it some sort of pathetic co-dependent thing, since they both had admitted to having big problems?

Maybe.

She realized, though, that she honestly didn't care. She was both delirious and relieved to see him again.

"You're here," she finally said, breaking the silence.

"Hey, yeah, I got the timing right today," he said, standing back and gesturing toward the bench. "So how does this work, exactly? Is there some sort of pre-bench ritual that happens? Chanting? Incense? Dance? Song?"

She laughed, astonished again by him. Handsome *and* funny?

"Nope, nothing that exciting," Lucy said with a smile and a shrug. "Honestly, I just sort of collapse. By the time I get here, I've already put in a long day on my feet. Sorry to disappoint you."

"Hmm. I really think you need to up your pre-park-bench ritual game," he said, still waiting for her. "But, okay, we'll do it your way. Come do your collapse maneuver and get off those tired feet."

Lucy started toward him again, but the moment felt huge, suddenly. Life-changing, even. Like if she sat down on this bench with this man, her life would never be the same again.

That was ironic, of course, considering her life was currently as rosy and warm as a burning barrel of garbage. Why wouldn't she *want* it to change?

But…no. This was selfish, right? She needed to focus on her mom. She couldn't let herself get distracted from caring for her mom and fixing her financial situation. Otherwise, she might never be able to pass the bar. She had no time for anything else.

Despite the doubts and fears that pummeled her mind like a hailstorm, she still approached the bench, shrugged slightly at her stranger, and slowly lowered herself down.

"There," she said. "I did it. Admit it, it was way more awesome than you expected, right?"

"No, but see, there was false advertising involved,"

he replied. "That was more like a feather floating gently downward than a collapse." He studied her for another moment before taking the spot next to her. "Are you a dancer or something?"

"No, not even close. But I…I have to tell you. As happy as I am to collapse on a bench with you, I…I still can't do this." She gave an awkward back-and-forth gesture with her hand. "This…whatever this is, it's just the worst possible time in my entire life for me to…."

Her voice trailed off. What was she even trying to say? *Oh my gosh, this is embarrassing!* Was she having a stroke?

"I get it, angel, I do," he said, cutting through her silent ramblings. "You're going through something, and you know I am, too. That doesn't mean we can't get to know each other. Start seeing each other, right? Just see where it takes us. Unless…wait, are you married?"

"No!" Lucy said, a lot more forcefully than she intended. "No, I'm not married."

"In a relationship? Wait, is it abusive? Is that why you don't want me to know your name?" A look of possessive anger raged across his face and erased the smile that had been there since she'd arrived.

"No! Geez, easy tiger. Relax!" Lucy said as a girlie bubble of happiness wafted through her at his alpha display. "I swear I'm not seeing anyone else. I'm not in some dangerous or abusive situation. It's nothing like that."

"Okay," he said, visibly relaxing again. "Let me try another guess. I'm attracted to you, but it's really not all that mutual, and you're just way too nice to tell me to get a clue and get lost."

"Oh no, it's like the opposite of that," she said with a smirk. "You're bad at this guessing thing, Yeti."

"The opposite? Meaning what?" he asked. "And why won't you tell me your name? Starts with an 'L'. What's the rest? No, wait—I'll try the guessing thing again. Umm…Linda? Lisa? Laura? Lulu? Layla? Oh, I've got it! LaToya?"

"So, like I was saying, this guessing thing is just not part of your skillset," Lucy told him with a laugh and a "there-there" comforting tap on his arm. "It's on par with your tree-chopping talents, really. As in phenomenally, earth-shatteringly bad."

"Just tell me your name, Lulu, or at least why you're being so secretive about it." He was clearly unable to mask his frustration even while teasing her.

"I know I'm being a weirdo and sending you all kinds of annoying mixed signals. I don't mean to, honestly. It's just…okay, here's the thing: I seriously have a *lot* going on right now. It's mostly to do with my mother, who's ill. And it's more than that, but that's the heart of the issue. Well, that, and the fact that I'm *it*. I'm her only family left. All the responsibility for caring for her and dealing with everything else that's going on…it's all me." She was surprised with herself as the words tumbled out. She hadn't really said any of this out loud since her ill-fated conversation with Mr. Fix-It-with-Flowers Stanley.

"I'm so sorry, angel," Tommy replied, turning to look at her directly. "I can't imagine going through that at all, let alone doing it by yourself. But I don't see why letting someone else in is a bad thing. Seems to me that maybe I came along at precisely the *right* time. No sense facing all of that alone."

"In truth, there are a lot of reasons," Lucy said, winding up her list of reasons in her mind, her legal background assisting as she mentally ticked through them, sorted them out, and lined them up. "First off, it puts too much gravity onto whatever this friendship is or whatever it could become. I'm seriously in a major life crisis. That puts weird 'Oh great, now I can't dump this pathetic lump, or I look like a jerk' pressure on the situation."

"I see what you're saying, but we all take chances when it comes to relationships," he told her as she continued organizing her thoughts. "Sometimes someone's the jerk in the breakup and that's just the way it goes. That's not reason enough to not even get to know each other or to never go on a first date, especially since we're both very interested in each other."

"It's not," she agreed, "but it's only part of it. There's also the fact that I'm so busy between work and caring for her that literally the only time I have each day is this short hour in the park. That's not exactly going to be enough for a real relationship…or, um…I don't mean to presume that's even what you're talking about here.…" She could feel her face getting red.

"That's exactly what we're talking about here," he said, a fiery heat igniting in his green eyes. "There's something between us I've never felt with anyone else. Like there's a magnet that's been pulling me to this bench ever since I first saw you. Is it one-sided? I know I've asked before, but put all your cards on the table here. Is that really what you're trying to say?"

"No, it's not," Lucy said with complete honestly. "I've never felt this chemistry before, either, and I'm dying over here because I want to get to know you and pursue this. But the start of a relationship is supposed to be the *fun* part. The exciting part. Y'know, with the chemistry and the sizzle of first glances and touches and all that. But I can't do it right now. I am, without a doubt, probably the most single-minded person you'll ever meet. When I focus on something, the rest of the world falls away. I can't focus on two big things at once. I can't take care of my mountain of soul-sucking problems and embark upon what might end up being a deliriously wonderful thing. I just can't pull those two things, with their polar opposite emotions, together at the same time. I mean, really, it's a miracle I can talk and sit upright at the same time."

He chuckled and ran his hand through his hair, wincing the way she'd noticed him doing before.

"So, you're telling me that no, you don't want to get to know me or keep meeting?" he finally asked after studying her face for another long, heated moment.

"That's the thing. I *do* want to get to know you. I just can't…I don't know. Maybe we could just meet and spend no-pressure time together on my bench? You know, without the intensity of names and specifics and dating and relationships. Can the rest of that, maybe, wait?" She was feeling particularly nervous as she asked this. "Like, say we just put thoughts of dating on hold? Give me time to take care of my mom and deal with my other problems and then maybe, if you haven't found someone else or gotten tired of me and this whole situation, maybe we could have all our firsts then?"

"I at least want to know your name," he said quietly but forcefully. "At least give me that."

"Okay, okay," she said. "I guess that couldn't hurt. Just first names, though. I like the idea of waiting to really and truly meet when I can freely give you my time and attention, does that make sense to you?"

"Yes, I think I understand. But I'm not going to

pretend I'm not disappointed."

"Thanks," she said with a smile. "You have no idea how much I appreciate your patience and understanding. It's, uh, it's Lucy."

"Lucy! I was close!" he said triumphantly.

"Lucy, LaToya. Yup, real close."

"Okay, if it's so extremely easy to guess a name based on a letter alone, then let's see how *you* do. Mine starts with a T...."

"T? Hmm, okay," Lucy said, studying his face closely. The green eyes. The soft brown curls on his head. "Umm, how about...Thomas?"

"What?" he said, his jaw dropping open. "How'd you do that? Are you psychic? Do you guess names at carnivals as a side hustle?"

"I was *right?*" Lucy crowed, laughing in delight as he tried unsuccessfully to scowl at her. "That's amazing! I should go play the lottery now!"

Then, realizing she had let her guard down once again, she worked to smother the laughter and regain control.

"So, Thomas, huh?" she asked.

"Yeah, although friends usually call me Tommy. Or Tom or just T. Kids in elementary school called me Tank Engine. That was fun," he said, still looking at her with shocked amusement.

"Okay, Thomas, now it's your turn. Without any identifying specifics, what had you wailing on that tree over there like a psycho?" she asked. "And how are you free to lurk in the park in the middle of the day—also like a psycho, I might add?"

"Okay, okay, that's fair. I admit I've given you lots of reasons to think I'm deranged, but, uh, the short answer is that I sort of got injured. At, uh...work. And I can't go back until I get rid of these headaches and pass the doctors' concussion tests."

"Oh no, I'm so sorry!" Lucy said, looking at the spot that kept making him wince when he touched it. "You got hit in the head right there, didn't you? At your job? So, what? You're out on short-term disability leave?"

"Um, yeah, something like that," he said, nodding. "If I tell you more, it'll be too identifying. I'm trying to respect your wishes here. Save knowing who I am for later and all that."

"Oh, yes. Okay, thank you, I appreciate that you understand."

"Honestly, I don't. Not fully, anyway. But I hear what you're asking, and I'm going to respect it. I won't pressure you, and this isn't meant to do that, but I just want to say upfront that my situation could change pretty suddenly. Right now, I'm just a guy with all the time in the world who's trying to rehab. But once the doctors sign off, I'll have to go back to…work. It'll likely happen suddenly. And when it does, it'll mean a lot of travel. You may show up one day, and maybe I'll just be gone. Can't we at least exchange numbers so that doesn't happen?"

"Oh. Travel? Yeah, I hear what you're saying. That complicates things," she said, as she rolled his words around in her mind. It was enticing to get his number, *very* enticing. She let the tantalizing thought dance through her brain a moment more before shutting it down, because she knew it was a trap her single-minded focus would fall right into. With a feeling of regret and a sigh she said, "I know myself Thomas. If I had your number, I think I'd want to text you all the time, or at least think about *not* texting you. That's not where I want to be right now, you know? I wasn't kidding or exaggerating about how focused I can get. Do you understand?"

"I guess so. Okay, I'll just…if that happens and I clear the concussion protocols, I'll try to get word to you or get here before I have to leave. Well, you know, if we're still talking when that happens."

"I feel like we will be," Lucy said, smiling as she stood. "Okay, well, I've got to go grab some lunch before I relieve the health care aide now. But…tomorrow, same time, same place?"

"I'll be here if I have any control over it at all," he said, also standing. "Stay safe, angel."

"You too. Feel better," she added with a smile as she turned to go. Then she turned back a moment later and saw that he was once again seated on the bench. She waved and headed out of his view.

She told herself that she'd gotten exactly what she wanted—a chance to continue seeing the handsome stranger without committing to the pressures of a budding relationship and the distractions it would involve.

So why did it feel like somehow she was making a huge mistake?

Chapter 10

"TOMMY! Hey, bro, it's great to hear your voice!"

"Thanks man, yeah, good to be heard," Tommy said to his friend and teammate as he stretched out on his couch, flopping his feet up on his often-abused coffee table with a thud. "How've you been?"

He and Dante were both rookies who had been brought up from the minors around the same time. The stress and pressure had bonded them quickly and tightly. Whenever he thought about calling someone on the team for a chat, Dante was always his first choice.

"Just laying low and trying to get in my playing time," Dante said. "You know how it goes. You been watching? They've been using me in right a lot with you out."

"Yeah, I've been watching. Don't you get too comfortable now," Tommy warned, mostly teasing—although he couldn't stop the stab of worry that shot through him. Would he, in fact, really be able to regain his spot on the team one day? Dante was a hell of a player. The team's right-field position was in very capable hands right now.

"Nah, man, that's your spot. Just keeping it warm for you," Dante said, as though he could read every one of Tommy's worried thoughts. "When you comin' back, anyway?"

"Not sure exactly. Still dealing with these headaches. Doctor says I'm out for the rest of this season. Aiming to rejoin by spring training at this point," Tommy admitted, frustrated by his slow progress. "Gotta be honest, though—I'm going crazy just laying around waiting for my bell to stop ringing."

"Yeah, man, I get it. But hey, speaking of that, did you hear Hiller quit the game? Left the Yankees, broke his contract and everything. Damn man, your hard head took out a legend!"

Tommy dropped his feet back on the floor and jerked into an upright position. "He did *what?*"

"Oh yeah, it's all over Twitter and ESPN," Dante continued. "Thought you said you were keeping up with things?"

"No, I hadn't heard." He rubbed his eyes in frustration. He really didn't need something else to worry about. *Thanks, universe.* "Huh, wow...I had no idea. I haven't really been following the news at all. Too busy feeling sorry for myself, I guess. But why would he walk away? He wasn't head-hunting with that pitch. Even I know that. It was a crazy accident." Tommy was saying all of this forcefully, as though he was trying to talk Dante into believing it. He just couldn't imagine Hiller walking away because there was no place for actual blame regarding what happened. "My parents even told him they knew it was an accident when he came to see me in the hospital."

"I don't know, my man, but the talk on the sports channels is that he just choked," Dante said. "Couldn't deal with the memory of you hitting the dirt the way you did. He hasn't thrown one pitch since that day, they say."

Tommy was stunned. Hiller really was a baseball legend. A sports god. Tommy didn't want to think that his own inability to get out of the way of a wild pitch had ended another man's career, especially one as meteoric and spectacular as Zach Hiller's.

"I hope he gets past it. I'd be happy to talk to him if I see him," Tommy finally said.

"Yeah, well, like I said, you'll have quite a hunt on your hands. The man split. Vanished. Went off the grid. Rumors are he left the country," Dante said, his voice was ringing with incredulity. "Man, I never thought a boss like Hiller would fly like that."

"No, me neither," Tommy said, still shaking his head.

"But hey, man, what are you doing with your time? Hitting on all those hot physical therapists they got working with you?"

"No, not at all. Actually, I, uh…I met someone," Tommy admitted. Dante couldn't see him through the phone, but a smile lit up Tommy's face as he pictured Lucy and how beautiful she'd looked when she was laughing at the park earlier. He had a feeling she didn't normally laugh much. Hopefully he could help change that.

"Ooh, T, nice!" Dante said gleefully. "Tell me all about this hot mama. And if she has a sister…."

Dante was a card-carrying player in every sense of the word, and a fun wingman when they went out after road games. But Dante was never seriously interested in any one woman. Of course, Tommy really hadn't been in the past, either.

"Uh, well, honestly, I don't know too much about her. Her name is Lucy. She's, uh, smart. Beautiful. Funny…," Tommy trailed off. He'd pretty much just hit the end of what he really knew about her.

"My man T sounds like he's in deep with this one!" Dante hooted with laughter.

"Yeah, well, I'd like to really get to know her more. A lot more, in fact. I feel like maybe we could easily hit it off for real. Who knows, maybe even get pretty serious. But, I don't know. She's holding back," Tommy caught himself about to run his hand through his hair. He really needed to get a handle on that nervous tic, at least until his head stopped throbbing every time he touched it. "She won't even tell me her last name."

That information sent Dante into a full-fledged laughing fit. Tommy rolled his eyes and held the phone away from his ear, waiting for the obnoxiously loud cackling to die down.

"I'm glad this is so hilarious for you," Tommy told him.

"Just enjoying the view from over here, T. Sounds like this one's not going to fall at your feet just because you're a pro ballplayer. No groupie, not this one. You better hang onto her."

"Yeah, well, she doesn't even know I'm a player. And I kinda doubt she's a sports fan in the first place," Tommy said as he mentally reviewed the few things she'd told him about herself. "She's got a lot going on in her life. Her mom's sick, and I think she's stuck caring for her full time."

"Aww, man, that's rough," Dante said, finally downshifting to a more sober tone. "Sorry to hear that, T."

"Yeah, me too," Tommy said ruefully. "I think it's pretty much the reason she's not exactly jumping into my arms. She's got too much reality to deal with."

"I get that. And, hey, speaking of reality, I gotta hit the weight room, T. But, man, it's great to hear your voice. I can't wait to have you come back so I can stop babysitting right field for you," Dante told him, then said his goodbyes and ended the call, leaving Tommy alone with his thoughts once more.

Chapter 11

TOMMY STARED at the phone absentmindedly as he leaned back again, thinking about his teammates and all he was missing. The camaraderie. The feeling of satisfaction that came with a monster blast off the bat or a diving catch in the field. He even missed the workouts, the weights, the drills, the stretching, batting practice, the ice baths…all of it.

He sighed and finally put the phone down.

He wished he could call Lucy. He told her he understood why they shouldn't exchange numbers, and it hadn't been a lie...exactly. But it was still frustrating. Was this whole thing crazy? Was she asking too much of him? Was he being a pushover by basically saying he'd sit around forever waiting for her to solve whatever mysterious problems she had? Or was he being a chump?

He needed another opinion. A *woman's* opinion....

He mentally scrolled through all the women he knew, wives and girlfriends of teammates, old school friends. He even briefly considered calling his mom. But in the end, he decided it would be easiest and simplest to go to Jenna. She already knew he'd met Lucy in the park and, more importantly, she knew precisely *how* he'd met her. Hearing about his meltdown at the tree would just upset his mother or potentially get back to the team if he went to anyone with Oriole connections.

He ended up leaving Jenna a message—she must be in class, he figured—then he threw himself into the exercises and stretches that the physical therapist and team trainer had ordered while they all waited for his head to heal. By the time his doorbell rang, he'd forgotten he'd made the call in the first place, so opening the door and finding her tapping her foot impatiently came as a complete surprise.

"Oh, Jenny J, hey," he said, wiping his face with a towel. "Didn't expect you."

"*You* called *me*, you dork," she said, brushing past him and into the kitchen, where she slid her backpack off her shoulders and dumped it loudly on the island. "So, what's up?"

"Okay, well, why don't you come in then? Have a seat. Abuse my kitchen counter even."

Jenna gave him a smirk, then got out a couple glasses and started filling them with water from the refrigerator door. Tommy watched her set the glasses on the island before sliding onto one of the stools that ringed it.

She looked up at him expectantly. "Well?" she asked, giving him the rotating hand gesture that also served as the universal sign for *Would you just spill it already?*

"I called you because, uh, I sort of need a woman's opinion on something," he said a little nervously. Was he going to regret confiding in this insanely annoying sister of his?

Probably....

But still, the enticement of hearing what another woman thought about his weird and mysterious situation was more powerful than the urge to dodge her relentless teasing.

He walked over and sat across from her, watching as her jaw dropped open in shock. He took a long drink of the water she'd poured. Too bad it wasn't something stronger.

"Is my big, obnoxious brother actually asking *me* for advice?" The shocked look on her face was priceless. "Are you dying? Am *I* dying? Do I have time to get my affairs in order?"

"Is now a good time to confess that I dropped you on your head when you were a baby?" Tommy asked.

"Very funny. But I feel like you dropped me on my head just now!" Jenna told him. "You have never asked my opinion on anything major before, but I feel like you're being really serious here. Is everything okay with your recovery?"

"Yes, everything's fine. Well, you know, everything's the *same*," Tommy confessed, his frustration wrapped tightly like a clenched fist around each word. "Still have the headaches. Still off the team until the doctors clear me. Which they aren't going to do. You know, because I still have the headaches."

"I'm so sorry you're going through this, T. I know you're terrified that you're not going to get back on the team. But you will. You worked way too hard for way too long. The team sees that. They *have* to see that. Come on, you were being considered for Rookie of the Year!" Jenna paused in her impassioned speech to take another sip of her water before continuing. "Is that what the advice is about? Not giving up? I know I came down on you hard about getting out of your whiny rut the last time we talked, but I said those things because I believe in you. Just keep going. Don't give up."

"It's good advice, Jen, and I appreciate the vote of confidence. But no, that's not all that's on my mind right now. Or, actually, *who* is on my mind right now," he said, looking up to see if she'd put the puzzle pieces together on her own yet.

"Who…ohhh! This is about your park stalker, isn't it?" Jenna's voice was getting louder and shriller with each delighted word that shrieked its way to his ears. "The psycho on the bench? You *found* her, didn't you? Tell me!"

"Hmm, not sure what you're referring to, Jen," Tommy said, the urge to tease her too strong to ignore. "I was just wondering if you have any show or movie recommendations? Anything I should be streaming and bingeing right now?"

"Shut up, you jerk!" Jenna said, her tone slightly less of a shriek and down to more of an exploding bubble of excitement. "Admit it! You found her, didn't you?"

"Yes, yes, contain yourself, woman!" Tommy replied with a laugh. "Yes, I found her, okay? Happy now?"

"Ecstatic. Now tell me what happened! What's her deal? Why is she being so weird and mysterious? Is she in the Witness Protection Program or something?" Jenna looked like she was just warming up and could potentially throw questions out all day if he didn't stop her.

"Stop, stop! I'll tell you. But I still don't know much, I'll say that upfront. And that's kind of why I wanted to bounce this off you. I want to see if you think I'm getting played here," Tommy admitted.

It didn't feel great to put that thought out there, as if saying it out loud could speak it into existence. Still…he really wanted to know what she thought about it.

"Okaaay. I don't like the sound of this already, but I'll listen. Hit me with the details," Jenna said, looking like she was bracing herself for bad news. "All that you've got up to this point. Everything."

"Fine. Her name is Lucy, and she lives with and cares for her mother, who is really sick. Whatever she has, it sounds very serious. As much as I can piece together, Lucy goes to work, takes an hour for herself on the park bench, then spends the rest of the day being a nurse to her mom. I also think a health aide stays with the mom in the morning so Lucy can work." Tommy thought back to the things Lucy had said about herself. The very few things she'd said.

"Oh, T, that's really sad," Jenna said. "Nothing in that infoblast leads me to think she's some sort of player, though. The opposite, really."

"No, of course not. But that's not the full story. The thing is...." Tommy stopped to nervously run his fingers through his hair and then instantly regretted it. Was he really about to talk about his feelings with Jenna, of all people? Still…the desire to get this all out seemed to propel the words into the air. "The thing is, I feel so drawn to her. In a way I've never experienced before. She's like a…I don't know, an addiction? A drug? I really want to be with this woman."

"She doesn't feel the same way?" Jenna asked softly. "Is that the problem?"

"Well, that's part of the craziness here. She says she does. And her body language says she does. I think we're both equally into each other," Tommy admitted.

"Then I must be missing some of the story, T, because I'm not seeing the problem at all. Actually, that sounds pretty great. I've never seen you particularly interested in one woman before, at least not since like high school or whatever."

"I know, I know, I'm getting there. And yes, it's special and unexpected and unusual for me. So, I'm kind of blown away by it, and she kind of seems to be too. But even though there's this powerful attraction, she says she doesn't want to pursue a relationship right now, or even exchange numbers or names or anything. I had to drag her first name out of her."

"What? Why?" Jenna asked, her face reflecting his own confusion. "Because of her mom's situation?"

"Yeah, that's part of it. She's given me a couple of reasons, actually. She says she has a lot of problems, more than just her mother being ill. She hasn't told me what they are, though." Tommy tried to remember the full list of Lucy's reasoning. "She also said she's not someone who can focus on two things at once. Like, she can't split her emotions between the pain of whatever she's dealing with and the excitement of starting something new."

"Okay, I guess. So…what? She just told you to take a hike? That's it?"

"No, she just asked if we could put the idea of the two of us getting to know each other on hold. Like, put thoughts of a potential relationship on ice until she can solve all her issues," Tommy explained. "She said all she can offer me right now is light, no-strings-attached, chatting on the park bench for an hour each day."

"Oh, wow, okay. I'm sorry, T," Jenna said, sympathy shining in her eyes. "I know that's not what you want."

"It's not. And it's not even the whole story. She asked if we could stay anonymous, too. No identifying information. No last names or phone numbers."

"Why in the world would she want that? Now

she's starting to sound like a psycho again. I'm not trying to joke about a very serious issue here, but…maybe those other issues she's not talking about are mental-health related?" Jenna asked, her tone gentle.

"That's the part I want your opinion on. Before I get in too deep here. Because on the one hand, when she's laying out her reasons, it all kind of makes sense. Like yes, I understand wanting to wait before jumping into a new relationship until you're able to do it happily. I get that. And since I really don't know what other issues she's trying to resolve, I guess I can't complain too much about her not having time to be dating. Who knows what's really going on?"

"Yeah, okay, I can see that side of it. So, what's on the other hand?" Jenna asked, her eyes narrowing in suspicion.

"The other hand is me being as suspicious and wary as you look right now. Like, is this some sort of intricate, in-person form of catfishing? Does she actually know who I am and is just setting up some sort of elaborate hoax? Will she be asking me to wire money to a 'sick' relative in Belarus or something? Is her name even Lucy? Does she reel in unsuspecting dopes for fun, and then laugh about it with her deadbeat husband as they sit in his mom's basement and eat Cheetos together?"

All of Tommy's worries were flooding out now, causing him to doubt everything Lucy had told him and everything he thought he'd felt when he was with her. Was any of it real? Any part of it at all? Man, he felt like such a sap.

He stopped talking and leaned back, rubbing his eyes with deeper frustration than ever.

"Wow," Jenna finally said, breaking the awkward

silence that had fallen between the two of them.

"Yeah," Tommy agreed. "Wow. Wow, as in, 'Wow, my brother is a chump'?"

"No," Jenna said, shaking her head. There was a kind smile creasing her face and pushing aside the concern that had previously been there. "No—wow as in, 'Wow, my big brother has it bad for his mystery woman'."

"Yeah," Tommy agreed. "If she wasn't holding back and throwing up roadblocks left and right, I'd be all in already. Both feet and no life preserver."

"I think maybe you already are," Jenna observed, taking another sip of her water while her words sank in.

"No, definitely not. There are too many unknowns. I don't understand her motives, at least not fully. And there's this persistent worry hammering away that I'm being played. That's why I wanted your opinion. What do you think? If I spent an hour each day during my rehab just chatting with her anonymously, with zero strings and no timetable, am I the world's biggest idiot?"

"I understand why that would worry you, T," Jenna started, then paused as if gathering her thoughts before continuing. "Let's look at this logically though. Had you ever been in that park before? At that time? Is there a chance she could have seen you before and decided you'd be an easy mark for catfishing?"

"No," Tommy said, thinking back. "No, I've pretty much just worked out here. I think the day of my meltdown was my first time in that park in a very long time."

"Okay, so she's sitting there on the bench, she sees you for the very first time drumming away on the tree like a weirdo. And in the time it took you to stop, see her, and walk over to her, she concocted this whole scheme? Does that sound even remotely reasonable? And a scheme that hinges, by the way, on the off-chance that you're going to feel major chemistry with her. That's what you're saying happened?"

"Well, no...of course it sounds stupid when you put it like that," Tommy said. "But yeah, I guess that's what I'm saying."

"Is she a total smoke show? Like the type of woman who routinely has men falling at her feet? The type who would confidently know that any old psycho in the park would fall for her crazy scheme instantly?" Jenna asked.

"No. I mean, she's beautiful. But in a quiet, studious kind of way," Tommy said. "She's not Park Bench Lolita or whatever."

"So, she's sitting there looking smart and studious and quiet on a secluded park bench in hopes that a rando will stumble across her, instantly fall for her understated charms, and immediately start wiring money all over the globe?" Jenna said, a devious smile appearing on her face. "That's your leading theory?"

"Holy hell, stop it already," Tommy said with a laugh. "Yes, you're right, that all sounds stupid. Of course it does. But maybe after she saw me throw my fit and we started talking—and the chemistry started flying—the scam just sort of came to her. Maybe she thought to herself that she knows a sucker when she sees one and started setting the trap from there."

"Oh, T. Yes, I guess anything is possible, really. But that goes for any relationship, no matter how you meet each other. There's always a chance that it's not going to work out. That's why dating can be hard and painful. There are never any guarantees. But sometimes a miracle happens, and it does work out. Based on how strong you feel the chemistry is between the two of you, it seems like it's worth taking the chance. Put yourself out there and see what happens," Jenna said, her affection for him clear on her face. And just when, he wondered, had his little sister turned into the kind of woman who had it all together and could dole out such sage wisdom?

"Thanks, Jen, I really appreciate it," he told her.

"Sure. And hey, given the fact that she's setting the world's slowest pace here, you'll have the time you need to get a better feel for the situation. If she really is a scammer, you'll figure it out. I would think maintaining the ruse of an in-person catfish would be incredibly difficult, if not impossible. So just take the chance and see what happens. Give her the time she's asking for. I think you're going to be glad you did."

"Yeah, that's kind of the way I was leaning anyway. But, I don't know, I just needed to hear if you thought I was being incredibly blind and stupid." He stood up to stretch; sitting on the kitchen stool for long periods wasn't exactly like sitting on a cloud.

"No stupider than you usually are," Jenna said with a smirk as she put their glasses in the sink and started gathering her things.

"Ah, yes, there's the little sister I know and love," Tommy said as he walked her to the door. "I wondered where you'd toddled off to."

"I know I tease you constantly, T, but you have to know I adore you and just want what's best for you." Jenna opened the door and went into the hall. "So let me know how it's going with the mysterious Lucy, okay?"

"I will. And I love you, too, Jenny J," he told her.

"Thanks."

He watched her disappear down the hallway before heading back inside.

Her words had made him feel better about his decision, sure. But he still had a feeling that no amount of his own fears or warnings from his little sister would have been able to stop him.

He'd be right back in that park tomorrow—if only just to catch a glimpse of his angel.

Chapter 12

"SO, ARE YOU an icy, stuck-up bitch or a clueless moron?"

"Er, what?" Lucy asked, the question jolting her out of the mental fog she tended to slip into at the diner.

Smile woodenly at the customers, take their orders, refill their drinks, bring their food, rinse and repeat....

Lucy tended to never really be *there* when she was working at the diner. Mostly her worries were, as usual, about her mom, who was home with the aide, Celia, each morning. Sometimes she took a break from that and fretted about the financial hole she was in, or about how that hole was really more like the Grand Canyon than, say, a pothole.

But in the last couple days, she found her mind was wandering straight to the park, wondering if Thomas was already there. Wondering what he was doing. What he was thinking. What he did when he *wasn't* there. And why his smile had the power to light her whole day....

"I asked if you're a bitch or a moron," her co-worker Mona repeated, again shaking Lucy violently out of her reverie.

"Oh. I...is there a third option?" Lucy stammered, confused by the sudden interruption of her thoughts.

She braced herself for the response as she studied the annoyance on Mona's face. Mona was a tough lady, the type of woman you couldn't picture ever having been young, sweet, or defenseless. She looked like she'd come into the world as the adult she was now, ready to fight a shark with her bare hands.

Mona was older by a few decades, Lucy guessed. Lucy honestly didn't know anything else about her. Until this moment, they'd never really spoken beyond whose section a customer would be seated in or whose order was up in the service window.

"I don't know, you tell me," Mona said. "You come in here day after day not talking to anyone like you're too good to be here. But guess what? You *are* here, and you're not showing any signs of getting out. So, what gives?" Mona emptied the last of the coffee and reached for the large container where the bags of fresh grounds were stored. They were constantly making coffee in this place.

"I…didn't. I don't know," Lucy said, lamely. She really didn't want to lay out all her problems to another stranger. Honestly, she just wanted this confrontation to end so she could get back to her mental fog and her happy thoughts about Thomas.

"You're a hard worker, I'll give you that," Mona continued. "And that's pretty much the only reason I haven't called you out on your crap before today. But after what you pulled this morning, the gloves are coming off."

"This morning? What did I do this morning?" Lucy asked, genuinely puzzled and shocked. She had come to work and clocked in like every other day, put on her ridiculous "Fork It Diner" t-shirt, and went out to get things started. Nothing unusual or special had happened, that she had noticed anyway.

Mona sighed, stopped what she was doing, and

looked Lucy in the eye.

"That's your whole problem. You don't pay attention to anyone around you. I'm older, and I don't care what you think about me, but some of these younger girls do care. Not sure why, but they've asked you time and time again to join their girl outings. They go out for drinks or shopping or whatever. I don't know. But they ask you to join them every single time. Usually, you just mumble something about being busy or having big plans, but today you just looked right through them like they were garbage and kept walking. As soon as I saw Tania start tearing up, I'd had enough." Each word that left Mona's mouth was pointed and flinty, like a barrage of knives being thrown Lucy's way.

Lucy was stunned. Had Tania really asked her to do something today? Had she even spoken to Tania? She honestly couldn't even remember.

"I'm sorry, Mona, I am. I never would have wanted to hurt anyone's feelings. Honestly, I don't even remember talking to Tania today." Embarrassment crawled up Lucy's neck and turned her face pink.

"Mmm-hmm. Well, there's your problem then. The people around you are insignificant like bugs, aren't they?" Mona asked, studying her face intently, a disapproving frown on her own. "No one here is worth your precious time or notice?"

"No, I don't think that at all. Seriously, Mona. I'm…I'm sorry. I've just been so caught up in my own thoughts and problems that I guess…I guess I haven't really allowed myself to be present in my life lately. If that makes sense?"

"Whatever. It's not me you need to apologize to or convince. But if I see you treating those girls that way again, you and me *will* have problems, you hear me?" Mona said with a scowl before heading back to her section of tables.

"Lucy, Table Five needs their check!" her boss, Pat, called from the kitchen.

Lucy straightened herself, shook off the confrontation with Mona, and slid it to the back of her mind. It needed to stay there if she was going to get through the rest of her shift. She'd have to think about it and deal with it later.

Mona's words stuck with her, though, and continued ringing in her mind as she went through the motions of her job. *Greet the customers with a smile. Take their orders. Serve their food. Refill their drinks....* On and on and on.

*   *   *

By the time her shift was over, and she was walking away from the diner, she was exhausted—emotionally, mentally, and physically. Mona's words were continuing to pound a staccato drumbeat through her head.

Was it true? Had she been so caught up in her own problems that she'd turned herself into an unfeeling bitch who made people around her cry? A person so heartless that she didn't even remember the conversation that had made that person upset in the first place?

Her mom and dad would be so disappointed in her. They'd always been very clear about their expectations for the type of person they wanted to raise. Smart and accomplished and independent, yes. But before everything else, kind and considerate. It was also what they had modeled to her throughout their lives. Kindness to everyone around them, that's what her parents had displayed, and it had been the way they'd lived every moment.

That message had come through loud and clear, as she was hoping to dedicate a huge portion of her professional life to helping others! And that goal was still very important to her. It felt like a way she could honor her parents, by giving back to others who couldn't otherwise afford legal services.

So how had she gone from a woman who wanted to devote herself to changing lives for the better to what she was doing at the diner? She wasn't showing kindness to the people around her. No, apparently, she was being so thoughtless and surly that she was making them cry.

What had she become?

Embarrassment and regret flooded through her. The truth was, she kind of *had* been a bitch. Mona wasn't wrong. She hadn't made any efforts to be friendly with her co-workers beyond meaningless greetings each morning. She didn't know much about any of them cumulatively. As usual, her blinders had been solidly in place as she soldiered through each day, wrapped up in her own worries and completely unaware of the world around her.

She had started working at the diner because it served a practical purpose. It offered her a regular morning shift that coincided with the times the home health aide was available to care for her mother. That was it. She needed the money to pay for basics like electricity and groceries. Her father's insurance money, the fund her parents had set aside for Lucy's education, and her mother's Social Security were all earmarked for her mother's care, which was only going to get more expensive. Lucy had to be frugal with the funds. She had no choice.

She hadn't entered the diner thinking it was a place where she could potentially make friends or plant any roots. She just wanted the paycheck and the tips, nothing more.

It took Mona's words to remind her that, despite the purpose the job served in her life, there were still humans involved. Yes, she was in a low spot in her life. But that didn't give her the right to treat the people around her like actors in her personal tragedy.

Is that what I've been doing to Thomas, too?

The sudden thought hit her like a blow. Was she brushing aside his feelings and being cruel by refusing to start a real relationship, even though it was something both of them seemed to want? Was she asking too much of him?

Yes, the more she thought about it—really thought about it in light of her conversation earlier with Mona—maybe she *was* just being selfish by wanting to see him without offering any part of herself. Once again, she was being cold and unfeeling.

An icy shard of regret spiked through her. Yes, she could see it now—she *was* being selfish.

Admittedly, her world was pretty small right now, so it didn't take much to move up in the pecking order of her quiet, solitary life. And, yes, she'd barely spent more than an accumulated hour or two in Thomas's presence. But when it came to this connection they'd forged, none of that mattered. Two hours or two decades; she was certain it didn't matter how much time they spent together. It just *was*: Thomas, in a few magical moments, had become vitally important to her.

Important enough, in fact, that she'd do anything to protect him, even if what she was protecting him from was herself. Lucy didn't let herself think more about it. It was decided. She needed to end this now before he got hurt. It didn't matter that she was definitely going to be annihilating herself in the process. She needed to end this before she destroyed anyone else's feelings, but especially not his. That was just about the only thing she knew for certain: Thomas was the last person in the world she'd want to hurt.

Chapter 13

SHE LEFT the walking path and entered the tree line, making the last portion of the journey to the bench. As she neared, she could see Thomas sitting there. A smile dawned on her face as she took him in, from the snug gray t-shirt that molded across his chest and did little to mask the muscles underneath to the worn and soft-looking jeans that covered his long legs. One arm was flung casually across the back of the bench like an open invitation for her to snuggle into his side.

She stopped and took a deep breath. *No one is going to be snuggling into anyone's arms,* she told herself. This was it—the last time she'd see him. She needed to let him know she didn't have anything to offer and that was it.

He hadn't noticed her yet, so she took advantage of the chance to soak the vision of this handsome, funny, and kind man into her mind. She had a feeling she'd be recalling this memory a lot in the coming weeks and months.

Finally, she took another deep breath and started walking again. *I can do this.*

Her sudden movement caught his attention, and Thomas turned to her with a lazy, sexy smile.

"Hey, beautiful," he said, standing.

"Uh, hi yourself," she said, unable to stop a smile from mirroring his.

"How was work?" he asked, sitting only after she

plopped down on the bench, the weight of what she wanted to say pressing heavily down on her. "Hey, are you okay?"

"I'm fine…no, no, that's a lie. I'm not. I'm the opposite of fine."

"So…not fine? Is that the opposite?" He was seemingly trying to tease a smile out of her. "Hey, angel, what's wrong? Talk to me."

She'd wanted to play it cool. Be frank but detached. Firm, clear, and decisive. But also kind and reasonable. All of those things would have been the right way to handle cutting Thomas free from her cesspool of a life. Instead, she went with the incoherent, half-sobbing, fully babbling route. *Sure, that could work too.*

"I realized today that I've been such an unfeeling monster, but the really monstrous part is that I honestly didn't even realize it. No, I had to be told by someone else what an insensitive jerk I've become. I didn't even remember talking to Tania at all, let alone making her cry! But Mona is right! I've turned into this robot with no feelings and no connections to any other humans. I just go to work, slog through my time there, and bolt to a lonely park bench for comfort. Who does that? And now I'm trying to do the same thing to you! And I can't hurt you like that. I can't! So, you've got to just go. Stop coming here. I don't want to hurt you, too. Not you. Especially not you." Her tangled words were now rolling out of her mouth faster than her brain could really process them. She didn't even know exactly what she'd just said, but hopefully Thomas understood the bottom line: She was in no place to be with him, at least not the way he wanted. He needed to go. Leave. Now.

"So, this is goodbye then," she added lamely, since

he didn't seem to be jumping up to leave.

"Wow, you've just settled an internal debate I've been having since I met you," Thomas replied, looking at her like he was happy about something.

At what point in any of the explosive word confetti that just erupted out of my mouth did I say something that would make this man happy?

"Wh…what?" she stuttered. "A debate? Let me guess, you've been wondering if I'm certifiably insane? Spoiler alert: I am." Suddenly, she felt unaccountably calm and in control of what she needed to say now. "Didn't you hear me? I'm a fairly awful person. Save yourself while you can."

"I've been wondering if you've got some sort of agenda here," Thomas went on calmly, his green eyes searching her face as though he were trying to uncover all her secrets. "Maybe trying to reel me in for some sort of scam. Refusing to tell me anything about yourself seemed suspicious, but after that little tirade, I'm letting those doubts go. You are what you say you are: You're a smart, beautiful, funny woman who's just doing her best to get through a really dark valley in her life, aren't you?"

"Don't give me any credit here," Lucy argued, a plea sharpening her tone. "Yes, I'm going through a lot right now. More than a lot. All of it. I'm going through all the bad things all at the same time. And no, I'm not trying to trick you into…what exactly?"

"Uh…I don't know. I hadn't sorted that out yet. A pyramid scheme? Wiring money to an off-shore account to pay off an imaginary blackmailer? Something like that?" There was a significant amount of humor evident on his face.

Lucy laughed and looked down at her hands,

studying them as though they held the answers to all of life's myriad questions.

"The truth is that everything has fallen down around me. And someone pointed out today that I've dealt with my problems by cutting myself off from the rest of humanity. I'm here, but I'm not *here* in my life." She realized she was trying earnestly to explain something she didn't fully understand, which only added to the challenge. "I've told you before that that's what I do. I focus pretty much to the exclusion of the whole world. But this person made me see that, in taking this approach, I hurt the people around me. People who just want to say hi or get to know me or maybe even share some of my burden."

"I'd like to be able to do that for you," Thomas told her quietly.

"I know. We barely know each other, and yet I know one-hundred percent, like I've known you my whole life, that what you say is true." Lucy looked again into his face. "But I need to work on myself. This is not who I am, or at least it's not who I want to be."

"I understand," Thomas said. "My sister recently pointed out that I've become a whiny, impatient, depressed lump ever since I got injured. Sometimes it's good to have someone hold up a mirror like that. Help us see what we're not seeing on our own."

"Yeah," Lucy said, nodding. "That's exactly what happened to me today. Mona held that mirror up and…wow, I really did not like the person I saw looking back at me."

"Okay," Thomas nodded. "So, we're both in a similar place. We both need to make changes. Come on, let's do it together. Let me be there for you, and you can be there for me. No pressure. No strings. Maybe it's true that neither of us is in a good place to start a relationship. But for some reason, I think I need you in my life anyway. And something tells me you need me, too. Stop trying to push me away, because unless you really want me to disappear—and I mean *really* want me to—I'm not going anywhere."

"Being with you helps," Lucy admitted. "Yes, you help me feel something. Every other part of my day is spent floating in a foggy paralysis. But the few times I've been with you? I'm suddenly alive again."

"That's good," Thomas said with a very genuine smile. "You do those things for me, too. I want to stop freaking out about being injured and just focus on healing. So, we'll both heal, together. Come on, let me walk you home. Or let me bring dinner over later? We can keep talking and really start supporting each other, the way we both clearly need."

"No," Lucy said emphatically. "I can't. I need to…no. I still just have this hour each day to offer you. That's it."

"Oh, that's ridiculous," Thomas replied. "I know you've got the responsibility of caring for your mom, but that doesn't mean we can't see each other or talk on the phone or something. Remember? We're trying to help each other through a bad time. How can we do that if we're never together and can't even reach out when we need to?"

But she continued shaking her head. "I have to do this on my own, Thomas. I can't rely on you to pull me out of it. Yes, it helps to have this time together to talk. To look forward to each day. But if I'm going to turn my life around and really make changes and find the elusive answers to my problems, I want to do it on my own terms. I don't want to move our friendship forward right now. Not while I'm feeling this way. Please—please try to understand."

"I'm not going to lie and say I'm not disappointed," Thomas told her, "but yeah, I guess I understand. Take the time you need. I'm slowly rehabbing and trying to get rid of these headaches. So, as long as I'm still on concussion protocols, I've got this time I can spend with you here each afternoon. But once I'm feeling better, that will change. I'll have to go. I want to make sure you understand that."

"Sure, I do. And when it does, then we'll figure it out from there, okay?"

"Okay, angel," Thomas agreed with a sigh. "For now, we'll stay on the bench."

Chapter 14

TOMMY'S REHAB didn't involve much. He was still hanging out in an apartment in northern New Jersey so he could be near his family—and close enough to Baltimore to be able to report quickly when the doctors finally released him. He was still doing his daily exercises and physical therapy routines. Days and weeks were slowly stacking up to create months, and yet all those things remained the same. The headaches were still there, but Tommy increasingly found he didn't care as much about the slow healing time, because Lucy was still there too.

After Lucy asked him to let her deal with her problems independently, Tommy decided to stop pushing for more from her. He heard what she was saying loud and clear, and he respected that she needed the time and space to figure things out on her own.

The problem was that time was marching on, and change was heading his way. Because those days were adding up to weeks and months, he knew their time together would soon be over. It was especially frustrating because he wanted a relationship with her while he was able to focus completely on building it. Solid relationships took work and time, as he knew from watching his parents and married teammates. Unfortunately, he soon wouldn't have much time that was his own at all.

All relationships were complicated, but the life of a

professional athlete was especially tough on them. From spring training in March—February for pitchers and catchers—straight through to the World Series in October, your time wasn't your own. Some players dealt with it by buying homes in their team cities and moving their families there. The convenience of having your family close when the team was playing home games was a wonderful perk.

The trouble with that solution, though, came when you got traded or your deal ran out, and you hit the free-agent market. There were no guarantees you'd land where you wanted to live. For players who had children, it might mean enormous and fast-moving changes: trying to sell houses and buy new ones, uprooting the kids from their schools and friends. Sometimes this happened every few years.

Other families tried to avoid all this by keeping a home in one place in order to give the kids stability. But the rigors of the long and unrelenting baseball season often meant the players were separated from their families until the kids went on summer breaks. Then the family could be reunited by spending those months renting another home in whatever city the player's team was located.

Thurman Munson, the beloved catcher and team captain for the Yankees in the 1970s, had tried to keep his family stable in their hometown of Canton, Ohio. He dealt with the separation by learning to fly and buying a small plane so he could frequently visit them on off-days. But what had seemed like an ideal solution to a really complex situation ended in tragedy for the Munson family, as well as for the Yankees team and fans: He died in a plane crash in 1979 on one such trip home.

It was clear that neither choice was ideal. Once a player found a life partner and started a family, both choices involved separation, change, and tough decisions. Yes, the money was good, and money could pave a lot of rocky paths. But it wasn't a simple life regardless.

Lucy didn't know any of that, though. She still didn't know his current home was in Camden Yards' right field and not in northern New Jersey where his parents lived. She wasn't aware of just how unusual it was for Tommy to be free like this. Even though it was only his first year in the Majors, he'd spent his whole life rigorously working in the middle of the sport, either in training or playing, and staying tied to the rise and fall of the long season.

Having unscheduled time to devote to developing a relationship was such a luxury. He hated that he could feel their unique opportunity slipping away. He knew that only a couple more weeks or, at best, months were all they had left. Then he'd be on a plane to the team's spring training facilities in Sarasota, or possibly Baltimore, depending on the timing and what the team wanted.

He remembered his excitement during spring training last year. He'd shown up in Florida in the best shape of his life, determined to prove to the team what he could offer them. His hard work and determination had paid off. He'd spent the entire time crushing the ball and making diving saves in the outfield. He could feel it, and the Orioles coaches and owners couldn't miss it. All the years of training, practice, discipline, and sacrifice were coming together. When he finally got the call that they were pulling him up to the Majors, he'd been   ecstatic...determined...driven...focused....   And most important of all, ready to grab the opportunity in front of him with both fists and never let go.

It felt absurd, then, that almost a year later part of him was dreading going back. How was that even possible? When he got hit with that ball, he'd been ripped right out of every dream he'd ever had and thrust into a personal nightmare. So why, then, had the actual end of his rookie season had such a minor effect on his life when it had finally, officially ended? Most of the worst-case scenarios he'd imagined after his injury had come true. His chances of getting back into the tail end of his rookie season had come and gone. He'd completely missed out on the end of the season. The playoffs were over. The World Series Champions had already been crowned and given their celebratory parade. Someone else had already been named the American League Rookie of the Year. Just a few months ago, any one of those things would have hit Tommy like a steamroller. He found, though, that all of those moments had basically tiptoed by, barely leaving a sting in their wake.

Oh, who was he even kidding? There was no mystery here. He knew there was only one possible reason that losing out on the end of his rookie year didn't have him panicked and rocking in a corner. That reason, of course, was Lucy, who daily was showing herself to be a funny, sassy, strong, smart woman—and one who always brought him up when he was feeling down. She had become his confidante and friend, someone he trusted implicitly, even though there was still so much they didn't know about each other, and her walls were still so firmly in place.

She had asked him to keep things light—and still frustratingly anonymous—between them, and he'd kept his word. But despite his best efforts, he knew he was falling for her. He stayed silent about it, though. He was firmly planted in the friend zone.

Since the day she'd had the confessional meltdown about the confrontation with her coworker, Tommy hadn't said another word about changing their relationship. She knew how he felt and what he wanted. But it wasn't about him. His problems would resolve eventually. She was the one who still had a lot to get through. It was about what Lucy wanted and what she needed right now, not what *he* wanted or needed.

She had been very upfront and honest with him from the start. She didn't want a relationship. She had no time or emotional bandwidth for it at this point in her life. He got it, and he was never again going to ask her for more until *she* was ready. Because of how open and honest they'd become with each other, Tommy was confident she'd let him know when things changed, either with her mother's illness or the way in which Lucy was learning to deal with her problems.

He knew she was still struggling against her instincts to shut out the rest of the world. But at least she was working on it. She'd proudly told him about conversations she'd started at work. Tidbits of information she'd gotten from talking to—and actually listening to—her coworkers. She'd been practicing greater kindness there, and it had been paying off. She even seemed to be getting close with Mona, the older woman who'd told her off a couple months ago. With her mom sick, Lucy was especially in need of Mona's tough advice and general presence. At least that's how it seemed to Tommy.

Yes, Lucy was making changes. And it would be soon, he felt certain, that she'd finally do the same where their relationship was concerned. She'd ask him to do something with her beyond the boundaries of the park. Maybe something simple like meet somewhere for lunch. He didn't care; he'd agree to it, whatever she asked. He was all in and definitely ready for something more.

He hadn't mentioned to her about how much better he'd been feeling lately, despite the level of honesty they'd achieved, specifically because he didn't want to pressure her. He felt certain the doctors were going to be releasing him from concussion protocols soon. Despite how fast it felt like time was moving, it was still the off-season, so it likely wouldn't matter to his daily schedule for another couple of weeks. But once it was time for spring training and the doctors cleared him…well, his days on the bench were definitely numbered.

Until that day, though, he was going to keep right on doing what he'd been doing—working out, resting, reassuring his worried parents that he was fine, and spending an hour each day with Lucy, at least when the weather allowed it. That was basically his life right now.

Of course, it was the hour spent each day with Lucy that made the rest of it bearable. If only he could be as much a part of her life as she was of his. He was impatient, but he was confident that day would come. It was that confidence that kept the worries and doubts at bay. He was sure he'd found the love of his life, and it was all going to work out for them in the end. He just had to continue being patient.

Someday she'd open that door to him. And heaven help him, he was going to walk right through it and never look back.

Chapter 15

"ORDER UP, Lucy!" Pat shouted from the kitchen.

Lucy rolled her eyes. *As if I can't see that it's in the window and ready to go.* The Fork It Diner wasn't exactly palatial. It was L-shaped and tiny, with booths lining the outer wall along the windows. A few tables were scattered around, and a long red and chrome-edged counter with matching stools wrapped around the inner wall. It was exactly like any other diner or truck stop café that you might see in the United States. Nothing less—and definitely nothing more.

"These plates aren't serving themselves," Pat snapped again as he glanced through the service window from his vantage point in the kitchen. "Let's go!"

"Oh, hold your pants on, old man!" Mona snapped, grabbing the plates as Lucy made her way toward the window. "Here you go, honey."

Lucy smiled in appreciation as she took the plates and delivered them to a booth around the corner. Mona and Lucy had certainly gotten off to a rocky start, but once Lucy began making the effort to be more aware of her co-workers and their feelings, Mona had displayed greater kindness of her own and was now quickly becoming one of Lucy's favorite people. Mona was still extremely prickly on the outside, but she was also a person who you knew could handle anything life threw her way. She was just plain tough, period. The kind of person, as Lucy's grandmother used to say, who could "chew up nails and spit out tacks." Lucy laughed to herself as the silly old saying floated through her mind. That was Mona to a T.

Under that hard outer shell, however, lived a kind and patient soul. Lucy had only recently begun to see glimpses of that hidden persona, and as a result she was growing to love Mona dearly. She had stepped into Lucy's lonely existence and given her friendship and guidance. Despite the work Lucy had put into expanding her focus beyond the limits of her own problems, those problems still surrounded her. Her mother, for example, was getting worse. Lucy couldn't even remember the last time her mom had recognized her. She now needed more supervision and constantly posed a safety risk to herself and others. Meanwhile, the extensions Lucy had received for her loans weren't going to last forever. That crippling debt was still sitting there, waiting to pounce.

And even worse than knowing she would soon have to start making exorbitant student loan payments was the knowledge that her time with Thomas was coming to a close. He'd warned her that he'd have to start traveling for his job soon. Lucy was so happy that he was feeling better—she hadn't heard him mention his headaches in weeks. That was wonderful news, of course. But selfishly, she knew it was also bad news. He'd soon be whisked away to the whirlwind of responsibilities that came with whatever his career entailed.

She'd often tried to guess this mysterious job that included so much travel. Pilot, maybe? She'd also wondered if he was in the military, but that didn't seem to quite fit him. He seemed very athletic and rugged.

She couldn't imagine that he was some sort of suit-wearing businessman, but the travel aspect would fit that. Her initial guess had been construction, but did people in construction travel a lot? Maybe he worked in constructions sites in other cities?

Obviously, she could solve the mystery simply by asking him. But something was still holding her back from moving their friendship forward like that. She thought about him all the time already. But if she could text him? Or go to his house or apartment? Forget it, that's all she'd ever want to do. It was all part of the fun of getting to know someone and falling in love with them. That rush of excitement and chemistry, and wanting to be together constantly, was what new relationships were all about.

He had been so patient with her. Once he'd agreed to her terms, he hadn't brought them up again. She was truly grateful for that, of course...but it also filled her with certain doubts. Had he changed his mind? Did he still want to push this relationship forward? Or had he already moved on? Maybe he was seeing someone else right now, and that's why he was so patient. But if that was the case, then why would he even bother to keep showing up at their bench each day?

She pondered these questions and quite a few others during her shift. Would he still be coming to see her if he was seeing someone else? Maybe he just felt sorry for her and awkward about walking away. Maybe he was counting down the days until he could whisk off to his mystery job and be done with her and her sadsack tale of woe? If she could just fly away from her problems, she certainly would in a heartbeat. She wouldn't blame Thomas one bit for wanting to do the same.

Once the shift was over, the questions were swirling through her mind like a tornado of doubts, and she felt more nervous than ever as she made her way to the bench. It felt like the stress her doubts were causing was thrumming away at her like a musician plucking guitar strings as she rounded the last corner, bringing the bench—and Thomas—into view.

Her eyes locked with his as he stood to greet her.

"Hey beautiful, how was work?" he asked. She smiled up at him, wishing she could just throw herself into his arms as she felt her nervous energy melt away. *But we can't do that because we're just friends*, she reminded herself—a status she had demanded. Not even friends, really. They were more like acquaintances. Bench buddies. That was it. That's what she wanted. That's what she needed.

Right...?

"Okay, I guess," she answered finally, flopping down onto her usual spot.

"Hey, what's wrong?" he asked, concern lining his gorgeous face as he sat on the opposite side, a careful space between them as always. "Your mom, is she...the same?"

"Yeah. Well, sort of, I guess. It's degenerative and pretty fast-moving. She's a little worse all the time," Lucy admitted. "She doesn't know me anymore."

"Wait, so it's dementia? That's what she has?" Thomas's empathy flowed off him through his kind and genuine tone, wrapping her tightly in its warmth. "I guess I always just assumed cancer."

"No...no, her body is actually very strong. It's her mind. Like I said, she almost never knows who I am anymore. Although sometimes she asks me if I've seen her baby. She gets lost in the past a lot, so in those times…well, at least she remembers she had *me*. Even if her version of me is still a baby." Lucy wasn't sure why she was suddenly unloading all of this on him, but it felt good to share a small piece of the burden.

"I'm starting to understand why you don't have spare time," Thomas said, a look of true understanding dawning across his face. "You don't just *want* to spend time with her. You have to actually watch her and take care of her."

"Right. She can't ever be alone. She could hurt herself or wander off and get lost. That's why I still don't have any free time. It's why I…we…." Her thoughts became tangled coming out of her mouth, and she just let them trail off before trying again. "Thomas, are you still…well, we haven't talked about it in a while. You've never nudged me in these months we've been meeting here, but maybe that's because you're seeing someone else? I mean, I would totally get it and understand if that's the case. You can tell me. I can take it."

"No," he said, smiling over at her. "I'm not seeing anyone else. There's no way. I feel such a connection with you, Lucy. I know it's crazy. We don't know anything about each other and haven't even really touched. And yet, when I see you, I see…endless possibilities. I see my healing and my hope and my future. I…I don't know. I'm not saying this well, but angel, as long as you feel the same way, I'm in this for the long haul."

Lucy beamed at him, nodding in agreement. "No, you said it perfectly. That was beautiful, and yes, you stated exactly what I see when I look at you, too. It feels like you're everything I want, Thomas. But now I just have to get myself to a place in my life where I'm able to reach out and take what I want. I just…I'm not there yet. I've got way too much baggage right now, and it's pulling me down and away from where I want to be."

"I still don't understand fully, angel. Your mom has dementia. That's terrible, but let's face it together. We can spend time at your place. I could help you care for her, at least before I have to go. What's holding us back from doing that?"

"I appreciate your offer, really I do. But my mom's health isn't my only issue," she said with a pained look on her face. "I really don't want to get into all of it, but it's to do with…I don't know. Lots of things. Money. Obligations. Career choices. Dead-end jobs. Lots and lots of things."

Thomas's frustration was evident as he blew out a long breath and raked his fingers through his hair. She noticed that gesture no longer made him wince in pain.

"I promised I wouldn't push you, so I'm dropping it," he told her. "I'm here for you, and I want to be more than acquaintances someday. That's the truth. And I'm not trying to add pressure by saying this, but I have to be honest since we're clearly putting all our cards on the table today. I'm feeling better now. The headaches are mostly gone. It won't be long before the doctors clear me. Once that happens, I'll be back at work. And I know I told you this before, but I travel a lot for my job."

"But you could still drop by to see me on days when you're in town though, right?" Lucy asked, still utterly confused about his work situation.

"Uh…that's the thing. The home, er…office for the company I work for isn't based here. I don't actually live in New Jersey. I mostly came here because this is where my parents and sister live. I wanted to be near them during my rehab from the injury."

"Oh," Lucy said, a panic filling her chest. "I didn't realize. I just thought you frequently traveled, but that this was your home base."

Thomas chuckled, but she wasn't sure what was so funny about what she said—a long-distance relationship was no one's dream scenario.

"Don't worry angel," he finally said, the amusement gone again. "We'll figure it out. When the doctors clear me, you'll be the first person I'll want to tell. We'll just take things from there, okay?"

Lucy nodded with a tiny smile. *Sure, okay,* she told herself. *It is all going to be okay.* Thomas still was single, and he was still interested in being with her. She just needed to get busy finding a way forward, and soon. All she'd accomplished so far in these months was making a few friends at work, and by doing so she proved to herself that she could remove her blinders and focus on more than her own problems.

That had been step one, and that was great. But all those issues remained. She still didn't have time to study, and until she could figure that part out, she was never going to pass the bar or secure a job that would enable her to pay off those loans.

As she thought about it when she walked out of the park a short time later, she was forced to admit that she was basically right where she'd started.

Chapter 16

TOMMY GLANCED at his phone as he set his protein shake on the kitchen counter. The name on the screen surprised him. Jack, his manager, was reaching out. Was this it? Were they calling him back to the team?

Wait, no, the doctors haven't cleared me yet. That makes no sense.

"Coach! Good to hear from you," Tommy said as he accepted the call.

"Hey, Tommy Boy, how're you doing? Still laying around like a lapdog?"

"Yeah, actually, that about sums it up," Tommy said with a laugh. "What's up, Coach?"

"The doctors say it should be soon, but I wanted to hear it from you," Jack went on, his booming voice causing Tommy to ease the phone back from his head. "Will I see that ugly mug of yours when spring training starts?"

"That's the goal, Coach," Tommy said. "And I think it's going to happen. Actually, I have a doctor's appointment tomorrow. This might be the one where they say they're lifting all the restrictions. I've been feeling great. The headaches are mostly gone, and my head's not even sore to the touch anymore. This is it; I can feel it."

"Excellent," Jack told him. "I'm proud of you, son. I know it was hard to sit back and be idle while the rest of your rookie year passed by. But this is your reward for sucking it up all these months. We want you to come to spring training and show everyone you've still got the skills."

"It *was* really hard," Tommy admitted as a vision of him attacking a defenseless tree in the park floated through his mind. "Especially at first. Not going to lie, I was a mess for a while there. But, well, things definitely got better."

"Hmm," Jack said thoughtfully. "Sounds like there's a story there."

"I'll never tell," Tommy replied with a chuckle. "But I really am looking forward to being back with the team, Coach."

"Looking forward to having you there, kid. Keep relaxing and recovering. That's your ticket home," Jack added before ending the call.

As Tommy set his phone down and picked up the shake again, he thought more about Jack's words. That conversation was all he'd wanted in the aftermath of his injury. Now? It just made him anxious to go see Lucy again. His time with her was almost over. He wanted to savor every moment he could.

He'd been hoping that at any moment she'd tell him she was ready to move forward. But after the last conversation they'd had, it sure didn't seem like things were going to be changing anytime soon. But if he was leaving, they were going to have to exchange numbers at the very least. Once spring training started, that would be it. He'd be in the thick of the rigorous Major League schedule until, at minimum, the beginning of October. He didn't want to be out of contact with Lucy for even a day, so the thought of endless months without any contact? No way. He'd have to stress again how important it was for them to exchange numbers soon. Unless she was lying when she said she eventually wanted to start a relationship with him….

Tommy gathered his wallet, keys, and phone, and headed to his truck. He needed his daily bench fix, and he needed it now.

*   *   *

He got there early, as usual, and sat down to wait.

What was it about this woman that had him so tangled up? So ready to wait for a relationship that might never even work out? What were they basing this on? They'd never even kissed. He'd never held her. Was he being a big sap and inventing some sort of fairytale situation in his mind? Was her admission that she had a ton of problems bringing out a hero complex in him?

Wait, was that it...?

Was he trying to be a superhero? A Prince Charming riding in to save the damsel in distress? If he was, he was the lamest one ever. His damsel was still dangling off a high rise, and he was just sitting around on a bench with absolutely no idea how to help her.

He considered this as he watched a couple squirrels chase each other through the trees, across the branches, and back down to the grass. There was a high-speed game of chase happening in his mind, too, as the doubts raced after each other. The thing was, when he wasn't with her, it was so easy to doubt everything. Her insistence at staying anonymous. Her refusal to exchange numbers or spend more time together. Her story that she couldn't tear herself away from her mother's side for more than an hour each day. None of it really felt like it made any sense.

During that one hour each day, however— somehow everything made sense then. All the questions and the worries and the doubts magically fell away the moment he saw her each day. He decided he was going to hold onto those feelings and try to forget all the rest of it. He didn't have any answers, but for his own sake he had to see this through anyway.

As though summoned by the power of his thoughts, Lucy appeared, happiness radiating from her face as she spotted him. Tommy stood and watched as she gracefully approached. Her expression changed slightly, a quizzical look crossing over the joy, as she moved toward him.

"What's wrong, Thomas?" she asked, her footsteps faltering. "Are you okay?"

"Dance with me," he replied, extending his hand and wrapping his fingers slowly around hers. A sizzle of awareness crackled between them. She let out a little gasp as her bag slid slowly off her shoulder, falling to the ground with a soft thump.

"There's no music," she protested with a laugh as he tugged her gently toward him and wrapped his arms around her for the first time.

"So put on a song," he said, looking down into her upturned face as they slowly began to sway.

"What's gotten into you?" she asked, smiling as he moved back and twirled her around before pulling her close again. "Do acquaintances dance in the park these days?"

"No, they probably don't," he admitted, loving the feeling of her in his arms. Once again, the doubts and worries melted away simply because of her presence. "But Luce, I'm leaving soon. We can't stay essentially nameless acquaintances any longer. We have to exchange numbers, at the bare minimum. I've got a doctor's appointment tomorrow. This is likely the one where they finally clear me to return to work. I'm about to fly away, angel. I need to get you to move us forward and out of the park."

"Oh, Thomas, I'm so happy for you," she said, a sheen of tears belying her words.

"So…those are happy tears then?"

"Yes! Very happy," she said, pulling her hand from his momentarily to wipe at her eyes. "I'm happy your problems are almost resolved. And I'm thrilled that you're healing and finally feeling better. But *my* problems? I feel like they're just getting started. It's like I'm floating in an ocean of them, but it's not a rescue boat I see on the horizon. It's a tidal wave."

"Well, you might be facing a tidal wave, but you're facing it with me by your side," he said as he leaned down slowly until their lips were a whisper apart. "I may be leaving, but I'm not giving up on this. And I'm not giving up on wanting us to be more. Are *you* giving up?"

Lucy's eyes widened as they studied each other. Their lips were so close together he could feel her breath on his face.

"Acquaintances don't dance in the park, and they definitely don't kiss, either," she said finally.

"Fact remains, I want to kiss you right now, and I'm pretty sure you want to kiss me, too," Tommy countered.

"I do, you know I do, but…." Lucy exhaled a soft sigh, as her brown eyes, filled with worry and regret, looked into his. She leaned forward then—he thought for a moment she was about to kiss him after all, and the chemistry between them arched and crackled. Suddenly, though, with a small cry, she pulled back, away from his almost-kiss and right out of his arms. "I can't do this. Not now. I still want to wait. I want to kiss you and be with you more than almost anything I've ever wanted in my life. But…I need to resolve everything. I can't take us forward yet, Thomas. I'm sorry, but I can't."

Thomas scrubbed his hands over his face. "I'm sorry, sweetheart, I really am," he replied. "Knowing that I'm leaving soon has me all tied up. I didn't mean to add pressure to your situation, I really didn't. But Lucy, I'm serious about the phone numbers. We're exchanging them soon, or there isn't going to be a way forward for us."

Lucy grabbed her bag from where she'd dropped it and took her usual spot on the bench, watching as he slid onto his side.

"I know. I agree," she said. "We'll exchange them when you're about to leave town, okay? Daily phone calls will replace daily meetings in the park."

"Well, yes, I'll want to talk to you, but I can't promise a certain time each day. My schedule will be all over the place. My time won't be my own anymore."

"It's okay," Lucy said with a small smile. "We'll figure it out. Although I won't be able to talk in the mornings because of work, of course."

"My afternoons and evenings will likely be full," Tommy replied ruefully. "This might involve a lot of texting."

"That's okay. I would do just about anything for a hot guy who dances in the park with me," she said as an adorable blush tinged her cheeks.

"Oh, come on, a woman as beautiful and smart as you? You probably have to make guys take a number like at a deli counter," he teased, hoping to see that cute blush again.

"No, no, nothing like that," she said, shaking her head with a smile. "Actually, I've always been studying or thinking I *should* be. No hot park guys. More like a few brainy library guys."

"I feel like there's an insult in there somewhere," Tommy said with a chuckle.

"No! I'm not saying you're not smart! I just think…I don't know. You seem like the type who was captain of the football team and king of the prom. Meanwhile, I was a member of the debate team and the band. I'm right, aren't I? You never even would have *seen* me in high school, let alone danced with me."

"Well, no, I wasn't the king of anything. But yeah, I was an athlete in high school for sure." Tommy wished he could pull her into his arms and close the gap between them again. "Can't imagine a world where I didn't notice you, though."

"What type of women do you typically date?" she countered. "Cheerleaders? Models? Actresses?"

"Uh…well, honestly, I don't really *date* anyone," Tommy admitted.

"You don't date them? Then you…wait, you're a *player*? Just hook-ups?" she asked, astonishment on her face.

"Kind of?" he admitted sheepishly. This was not the conversation he thought they'd be having. "In my job there are a lot of, uh, women around who…just…well, no I don't really *date* them."

"Women hanging around your job? What are you…wait a minute, are you talking about *groupies*? Are you a musician? Oh my gosh, have I been sitting next to a rock star this whole time without knowing it?" The incredulity was plainly evident on her face. "What the heck, Thomas?"

"No, listen, I'm not a musician. No groupies…sort of. I don't know. I'm pleading the fifth," he said with an embarrassed laugh. "Anything else that I say will either get me in trouble with you or reveal who I am."

"Oh no, now I'm dying with curiosity. Are you a pimp? In the mafia? Something I'm really not going to like?" He couldn't tell if she was teasing or serious at this point.

"Angel, no," he said, reaching out and grabbing her fingers in his own. She looked at their joined hands, then back up to his face. "Trust me, it's nothing awful. But it does involve a different kind of lifestyle than your typical job. I'm not going to lie to you."

"Oh, okay. Sure, I get it now," she said, pulling away and standing. "I guess my time is up for today."

"You get *what*, exactly?" Tommy said, his eyes narrowing as he stood, too.

"You're going back to this groupie lifestyle, and you're being upfront and honest about it with me. I…I guess I just really appreciate your honesty," she said, the sad look on her face not matching her words.

"Lucy, when I told you I'd wait for you, I meant it. I'm going back to my job, but I'm not going back to that life, okay sweetheart? You and me, exploring what we might become together. This is where my future is."

"Okay, sure," she said softly. "I believe you. See you tomorrow?"

Tommy watched as she turned and walked away, once again assailed by the doubts that were only at bay when he was with her.

She had believed him, hadn't she?

Everything was going to work out…right?

Chapter 17

"HEY, LUCE, how are you doing?" Tania asked, walking past her with a stack of dirty dishes. "Have you had your break yet?"

"No, have you?" Lucy asked, too exhausted and weary to decipher where Tania was going with her line of questioning.

"I really think you should take your break now," Tania replied, a devious look on her face as she dumped off the dirty plates. "Like, *right* now."

"Okay, I'll bite," Lucy said her eyes narrowing in good-natured suspicion. "What are you up to? Why is my taking an immediate break so important to you?"

"I just think it's so critical for you to rest after the long morning we've had. I'm looking out for you," Tania said with a now-impish look. "Plus, Mona just seated a super-hot guy in your section, and I'm dying to check him out."

"Ah ha! I knew you weren't concerned with my tired feet," Lucy said with a laugh. "I'll agree to it only after I've checked out this guy for myself."

"Trust me girl, you won't be sorry you did, but you're probably not going to give me that table now, once you see him," Tania said, her face scrunching up with disappointment. "He looks like that actor named Chris."

"Hemsworth?...Pine?...Evans?" Lucy rattled off, enjoying this ridiculous exchange now. "Or, no, wait—

let me think...um, Pratt?"

"Yes," Tania nodded solemnly. "All of them."

"This I've got to see," Lucy said as she headed toward the swinging door of the kitchen. "Which table?"

"Oh, you'll know," Tania replied, following close behind.

Lucy pushed the door open slowly, peering out like they were on an undercover mission. Her gaze traveled down the line of booths in her section. There were two older women who came regularly after taking morning walks together. Then a couple of teenagers who probably should be in school. After that was an empty booth, followed by a gorgeous woman with long, light-brown hair streaked with blonde just like a sun goddess. She was talking to a man whose back was toward her and whose face Lucy couldn't see. Was he Tania's hot guy? She looked closer. He had broad shoulders; huge and muscle-bound arms; and brown, curly hair.

Curly hair? She looked closer then.

It couldn't be. Was it...?

Just then the mystery man turned his head slightly so she could see his profile.

Oh no...Thomas.

Yep, it was him. With a gasp, Lucy stepped backward and, in her haste to retreat, collided with Tania.

Thomas can't see me here!

She had to hide. She had to...take that break Tania suggested.

She wasn't embarrassed about working as a waitress. Not *exactly*, anyway. It was honest work, after all. On the other hand, it wasn't who she was. And it certainly wasn't who she *wanted* to be. But all that aside, she just couldn't stand there and cheerfully serve him and that gorgeous beauty coffee and pancakes while pretending everything was okay. *Nothing* about this was okay.

"Yep, Tania, that table is all yours," Lucy said, turning toward the back room. "I'm on break."

"Thanks! You're crazy for not taking it, but I owe you one!"

Lucy all but ran to the break room, with its fluorescent lighting, broken-down lockers, and solitary table circled by a few wobbly chairs. She collapsed on one of those chairs and put her head down, struggling to calm herself. She'd never had a panic attack before, but this kind of felt like it might be one.

What was Thomas doing here, and with that entrancing woman? It was a date, she guessed. It had to be a date, right? Didn't he just get done telling her he was Mr. Hook-Up, living a life constantly surrounded by all those "not-groupies"? Was that glorious creature one of them? Was this a late-morning brunch after a wild night of crazy monkey sex? But wait, didn't he say he had a doctor's appointment today? Was *that* his doctor? No, that's crazy. Doctors don't make diner calls....

Wild, irrational questions and theories were pinging all around her mind, filling her with doubts and self-recrimination. *This is my fault, all my fault.* Thomas had asked her to go on dates and start a relationship, and she was the one who'd refused. He wasn't doing anything wrong. He tried to get her to commit to something more, and she had said no. Now he was just living his life. He certainly didn't owe her anything. They weren't together. They weren't even really friends. They weren't...*anything*, really. *I don't even know his last name.* The blonde goddess probably knew his name, though, she thought ruefully. Or, heck, maybe she doesn't, if he's the kind of player he had claimed to be.

Maybe this was his pattern! Maybe he picked up lonely women in parks, promised them the world, then ditched them once they slept with him. Maybe the only reason he was still coming to the park to see her after all this time was because she was still a challenge.

"Ugh!" Lucy said as she sat up again, only to see Mona standing in the doorway looking at her with a combination of concern and amusement.

"What's gotten into you?" she asked after studying Lucy's panicked face. She pushed off the doorjamb and took a seat across from Lucy. "We can't leave Tania out there alone too long, so make this quick and just spit it out, girl."

"The story of what's going on here is too long," Lucy said, shaking her head. "Too long and complicated for a quick summary. But I guess the short version is 'man trouble'."

"You seeing that handsome man out there who's got Tania all in a flutter? Is that what's going on?" Mona asked.

"Sort of. He's interested in me, or at least that's what he says. But with my situation…well, I told him I can't date him now, or…even really get to know him better." Lucy looked down at her hands to escape Mona's fiercely knowing gaze.

"And what situation would that be?" Mona asked sharply.

"Well, you know parts of my story. It's the reason I'm working here. I graduated from law school recently. My dad died, and my mom's got severe dementia. She has to be watched constantly. When I'm here, she's with a home health aide. I thought at this point in my life I'd be studying full time for the bar exam so I could start my law career. But I don't have the time or the resources. My parents' savings is now for my mom's care exclusively, so I got loan extensions on all my debt. I'm…stuck."

"I'm sorry about all of that, Lucy," Mona said sincerely, "but what does any of that have to do with your young man?"

"I'm at an all-time low in my life, Mona. I don't have even a free minute to study for the exam—the one that would help me secure a job that would allow me to pay off my debt. And trust me, preparing for that test is a full-time job. I can't focus on starting something with him when I've got all these burdens and problems and no time in my life to solve any of them. It really wouldn't be fair. And I'm just not wired that way. I can't split my attention like that."

"That's stupid," Mona said then, a look of sheer disappointment creasing her face.

"I…what?" Lucy asked, startled by the blunt response. "It's not stupid! It's the truth. I've always been that way. I focus on one thing to the exclusion of everything else in my life. That's what I was doing when you got mad at me, remember?"

"Based on the full-blown meltdown I witnessed when I walked in here, you clearly are attracted to that man. And he said he wanted to date you? From where I'm sitting, the only roadblock to your happiness is the person I'm looking at right now. Stop creating foolish excuses and just live your life, child."

Mona stood and headed for the door, then stopped and turned back. "When you've lived as long as I have and seen as much as I've seen, you'll understand why this is so clear to me. Life doesn't give us that many chances for happiness, girl. Grab them when you see them and don't let go."

"It's not that simple," Lucy said, shaking her head, frustrated that Mona clearly didn't understand everything she was saying.

"Lucy, hear me when I say this," Mona countered, the woman's steely gaze drilling into her now. "*Make* it that simple, or you're going to live a life full of nothing but regrets."

"Thank you, Mona. I appreciate that you care about me, I honestly do," Lucy said. "But it really just isn't as simple as you're making it seem."

Mona let out a frustrated sigh but said nothing further.

"Can you cover for me until he's gone?" Lucy asked, not sure if Mona would comply with such a request. They'd been extremely busy all morning. Covering for her today was a big ask.

Mona appeared to think it over for a moment. Then she said, "You owe me," before shaking her head, rolling her eyes, and walking out.

*   *   *

After Thomas left, Lucy spent the rest of her shift in a nervous trance. She hated how jealous she felt about Thomas dining with other women, but there was no arguing that it was her own fault. This was the bed she'd made, so now she needed to just roll around in it and get comfortable.

"Thanks again for letting me have the hottie's table," Tania said, snapping her out of her hazy fog of regrets, as they were cleaning up at the end of the shift. "Not only is he beautiful, but he's a great tipper, too."

"Oh, good, I'm glad," Lucy said and was suddenly

struck with curiosity. "Did he use a credit card?"

"Huh? No, cash. Why do you ask?"

"Just wondering. Wanted to know if you got his name."

"Sadly, no," Tania replied. "And since he was with that beautiful woman, I didn't try to get his number, either."

"Did they seem like they were on a date?" Lucy asked, terrified to hear the answer but also so curious she couldn't stop herself from asking the question.

"Uh...I guess? They seemed like they really knew each other well. Lots of teasing and laughter. That sort of thing." Tania looked thoughtful for a moment. "Definitely too familiar with each other for a first date, that's for sure."

Lucy was crushed by this. Was that woman a steady, long-time girlfriend? Her heart was beating wildly as she tried to ask her next question with an air of disinterest. "What makes you say that?"

"Oh, I don't know. Just some of the things they said. Like he asked if she was going to get her usual. That sort of thing." Tania gave the counter a final wipe as she glanced up at the clock. "Guess it's time for us to head out of here. No more dreaming about hot guys who look like they wandered off a movie set straight into this dump."

She watched Tania walk toward the break room as her words bounced around Lucy's tired mind until a lightbulb turned on...*Is Thomas an* actor?

He certainly was gorgeous enough to be one. Hadn't Tania just this morning compared him to all those first-name-Chris actors? And only yesterday hadn't he told her that his job came with a certain lifestyle that included women hanging around wanting to sleep with him? She could totally picture that happening to an actor. He also told her that he traveled a lot—movie set to movie set?—but that the main headquarters was somewhere else. Somewhere…like Hollywood?

It all fit like puzzle pieces snapping into place to create a bigger picture. This was it. He was probably an actor. Or…maybe a stuntman? From the very first time she saw him, he seemed like someone who worked outdoors and likely did something physical for a living. Stuntman fit that description. And he had gotten hurt on the job after all, which surely happened to stuntmen all the time. It was a job he couldn't return to until he cleared what was apparently extremely strict concussion protocols. That would also fit with him being a stuntman. No movie producer would want the liability of an already-injured stuntman getting hurt further. And it fit that he was worried she'd recorded his outburst in the park and posted it to social media. Anyone associated with Hollywood would be afraid of that kind of bad press, surely.

She smiled with satisfaction at her detective work, but then the smile slowly fell away. What did it even matter that she'd likely figured out his career? That didn't change anything between them. She was still stuck in the rotting landfill her life had become. And he was mostly healed up and ready to leave soon. Which meant he was free to have fabulous meals with fabulous people whenever and wherever he wanted. She had absolutely no right to be jealous. Thomas was leaving soon, and she was going to have to stay here stewing in her own heartache while she watched him fly away to his old life.

A life that probably would never include her.

Chapter 18

TOMMY CHECKED his phone again in frustration. This appointment was supposed to be over by now. He should already be sitting in the park. Instead, he'd arrived in plenty of time only to wind up spending more than an hour hanging out in a packed waiting room while the minutes ticked by. The doctor became backed up due to some sort of emergency, or so the receptionist said. Now it was looking like he was going to miss today's time with Lucy entirely. It was especially frustrating since they had so few days left to spend with each other.

"The headaches are completely gone?" Dr. Singh asked him, shaking Tommy out of these thoughts. He watched Singh typing into his notes before looking back to await Tommy's response.

"Well…*completely* gone is a stretch," Tommy admitted, trying to think back to the last couple headaches he'd had. "I'd estimate they're down to maybe two or three a week? Something like that."

"Hmm, well, that looks to be a significant improvement from the last time we spoke. Then you said they were still happening daily. To confirm, they are no longer a *daily* occurrence?"

"No, definitely not daily. I don't think I've had one since…Sunday? Maybe Monday?" Tommy tried to think back. "I was logging them for a long time, but I stopped when they weren't as frequent."

"And the nausea? Are you still experiencing that?"

"Nope, nothing and not for a while now," Tommy replied. "Really, other than the occasional headache, I'm feeling great."

"Well, I'm happy to say the MRI results agree with your assessment. I think it's time, Thomas. I'm officially releasing you to the care of the team doctors and signing off," Singh said with a smile as he stood up and reached to shake Tommy's hand. "Congratulations. You took this time of healing and rest seriously, and now it's going to pay off. So just wait here a few more minutes while I find out if there's anything further the team needs in order to make things official."

"Oh okay, sure, yeah," Tommy said as he glanced at his phone again. The only thing that was official right now was that he wasn't going to make it in time to see Lucy. She'd be leaving their bench in about ten minutes, give or take. But still, he had just received great news, which he knew he needed to share despite not being able to reach the one person he wanted to tell the most.

Still...Lucy knew I had an appointment today. Hopefully, she figured out that I got held up here.

He took a moment to text his parents and his agent. Then he texted Dante and a few other teammates too. As an afterthought, he updated Jenna as well, although he'd already told her days ago that he was likely getting the doctor's sign off today. She'd wanted to celebrate early, which is how they'd ended up grabbing breakfast at a nearby diner before his appointment that morning. He'd hoped he could fit everything in, but all it had taken was one backed-up doctor's waiting room to annihilate that plan. He'd have to wait to give Lucy his good news tomorrow.

Tommy smiled as congratulatory texts started to light up his phone. Everyone was thrilled that he'd found his way through his injury and was able to rejoin the team when spring training began in a few weeks.

Singh returned to tell him he was all set. Tommy looked at his phone for the hundredth time, confirming it was too late to see Lucy. But he decided to head to the park anyway. *Who knows,* he thought, *maybe I'll luck out. Maybe today she'll wait a bit longer so I can tell her how the appointment went....*

*   *   *

Buzzing with an energy that should have been fueled by the excitement of rejoining his team but was mostly about seeing Lucy, Tommy got on the familiar walking path and headed toward the bench. He could find that bench in his sleep at this point. Muscle memory guiding him there, he answered his phone without even glancing at the screen when he felt it buzzing in his pocket.

"Hello?"

"Tommy Boy! You did it!" Jack's booming voice caught him by surprise, causing Tommy to hold the phone away from his ear with a laugh. "The doctors tell me you got the official stamp of approval, and you're ready to head down to Florida with the team in a few weeks."

"That's right," Tommy said. Hearing Jack's voice made it finally seem real somehow. Suddenly he could feel that old familiar drive to play the game he loved once again thrumming through his veins. These weren't empty words, either—he really *was* ready to play again. "The headaches are down to an occasional nuisance," he went on, "and I'm feeling great, Jack. I'm ready to prove to you...to myself...to everyone, I can do this."

"That's terrific, Tom. Just what we wanted to hear. But you know your place on the team isn't automatic, right son?" The coach paused for a second to let his words soak in before continuing. "You're still, for all intents and purposes, a rookie. You're going to have to show up in that camp with absolute focus, drive, and intensity. No distractions. No messing around. The team's going to want to see that and more from you before they fully believe that you're back to one-hundred percent. I'm rooting for you, kid, I really am. I'm on your side, but you're the one who's going to have to make it happen."

"Thank you, and yes, I hear you loud and clear," Tommy said confidently, even as he was hoping he could live up to Jack's expectations. He did plan, after all, to be regularly distracted with calls and texts from Lucy. Would having her in his life more fully help him and make him stronger, or would she keep his mind off his goals?

"One more thing, kid," Jack added, "and then I'll let you go celebrate. Don't take your eyes off the prize now. Just because the doctor took you off those protocols doesn't mean you can be out partying and living it up in these next few weeks. I don't care what he said or what the team doctors say; as far as I'm concerned, you're still taking it easy. No stress, no parties, nothing that's going to get in the way of your success at camp. You got me?"

"Sure, Coach, I hear you," Tommy said with a chuckle. "I'm not exactly sure I could find a wild time here if I even wanted to, though. My life has been really quiet since I got here, and I see no reason why that would change in the next few weeks."

"Make sure it doesn't, or you're going to hear

about it from me, son," Jack said. "I don't want you tripping at the finish line."

"I won't," Tommy replied just before they ended the call. "I promise."

*   *   *

The park bench was in view now, and Tommy was disappointed to see it empty. Lucy had left for the day.

He hadn't actually expected her to be here, but he still felt annoyed all over again at the delay that had caused him to miss her. *It seems like something is always standing in our way,* he thought as he sat in his usual spot. Most of those roadblocks were coming from Lucy herself and her desire to deal with her mysterious problems alone. Now his career was going to be yet another hurdle in their path. If it was this hard to be together, maybe they really weren't meant to be. Maybe the universe was screaming at him to just make a clean break and start fresh.

Wait, what? Did I just use the phrase "meant to be"?! Did he even believe in fate and finding The One? He never thought so in the past. But now....

Before he met Lucy, he likely would have laughed at such ideas. He hadn't been exaggerating when he told Lucy about his previous experiences with women. He'd always pretty much been a "love 'em and leave 'em" type. No ties. No commitments. No dates or romance. He wanted to focus on the game and his career with nothing and no one tying him down. Ever.

But with Lucy everything was...different. With all that had happened, *he* felt different. Suddenly he was a romantic sap who danced with her in the park even though there was no music while simultaneously angling for a bigger commitment. He'd never done anything even close to this before. This wasn't who he was. Lucy had come into his life and rearranged everything, all without ever lifting a finger or, quite frankly, leaving her park bench.

Yet he couldn't lie to himself—it *did* sort of seem like circumstances were conspiring to keep them apart. Finding a way to be with Lucy wasn't exactly the safe and easy road to take here. He could jet off to Sarasota without another word, and she'd have no way to find him. What they had together would simply cease to exist. Surely that was the *easier* path. Then he wouldn't have to worry about the distractions Jack was telling him to avoid. In that scenario, he'd have absolutely nothing but the game of baseball and his drive to succeed in it. Thanks to all of Lucy's rules and demands, it would be the simplest, cleanest break in history. It would free her up to put those blinders on that she loved so much and fully focus her attention on her mother and whatever else was going on in her life.

The fact that she still hadn't shared the rest of her burdens with him still bothered him. That was the other part that made breaking things off seem like a smart option. What was holding her back? Why not just tell him all of it? Those unanswered questions were troubling. In most ways he fully believed she was exactly who she said she was. But when he thought too long about her persistent secrecy? Well...there was a part of him that couldn't help wondering, even now, if he was somehow getting played. He had no idea what she would possibly gain from such a scheme, but the doubt persisted. If he walked away, those worries would disappear right along with everything else.

Even as these thoughts and options swirled around his mind, Tommy knew there was no way he'd just take off and never see her again. Because ending it with her was anything *but* the easy option here. That was a joke. Leaving her now was already going to gut him, even if they did exchange numbers and stay in touch to continue their...friendship or whatever was the correct term for what they had. But to simply disappear with no hope of a further connection? To know he'd never see her or hold her again...? Tommy's pulse raced at the thought of it.

No, he decided as he stood up and started making his way back to the path. The universe might not want to make this relationship easy for either of them, but that was too bad. He was going to see it through no matter the obstacles.

"Bring it on," he said out loud as he walked away from the empty bench.

Chapter 19

"HEY, LUCY, if you're hoping these plates will serve themselves, you're in for a long wait!" Pat snapped at her from the kitchen window. "Move it!"

"Yeah, yeah, sorry," she said, shaking her head in frustration as she went to retrieve the orders. It had been a long and miserable morning filled with lots of mistakes and very unhappy customers. And it was only a couple hours into the shift, which now felt interminable.

"Okay, what gives?" Mona asked as Lucy went behind the counter to find a replacement ketchup bottle. "Looks like Mona's therapy couch is going to get its daily use."

"I…no, it's nothing," Lucy answered, shaking her head as she snagged the bottle and turned to head back to her table.

"Don't play games with me, Lucy. I can see something's bothering you. And so can every single other creature in this place, by the way, including the customers and all their broken dishes. Make this easier on everyone and just get it off your chest."

"Honestly, it's nothing, really. I'm just extremely tired, Mona, that's it. I couldn't sleep at all last night. My mom was incredibly restless, so I was up and down worrying and checking on her. Plus…well, I have a lot on my mind anyway. Even when my mom was calm and able to sleep, I wasn't."

"Okay, alright. I'm sorry to hear that. Now go deliver that ketchup and try to finish this shift without killing anyone. But before you leave, I want you to tell me what's got you so tied up that you can't sleep, do you hear me?" Mona's eyes narrowed as she studied Lucy's face. "Promise me."

"I…okay. But why are you being so kind to me?" Lucy asked, genuinely puzzled. Hadn't this very woman called her a moron a few months ago?

"I'm stepping in for someone," Mona answered.

"What?" Lucy asked, puzzled. "What do you mean? Who are you stepping in for? And stepping in for *what* exactly?"

"I'm stepping in for your mother," Mona said simply before picking up the coffee pot and heading to her section.

Lucy was stunned. Mona presented herself as such a tough character, but here she was trying to give motherly advice to Lucy when her own mom wasn't able to fill that role. A wave of love sloshed through her as she eyed Mona through a sheen of tears.

"Lucy? The plates still haven't sprouted legs. What's your next move?" Pat yelled, shaking her out of her dazed reverie.

With a sigh and a swipe at her eyes, she took a deep breath and turned back toward her section, the ketchup bottle still in her hand. Through sheer grit and determination, she managed to make it through the rest of her shift without collapsing or dropping anything else. She wasn't even sure she would be able to go to the park after work. And, honestly, she wasn't sure she wanted to anyway, considering what happened the day before. She'd sat there alone on that bench waiting for Thomas while he was out with the sun goddess, no doubt having sex all afternoon. Their trip to the diner was probably just a break so they'd had enough energy to keep going.

She'd been devastated when he didn't show up, especially since she'd just seen him having a great time earlier that day. So obviously he wasn't sick. Clearly something else had happened. Was this the end? Was the little park-bench fairytale over now? Was he tired of her demands and limitations? Had he been cleared by the doctors, paving the path for him to immediately reunite with the sun goddess and jet back to Hollywood?

And will I ever see him again?

She felt like such a sap. A huge part of her had believed he'd arrive and share some hilarious tale about how he'd gotten stuck having a late breakfast with someone to whom he wasn't attracted at all. Or maybe he'd talk about how he had taken her out to breakfast to let her down easy and explain that he was in a solidly committed non-relationship with a bench lady whose full name he didn't know.

Lucy rolled her eyes at her own stupidity. These were *her* terms and *her* limitations. Thomas had done nothing wrong, no matter where he was right now and what—or who—he was currently doing. She had absolutely nothing to be upset about, and no reason that she should be up all night fretting.

And yet....

She grabbed her bag and sweater out of her locker and turned around to find Mona waiting patiently.

"I got things to do, missy. Just get it off your chest and don't make me yank it out of you word by word," she said impatiently, looking at her watch. "Let's hear it."

"Okay, okay. It's just that…Thomas…the guy I was telling you about. The one who was here yesterday…."

"Yes, yes, I know who you mean. Go on."

"Well, you know he was here yesterday with a stunningly gorgeous woman who looked like she just walked off a runway in Milan," Lucy said, playing with her bottom lip nervously now.

"Okay…," Mona prodded.

"Well, he and I always meet at noon in the park, but yesterday he didn't show up. So, then it made me think he was probably still with the runway model. He's been telling me for a while that he'll be leaving soon." Lucy hesitated here, not liking the words as they left her mouth, as though she might actually be speaking her worst fears into existence. Still, she'd come this far, so she may as well say it all. "So…you know…maybe that's it. Maybe it's over. Maybe he's already gone. You told me yesterday to grab my happiness, but, well, it might already be too late. I think I blew it, big time."

"Yep, you might be right," Mona said, an abruptness clipping each word.

"I…what?" Lucy asked, startled that Mona wasn't trying to comfort her more. *This was her motherly advice?!*

"I told you the games you were playing might not end well for you," Mona went on, shaking her head as Lucy struggled to fight against a fresh round of tears. Mona studied this for a moment before a softer look crossed her face. "But don't tell me that you're just giving up. I mean, come on—that's it? You're not going to go back to that park every single day until your man shows up with an explanation? That's not the Lucy I've come to know."

"I'm just so *tired*, Mona. And I don't want to be disappointed again today. Not when all I'm running on is fumes and despair. I still have the rest of the day and night with my mom to get through, after all." Lucy shook her head and exhaled deeply.

"Listen, get your tired butt over to that park and try again," Mona said. "And when the time is up, come back over here and pick me up. I'll come with you to watch your mom while you get a few hours' sleep. How does that sound?"

A tear that Lucy had been struggling to hold back trickled now down her face. She wiped at it as a small smile crept onto her face. "You'd really do that for me? Mona, a minute ago you were impatiently checking your watch. You clearly have better things to do. Plus, it's a huge thing for me to ask of you. My mom can really be a handful when she gets stubborn about something."

"If you ask me, those stubborn genes of hers ran mighty strong, and you're not the one asking anyway. I'm the one offering. So go on," Mona said as she made shooing motions with her hands. "Get moving, and I'll see you…when? In an hour?"

"You're the best, you know that?" Lucy said with a sniff. "Okay, okay, I'm going to take your wonderful gift, but I'm not sure that I could repay it in a million years."

"Not asking you to, child," Mona said, sounding affronted. "Now, I'm not telling you again, get on out of here."

Lucy let out a hiccupy laugh and then did what Mona was urging her to do: She left immediately and headed straight for the park.

Hopefully, this time Thomas would be there.

Chapter 20

PLEASE, *please, please....*

This silent chant bounced through her worried mind as she all but ran through the park, nerves fueling her and propelling her exhausted body forward.

Please, please, please....

She stopped before the final turn toward the clearing that held their bench and inhaled, trying to slow her breathing and relax her nerves. It would be okay. She would be okay. Whether he was there or not, she would survive. Everything was going to be fine....

Satisfied with her internal pep talk, Lucy stood straight, took another deep breath, and rounded the corner to find...Thomas.

Happiness fluttered through her, causing a smile to slowly appear on her face. Even if he was there to tell her he'd eloped yesterday with the goddess, he was still here. She had a chance to see him again, even if it was just this one last time.

She hadn't realized until that moment precisely how crazy she was about him. *Boy am I in for a rough landing when he leaves town*, she thought.

"You're really here," she said as he spotted her. She slowly approached the bench as she added, "I'm so happy to see you again."

"Of course I'm here, angel," he said, rising to greet her. He looked like he wanted to hug her, or maybe that was her own desires she was projecting onto him. She hesitated to move too close, however, as her earlier doubts and fears were still rattling around in her weary mind. In the end, they just stared at each other for a long, intense moment before she finally broke the gaze and lowered herself onto the bench.

"Lucy, what's wrong?" he asked. "Is this about yesterday? Because I didn't show up?"

Lucy watched him sit down next to her, angling his body in her direction.

"Yes?" she finally replied, hesitancy causing her to say the word like it was a question.

"Believe me, I was plenty frustrated that I had to break our bench date," he said as a cloudy look crossed his face. "The doctor's office was backed up with some emergency. I sat in the waiting room forever, watching the time tick by and worrying I'd miss you. When I finally got here, you were long gone."

"You came here anyway?" she asked, feeling a small surge of happiness. "Why?"

"Hoping maybe you'd waited for me," he said. "I had some great news to share with you."

"Really? What's your news?"

"The MRI looks good. My headaches are mostly gone. So, this is it. The doctor cleared me. I'm approved to return to my...my job."

"Oh, wow, Thomas, I'm so happy for you, I really am." Lucy's heart felt like it was splitting in two. "When do you have to leave?"

"In a couple of weeks. And before I go, you're giving me your number so we don't have anymore of these misses and misunderstandings, okay?" Thomas asked in a decidedly urgent tone. "We don't need any extra problems between us. We're all set. We've got plenty."

"True," Lucy replied with a small, rueful laugh. *This was good*, she told herself. He was still here and seemingly still wanted to pursue at least a long-distance friendship. She hadn't thrown away her happiness the way Mona predicted. It was still right here in front of her. *He* was still right here in front of her.

And yet….

"Why do I get the feeling that you've still got more on your mind?" Thomas asked as he looked closely at her face. "Are you feeling okay? You look worn out."

"Yeah, I *am* worn out. I had a terrible night," she confessed. "My mom was up and down a million times, and I just couldn't get my brain to shut off so I could relax."

"I'm sorry to hear about your mom. I can only imagine how difficult it is to care for her full time," Thomas said. "And I know you've said you've got a bunch of other issues to deal with. Are those the things that were keeping you up all night?"

"Well, no…," she said, trailing off. Should she bring up the runway model? Clearly Thomas still wanted to spend time with *her*, despite whatever relationship he had with that other woman. Was it enough to know he still cared and was committed to their friendship? Should she just let it go?

"Then what's wrong?" he asked, reaching over to grab her hand. She looked down and watched as his strong fingers laced together with hers. A feeling of warmth and security coiled through her at his simple touch. "You can tell me anything."

This was it—her opportunity to ask him about that brunch yesterday. Wouldn't it be better to know what he had to say about it than letting the worries and doubts continue to fester? She didn't want him to think she was a clingy, desperate type, but still....

She looked up from their joined hands to study his kind, green eyes. Indecision held her back a moment before the words tumbled out of her mouth before she even realized she was about to speak.

"I saw you," she said. "Yesterday."

"You did?" he asked, surprised. "When I came to the park late? You should have said something!"

"No, no, I left at my usual time." She still wasn't sure if this conversation was the right one to be having. *Sorry...too late now,* a voice in her mind told her. "I saw you earlier. When you went to the diner."

"Okay, I'm still lost here. Why didn't you stop and say hi?" Thomas asked, confusion marking his handsome face. "Wait, is this part of your rules for keeping me at arm's length? You didn't want to say hi because we weren't on this blasted bench?"

"I...no!" Lucy said, surprised by how quickly his tone had turned to irritation or maybe even anger. "No, I didn't approach you because...well, you were with that beautiful woman. I didn't want to interrupt your...well, your date, I guess."

A sunny smile broke slowly across his face at that moment, his white teeth contrasting vividly against the golden skin. He squeezed her hand and sat back, looking smug now. "You're jealous."

"No! I wasn't jealous at all," Lucy said, thrown into sarcasm by his reaction. He wasn't exactly tripping over himself to reassure her here. "I enjoyed very much knowing that you're doing your part to keep the sun-goddess population fed. Thank you for your service."

Thomas chuckled, squeezed her hand again, turned to face her once more, then lifted his other hand to her face, lightly tracing his finger down her cheek. "You're beautiful, angel. And I love that you got so jealous. It tells me you feel as strongly about me as I feel about you. Because if I saw you out with another guy, I'd probably be flipping tables."

"Okay, then who is she?" Lucy asked. "Why shouldn't *I* be the one flipping tables right now?"

"Aside from the fact that there aren't any tables around here?" he teased.

"Yes. My tables are metaphorical tables," Lucy countered. If he was teasing her this much, the goddess couldn't really be much competition, could she?

"Well, you missed an opportunity yesterday to meet my baby sister, Jenna," he answered finally. "She's the sun goddess, and we were out celebrating my imminent release from the concussion protocols. I've told her about you, you know. She would have loved to meet you."

"Your…your sister?" Lucy sputtered in response as she processed this information. "Jenna?"

"My sister. Jenna. Yes, she's my sister." He repeated all this very slowly, as if she was a complete idiot, the teasing smile still firmly in place. "I've told you over and over that I want us to move our friendship beyond a friendship, off this bench, and straight out of this park. I meant every word, angel. I'm not off secretly dating other women. I've been focusing on two things in my life: recovering and spending time with you. That's it."

Lucy searched his eyes for any traces of deception, but her heart already knew there weren't any. "I'm so sorry, Thomas," she said. "I saw you and every doubt, regret, and feeling of jealousy in the world just came raining down on me. I almost didn't even come here today. I figured you'd gotten cleared by the doctor, grabbed your beautiful breakfast date, and took off for the future."

"I've been filled with worries and doubts myself, angel. I'm not going to lie to you," Thomas said. "Part of me wondered if I should take the easy path after the doctor cleared me and cut ties with you. Focus exclusively on rebuilding my career in the wake of this extended time away from it."

"You did?" Lucy asked, her heart stuttering. He'd just given voice to every fear she had. "What stopped you?"

"*You* did," he said with a sexy half-smile on his face, which pulled her focus down to his lips for a moment as he continued his explanation. "Leaving you could never be the easy way for me, even though you drive me crazy with all your secrecy and rules."

"Yeah, well, a wise woman told me I need to make things simpler between us and grab my happiness while I can," Lucy replied, looking back into his eyes once again.

"Mona?" Thomas guessed. "Your beloved co-worker and current Zen master?"

"Yep," she said. "I guess she's right. My stalling and holding back isn't actually fixing any of my problems, it's just creating new ones. But since you're leaving soon, I don't want to…well…I don't know. Let's just keep things as they are for now. I need to think about this more when I'm not so tired. When you're ready to leave in a couple weeks, we'll exchange numbers at the very least and then see where life takes us, I guess."

Thomas's smile faded a bit, but he said, "Okay, I guess that works."

"I'm sorry I'm still holding back, Thomas, really I

am," Lucy replied, desperate for him to understand. "It's not that I don't want to jump into a relationship with you immediately. It's just that…I don't know, I still have so much to work through. So much to figure out. I just need a bit more time. That's it. Can you give me that?"

Thomas shrugged. "I guess I don't have much choice in the matter, do I?"

Lucy squeezed his hand in response. She simply needed to think everything through. Surely he could understand that. She was too exhausted right now to make any real plans, changes, or decisions anyway. It was plenty that he'd explained what she'd seen yesterday. He wasn't dating anyone. He hadn't meant to skip their time together. She believed him about all of that. He was simply healed up and feeling better and looking toward the next chapter of his life. And yes, he was on the verge of returning to his old life without her. But he was also taking great pains to ensure he had a way to keep in touch with her. What more could she ask from him?

As for what *she* wanted? Everything was the same as before: She wanted a few stolen moments of sunshine in her otherwise gloomy world. Simple peace and quiet on a secluded bench. She wasn't letting her chance at happiness slip through her fingers, though, like Mona warned. No, her future was still sitting right here on this bench with her, his hand still holding hers.

For now, it was going to have to be enough.

Chapter 21

THE THUD OF his sneakers hitting the pavement in a steady rhythm matched the pulsing guitars and drumbeat of the song currently wailing through his earbuds.

Classic rock and metal had always been his genres of choice, especially when he was out running, something he typically did almost every single day. Well, something he *used* to do almost every single day. The doctors had severely limited his physical activity since the accident, so now that he was cleared by Dr. Singh, this was the first time since he'd been injured that he was free to run.

Freedom. That's what running felt like to him. Cool morning air. Quiet roads not yet full of honking commuters heading to their jobs or shouting kids walking to school. Nope, just him and his thoughts and the tunes randomly popping up on his playlist.

The driving rock song he was listening to ended then, and the quiet opening strains of a slower song began. *Patience,* he thought, easily identifying the familiar Guns 'N Roses song. Easing his pace to match the softer rhythm of the song, he listened as Axl Rose's familiar voice filled his ears.

The lyrics automatically wove their way into his thoughts about Lucy. Since they'd met, there had been plenty of times when he hadn't been sure about her. Her hesitation to share almost any part of herself had filled him with doubt. But after their conversation yesterday—after he saw how jealous she'd become after seeing him with Jenna? Well, she had set his mind at ease, just like the song said. She definitely had worked her way into his heart. He felt more for her—a woman he knew next to nothing about—than he'd ever felt for anyone. It wasn't even close. Yes, they had many obstacles in between them. But Tommy couldn't imagine walking away or giving up now.

Patience. That was the key here. He had to keep being patient. *I'm taking advice from rock songs now,* he thought with an internal laugh. But hey, rock song or not, it was good advice. He *did* just need to keep being patient and give Lucy the time she wanted. Things were going to work themselves out in the end, he was absolutely confident of that. After all, look how his own problems had finally resolved themselves. A few short months ago, he couldn't even turn his head without wanting to throw up. And now he was running again, the pain and headaches practically a distant memory. He was going to rejoin his team in a few short weeks, throw himself into spring training, and give the team absolutely no room for doubt that his rightful place was as the starter in right field. It was all there in front of him. He just had to reach out and grab it.

As the song ended, he heard a call coming in. So, he slowed his pace, came to a stop, and bent over to catch his breath as he checked the screen. He wished for the hundredth time that Lucy had his number and that it might be her calling....

But no, it was Dante. His buddy from the team was calling. Tommy straightened up and answered it.

"Hey, D, you got my text with my big news?" Tommy asked, gaspy and breathless.

"I did my boy! Congrats!" Dante said. "Just wanted to see what we can do about celebrating. You heading to Sarasota early by any chance? We could light it up before training kicks in."

"Nah, man, sorry. I'm not heading there until I have to report, day one," Tommy replied, wiping the sweat off his forehead with the bottom of his t-shirt.

"Oh yeah? I know what this is. That hottie who wouldn't tell you her name still has you on the hook, twisting in the wind, doesn't she?" The glee was evident in Dante's playful tone. "You with her now?"

"No…yes…I mean, I don't know, man," Tommy said, as Dante's laughter pealed out. "Not going to lie, I still don't know much about her—even her last name. She just wants to take it extremely slowly while she works some problems out. I'm really into her though, D. Hook, line, and sinker. She wants me to wait? I wait."

"Hmm," Dante's teasing tone was gone now. "I don't know, man. You sure she's not playing you? Stringing you along while she dates other guys or something? I don't like the sound of this."

"I know, I know. I've had my doubts along the way, too, trust me. But…I know this makes almost no sense, but I'd be willing to bet any amount of money she is exactly who she says she is."

"Okay, I'll bite," Dante replied, skepticism still lacing his words. "Who does she say she is?"

"She's someone who's stuck in a terrible time in her life," Tommy explained. "No laughter. No friends. No fun. She literally goes to work in the morning, sits with me for an hour in the park, then spends the rest of her day watching her mom like a hawk because the woman has severe dementia and might injure herself if she's not supervised."

"That's terrible, Tommy," Dante said, his tone softening now. "And there isn't anyone who can step up and help her?"

"No, there's no other family. But…I don't know. She's got this, I think. Whatever it is. She's so strong and independent. Honestly, that's one of the things that I really love about her." Tommy paused, shocked to hear the word *love* come out of his mouth but not able to examine the idea further at the moment. "I don't know—I've offered to be there for her more but, well, she wants to do this by herself, and I guess I have to stand back and respect that. My current plan is to give her all the space she needs. When she's ready, I'll be here."

"She knows you're leaving for Sarasota, though?"

"Yes. Well, no, not Sarasota specifically," Tommy said. "We still haven't discussed the details of our careers with each other. She still doesn't know I'm a professional athlete."

"I don't know man, I'm still not sure this sounds on the level. But, hey, if she's making you happy, I guess that's what counts. So, back to the reason I called, when are we going to get to celebrate your recovery if you're not showing up here early?"

"No celebrating for me," Tommy replied with a shake of his head. "I promised Jack I wouldn't do anything crazy to jeopardize my return. He said as far as he's concerned, I'm still relaxing until I report."

"We'll see about that," Dante said, the teasing tone back in his voice.

"Oh no you don't," Tommy said with a laugh. "You're not distracting me here. Eyes on the prize. I'm chilling for the next two weeks, going back to camp, and then I'm getting my old spot back. When they tell me I'm back with the team, that's the day I'll celebrate."

"Okay, okay, T," Dante said. "I'll let you go now, but I'll be seeing you real soon, my man. *Real* soon."

Tommy shook his head with a smile as he slid his phone in his pocket, his thoughts about the things he'd told Dante as he started walking in the direction of his apartment. He needed to get home to finish his workout before hitting the shower. He had to make sure he was ready to meet Lucy on time. With their days together quickly coming to an end, he didn't want to do anything that would jeopardize a single moment with her.

He thought more about the conversation he'd just had. He completely understood why Dante seemed so skeptical about the relationship. He knew exactly how crazy it all seemed. But all of that would melt away the minute he saw her, and that's what mattered. At some point, every relationship came down to trust, right? Trust that the other person really cared about you and had your best interests at heart. Trust that the things they said were always true. Trust that there was no one else. It was a gamble everyone took when they put themselves out there in the dating world, right? This situation just called for a bit more trust than most. That was it. He just had to keep being patient....

When Tommy got back to his apartment, he downed a bottle of water and finished his workout. By the time he was showered and dressed, he was ready to hop in his truck and head to the park. As usual, his time in the park was what he looked forward to most, and he couldn't wait to see Lucy again. When he was with her, absolutely everything made sense, and almost anything seemed possible.

Chapter 22

WHEN HE GOT to the park, he went to the bench and waited. Closing his eyes, he allowed himself to relax as happy thoughts bounced through his mind. There was relief he'd been cleared by the doctor. Determination to get back on the team. Happiness that he'd found Lucy. Hope that soon her life would also turn around for the better. And he believed *their* luck would turn soon, too. He could feel it. Good times were heading their way.

"What's got that satisfied look on your face?" she asked, her voice wrapping around him like a caress as he opened his eyes to watch her approach.

"You. Us," Tommy said, standing and extending his hand to her. She hesitated a moment, then reached for it. He drew her closer then, and they stood silently a moment, lost in each other's eyes.

"Hey, beautiful," he said finally, "glad you're here. I've been thinking about you all day."

"No, come on, something's gotten into you. Something's different," she said, a cute, puzzled look on her face as she studied him. It was as though she could read his thoughts if she only looked closely enough.

"Yeah, I guess I'm pretty amped up. Today *has* been different. I got to go running this morning for the first time since my injury. It felt amazing." He broke their gaze and gestured toward the bench. "Here, sit down. I know you're usually exhausted when you get off work."

"Yes, I am," she replied, squeezing his hands before pulling away and sliding into her usual spot on the left side of the bench. "I wasn't the one working out all morning though. So, you're a runner, huh?"

Tommy sat next to her and nodded. "Always have been. It's great cardio, of course, but mostly I just love how free it makes me feel. Like I could go anywhere or do anything. My mind wanders, and I listen to the music in my headphones, and…well, I guess nothing's bothering me then. Nothing's holding me back."

"That sounds amazing," Lucy said, her tone wistful. "I'm glad you were able to return to something you love so much. I am so *not* a runner. But it fits you somehow. From the first time I saw you, I guessed you were the kind of person who liked to be outdoors and doing something physical. You never struck me as an office person."

"You got that right. No spreadsheets and data reports for me," Tommy said. "How about you?"

"Yes to all of it. Spreadsheets, data reports. That's me," Lucy said with a short laugh before a look of frustration clouded her expression. "Well, maybe someday I'll get myself into an office job, that is. I'm not there yet, that's for sure."

"What are you doing now, then?" he asked.

"Just doing what I have to do in order to pay the bills I guess," she said with a shrug. "Getting through things one day at a time. Definitely not in my dream job, though."

"I get that," Tommy said, sorry he'd put that melancholy look back on her beautiful face. "So, I told you about running and how much I love it. What's your version of that? What makes you feel free?"

"Oh, I don't know," she said, looking at her hands now, watching as she twisted them nervously in her lap, then lifting her eyes to meet his again. "This bench and time with you, mostly. The thing is, mainly what's imprisoning me right now is my mom's health situation, which there isn't a cure for, you know? So…well…what would free me would be…well, honestly, it would be a permanent end to her suffering, but I don't want that! She's my mom! How could I possibly want to lose her forever just to put me out of my *own* misery? It's so selfish and too horrible to even think about, and yet…well, I don't have any feelings of freedom right now, and I don't even want to think about that. Does that make sense?"

He nodded. "Of course it does. You're a wonderful daughter and a loving person. I understand that there would be guilt tied to your current situation and any feelings you might have about being free from those responsibilities. Of course you don't want her to suffer but also don't want her to go," Tommy said, feeling terrible for her now. *What would that be like?* he wondered. To be alone and trapped in a situation with the only end in sight being the death of someone you loved?

Suddenly he wanted to change the conversation and take that pained look from her eyes.

"What about when you were a kid?" he asked. "What gave you joy and freedom then?"

"Well, I don't know really. I guess I always loved to read. And from my earliest memories, I had this internal drive to succeed in school, so I was a studious little thing, even in elementary school." Her face was slowly becoming sunny again at these memories. "But freedom? I don't know about that. My parents were older when they had me, and I was their only child. I spent those years pretty much carefully packed in bubble wrap."

"Oh, wow, my childhood was basically the opposite," he said, a small half-smile creasing his face as he thought back. "My life was all about my little pack of neighborhood friends, wheelies on bikes, playing street hockey, and finding the best skateboard parks. I was either jumping off things or breaking them."

"You must have driven your parents crazy with worry," she observed, a cute little furrow appearing between her eyebrows.

"Yeah, well, they decided they needed to find a way to channel all my energy, so…well, that's probably a story for a different day. Short version: Yes, they had their hands full with me."

"How many ER visi…wait, oh wow, you just made me think of something I haven't remembered in forever!" Lucy turned to him, her eyes wide with shock. "I actually have a 'jumping off things and breaking them' story of my own!"

"You? Miss Studious?" he teased.

"Yes, me! I can't believe I forgot about this! We went to a lake in upstate New York one summer, and there was this gorgeous climbing tree," she explained. "You know, like the kind of tree that has tons of sturdy branches just begging to be climbed by a kid?"

"Yeah, okay, I can picture your climbing tree," he said, nodding.

"Our whole week there I just watched that tree, picturing myself climbing up to the very top. I built an imaginary tree house in its branches. It was such a great tree, but I'd always been such a cautious kid. I don't know…I was nervous to go climb it, but I was dying to do it, too."

"So, what happened?"

"On our last full day there, I gathered up the nerve, walked right over to that tree, somehow scrambled up to the first big branch, and then I kept climbing as high as I could go. That tree was everything I'd hoped it would be, so I kept climbing and climbing."

"Is this where you tell me you got to the top, a branch cracked, and you came rolling right down again?"

"You'd think that's how this story ended based on how I've described my childhood for sure," Lucy said. "But here's the crazy part of the story and the reason I can't believe I forgot it for so long: I didn't fall out of the tree, I *jumped*."

"Wait, what? You jumped out of the top of a tall tree?" The little daredevil she was describing definitely didn't fit with his mental picture of her. "Why?"

"I don't know. I got up there, looked down, and just thought…I'm going to fly. For one thing, I don't think I realized how high I'd climbed. But, well, I steadied myself, counted down from three, and just…jumped. For a moment I felt that freedom you were describing before. It was so exhilarating…until I landed and sprained my ankle and fractured my wrist," Lucy said, shaking her head now at the memory. "I paid for that freedom with a lot of pain and weeks of itching inside a cast."

"Wow, what a story," Tommy said, shaking his head and eyeing her thoughtfully. "We need to find something that makes you feel happy and free like that but doesn't involve such a hard landing. I think that should be our new project."

"Our project?"

"Yeah, you know—a way we can help you deal with your current issues, at least as a stress reliever. You need a release valve, Luce. I want to know that after I'm gone, you've still got a way to find some happiness each day. I know you find peace here, but will the park bench still offer that to you once I'm gone? Is it going to be enough? Will you keep coming here to find peace and relaxation?"

She shrugged. "I don't know. It might just make me miss you too much, Thomas. But, well, I think you're probably right. I'm going to need something more. I mean, clearly jumping out of trees won't answer any of my problems, but I do need find some sort of relaxed happy place for my own well-being. I can't keep living at this maximum stress level forever. And I've said this before, but I've got to find a way to take my blinders off. Something in my life has got to give."

Thomas leaned back, satisfied that he'd finally found a way he could help her. No one could keep up such a steady slog of misery without losing their mind. She had to find a way to release her inner tree jumper again. It may not completely release her from all her worries, but she had to find a way to feel that freedom again.

He studied her face carefully as he turned the idea around in his mind.

Yep, he thought happily, *change is coming*.

Chapter 23

"SO, LUCY, Mona tells me that you're finally coming out with us for girls' night!" Tania said, her words tumbling after each other in a squealing rush. "We're so excited! My friends Kelly and Izzy and me—and you, Miss Busyallthetime—we're all going to dance and drink and check out hot guys and stuff our faces with amazing things like guacamole and chips and...I don't know, but it's going to be amazing! Wear the tiniest, tightest, sexiest thing you own because we're going to be turning some heads tonight!"

"Mona? Said I'm coming?" Lucy parroted, confused and startled. She pulled her phone away from her ear and looked down at it as though it would suddenly answer all of life's mysteries for her. "Guacamole? Tight clothes? Um...I'm sorry Tania, I'm sure you guys will have a fabulous time, but no, it's going to have to be without me. I'm home and taking care of my mom tonight. There must have been some kind of misunderstanding."

"Nope, not a misunderstanding at all," Tania said, with a short laugh. "Mona told me you'd fight this. She said, and I quote, 'You tell that girl to get herself prettied up, and I'll be at her house to stay with her mom by nine.' So, you see? Mona says it's happening? Girl, it's *happening*."

"Oh, I...wow, I just...." Lucy found she couldn't form an articulate thought, let alone a complete sentence. This was a wonderful gesture by Mona, of course. But honestly, if she had some free time to herself for the first time in ages, she wouldn't spend it dancing and drinking. She'd rather use the time to study for the bar. Take a long bubble bath, maybe. Or, even better, spend time with Thomas—if she could ever get over herself and just exchange numbers with him like a normal person, that is.

But even as those thoughts floated through her mind, she knew there was no use in fighting this. She was an idiot for not having Thomas's contact information yet, so she couldn't be with him this evening even if she could plead for a change in plans. And Mona was a steam roller when she made up her mind about something anyway. Tania was right: If Mona had given this plan the green light, it was happening. "Okay, fine. So, am I…meeting you somewhere?"

"Nope, we'll come to get you a little after nine. We'll give Mona a few minutes to get settled in, then we're off to light up the town. Don't worry, she already gave us your address…." Then Tania ended the call before Lucy could formulate any further protests.

"Great…thanks…," Lucy said into the now-silent phone before tossing it on the counter and looking over at her mother, who was entranced by a Spanish novella on the television. Her mom didn't speak Spanish, but, for whatever reason, she appeared to be enjoying the bright colors and loud music and high drama.

She was having a good day, thankfully, so Mona shouldn't have too much trouble caring for her. Lucy had been able to nap for a few blissful hours the day before while Mona sat with her, and it had all worked out fine. So, this should be okay, too. Still…Lucy couldn't quite figure out why, but she felt uneasy about this plan. She honestly didn't want to be doing this whole going-out-on-the-town thing at all. Sure, she knew Mona would care for her mother as if she were her own, and yet....

She shook off these worries—which were so vague that she couldn't even explain them to herself—and headed to her closet, certain even as she walked toward it that she wouldn't be finding much to match Tania's "tight, sexy, and tiny" demands. She did her best and ended up with a black cocktail dress she'd bought for social events when she was interning at the law office. It did not scream "young and sexy" at all. It hit more of an "I'm mature and shop with coupons" vibe. Oh well.

Hey, maybe next time they'll give me more warning, she thought with an eyeroll as she examined herself in the mirror.

She wasn't sure what to do with her hair. It was long enough to gather up into all sorts of amazing and dramatic up-dos, but she'd never been one to play and experiment with it much. She mostly left it hanging. It fell pin straight without needing a flat iron. She eyed it a few moments longer, but in the end, she just pulled it back in a low ponytail before examining herself again.

Yeah, she thought, *good enough.*

She took a peek out at her mother, who was still watching the television. *Okay for the moment....*

Now...make-up. This was another area where she'd never really played around much. As a lifelong glasses wearer, she had always figured why bother? She tended to only put it on for big occasions. Although she wouldn't exactly call this surprise outing a major life event, she still leaned over, opened the vanity drawer, and pulled out a small bag that contained her tiny collection: a few eyeshadows, a blush, an eyeliner, and a mascara. Just the basics. She played with it a while, trying to give herself a subtle, smoky eye effect before deciding what she had done would have to be good enough.

She put her glasses back on, stood back, and inspected the results of her efforts. Truthfully, she looked...tired. And she still couldn't shake the sensation that she really didn't want to be doing this. That she really *shouldn't* be doing this. Was it because of her mother? She pondered that for a moment. *No...I don't think that's it.* She knew Mona would take excellent care of her. Was it because she naturally didn't like distractions? Sure...that was probably part of it. But was there more to this feeling? Something that had to do with Thomas, even?

Yes...actually, I'll bet that's exactly where these feelings are coming from.

She'd been telling Thomas for weeks and months now that she had no spare time in her life. And she really didn't. But she hadn't counted on Mona sledgehammering her way into the situation and shoving her into the world again.

Should she call Mona and beg for her to understand how exhausted she was and how much she really wasn't in the mood for drinking and dancing? Mona didn't strike her as a romantic, exactly. But surely if she just explained that it really wasn't fair to her and her, um...*boyfriend?* No, that wasn't right. Thanks to her own roadblocks and hesitations, he wasn't a boyfriend. *Crush?* No, that didn't fit, either. Her feelings for Thomas were so much more than a simple crush.

Thomas was...her *person.* The One.

She'd never let herself really label her feelings for

him before that moment. And yet even as these new thoughts floated through her mind, she knew they were absolutely true. However you wanted to categorize it, Thomas was *it* for her. She was certain of this even though she'd built barrier after barrier between them. Despite her fears and worries and problems, he'd patiently understood and supported her. He'd even been talking about working together to find a way for her to relax and once again "find freedom," as he'd called it. If he understood that she desperately needed a way to gain peace in her life, especially now that he was leaving, he'd surely understand why she was going along with Mona and Tania's scheme to help her get out of the house, right?

Yes, definitely.

She'd tell him all about it tomorrow. If he could understand why she'd asked him to wait this long, there was absolutely no reason in the world why he wouldn't totally get this too.

Thomas would understand.

Chapter 24

SHE WANDERED out of the bathroom and settled onto the end of the couch opposite her mother.

"May I help you?" her mother asked, turning toward her quizzically. "Who are you?"

"Just wanted to watch the show with you, Marie," she said, careful not to call her *mom*. She found that it tended to stress out her mother, who mostly thought Lucy—if she thought about her at all—was still a baby. "But can I get you anything to drink?"

"Oh, no, don't trouble yourself, dear," her mother said, turning back to the television and ignoring Lucy now.

The sound of the ringing doorbell startled her just then.

Here we go, Lucy thought with a sigh as she walked over to answer it. She took a deep breath, smoothed a nervous hand over her dress, and pulled the door open. Both Tania and Mona were there. At first, they both smiled in their greeting, but a slow-moving look of horror overtook Tania's features as she examined Lucy more closely.

"Oh girl, no," she said, breezing in, a huge tote bag over her shoulder. "Good thing I brought supplies. I had a feeling you weren't going to follow my directions."

"What?" Lucy asked, giving Mona a wide-eyed *help-me* look as the older woman walked past her with a shrug and moved toward the couch. Lucy's mother, meanwhile, never broke her gaze from the television.

"You're on your own, girl," Mona observed as she sat quietly.

"Come on now, we don't have much time and wow do we have a lot of work to do!" Tania said, tugging on Lucy's hand. "Where's your room?"

Lucy looked over again at Mona and narrowed her eyes in accusation. Mona merely smiled and waved. She apparently wouldn't be getting any reprieve from whatever horrors Tania had in mind. Lucy sighed, then, and begrudgingly led Tania to her room.

"What's in there?" she asked, eyeing the bag suspiciously as Tania dropped it on her bed.

"Everything!" Tania said cheerfully as she began to pull out a wild array of dresses and heels along with make-up, hair clips, brushes, and more.

"Come on, Tania, I put a dress on just like you asked," Lucy said, knowing even as the words left her mouth that the style of her dress did not scream *party*.

"Girl, *what*?" Tania said, looking at her critically again. "You look like you should be handing out lunch detentions, not releasing your inner wild child."

"I don't *have* an inner wild child," Lucy said, even as she unzipped the offending dress and let it pool at her feet. "There. Now what?"

Tania made a happy, clapping gesture and started pulling out an assortment of the tiniest dresses Lucy had ever seen. Then she held them up one by one against Lucy, a thoughtful look on her face as she considered the options.

"Those are way too skimpy and revealing!" Lucy protested. "No way!"

"Way." Tania thrust a shimmery red thing at her.

"I don't even have the right kind of bra for something like this," she tried again, even as she saw the tight, strapless bodice had a bra sewn right into it.

"You're good!" Tania chirped as Lucy rolled her eyes and tugged it on, pulling her bra off as she yanked the bodice into place.

She turned toward the mirror to study the results. *Ugh, I can barely breathe....* And the dress, which was essentially a wide rubber band cinched around her midsection, was ridiculously short. She'd never be able to sit without flashing the room, and her chest was pushed up like something on a Victoria's Secret model. She may not feel like herself, but she couldn't argue with Tania's results, though: She'd definitely never looked this sexy before.

"Wow," she said as she met Tania's eyes in the mirror.

"Wow is right," Tania replied, smiling her approval. "I figured we'd be about the same size, but damn girl, I never dreamed what a total hottie knockout you were going to be! Now let me do your hair and make-up!"

Lucy shook her head with another eyeroll and a laugh, then turned herself over to Tania, who went into a fast-paced beauty overhaul the likes of which Lucy had never experienced before. Curling wands and brushes and bright palettes of shimmering shadows and blushes all marched their way through Tania's hands as she worked through her ministrations. Lucy didn't look in the mirror, instead letting her mind wander as Tania did the fussing. Lucy couldn't help but wish that all this effort was going into a first date with Thomas. *Where would he take me?* she wondered. What would they do? Something traditional like dinner and a movie? Maybe something more romantic like a walk on the beach? She liked the thought of that—her hand in his as they walked along, barefoot in the wet sand, without a care in the world....

Unfortunately, Thomas wasn't coming to take her out, and he wouldn't be seeing her in this ridiculously sexy dress, either. She sighed and looked up to find Tania had already stepped back to evaluate her work.

"You look gorgeous, you know, and we are going to have a blast tonight," Tania said. "So why did it take so long for us to get you out? Because of your mom?"

"Yes, I've basically devoted my life to her care," Lucy said with a shrug. "If Mona wasn't willing to stay with her, this would be impossible."

"Well, I'm so happy she was so willing, then. We're going to go absolutely crazy tonight. And who knows, maybe we'll even find you a man like Cinderella at the ball.... Hmm, I wonder how long Mona would be willing to stay...?" Tania said, a devious look on her face.

"Oh no you don't!" Lucy replied quickly. "No hook-ups with Prince Charming for me. I...I sort of have a guy who I...well, it's special." She couldn't help but stammer awkwardly when talking about the odd non-relationship she and Thomas had formed.

"What, really? But...when do you go out with him?" Tania asked, clearly surprised.

"I don't, that's the problem. I've been putting him off for a while now. I never even dreamed Mona—or anyone else, for that matter—would want to help me in this way. I never even considered it. Now I wish I'd spent more time with him. Turns out, I've pushed him away for no good reason."

"Come on," Tania said, "now that you have the

idea, I'm sure Mona would help you out again."

"It's too late," Lucy went on. "He's leaving town, so it'll be a long-distance thing anyway."

"Well, then, you're just going to have to take this night as the one-off gift that it is," Tania said, her eyes sparkling as she rotated Lucy toward the mirror. "Now, take a look."

Lucy had closed her eyes. Now she took a deep breath and opened them again to see a beautiful stranger looking back.

Her hair was stacked high in a cascade of wispy curls. Her make-up was dark and dramatic, accentuating her cheekbones and causing her light brown eyes to pop and sparkle. She was a glittery goddess; Tania must have cast some sort of spell to make her look this ethereal.

"*Wow*...you should do this professionally, Tan," Lucy said, turning around to face her. "I don't even recognize myself. Seriously, you're a miracle worker!"

"Actually, this is *exactly* what I want to do someday," Tania replied. "Now pick out some heels, and let's go! The girls are waiting for us!"

"No way, I'll kill myself in stilettos!" Lucy said as Tania was eyeing her selection and handing her choices. "How do you even know my size?"

"My girls contributed so I could bring a range. Now choose!" Tania insisted.

Lucy protested some more as she tried on the selection, eventually settling for a shoe with a wedge heel that she thought would at least give her some stability.

By the time they met up with Tania's other friends and walked into the club some thirty minutes later, Lucy had decided to surrender herself completely to the evening. No, she wasn't in her comfort zone. And yes, she still felt vaguely guilty that she was doing precisely what she'd told Thomas she couldn't do at this point in her life. But, well, he had insisted she needed to find a way to release some of the pressure that was constantly weighing her down. She felt pretty. She felt young. And she felt *free*. Allowing herself to enjoy those feelings would accomplish exactly what Thomas wanted for her.

So, she did exactly that. She drank. She talked. She laughed.

And when a group of gorgeous guys at a neighboring table asked them to dance, she said yes.

Chapter 25

Yeah, it was the sound of someone knocking at his door. He rarely had visitors, so it took him by surprise.

Who could it be? Tommy thought idly as he padded out of the bathroom, where he'd just showered after a workout. It'd been a long day, between his morning run, his time with Lucy, and an afternoon of intense exercising. His muscles were thrumming with exhaustion, but so was his mind. He knew he needed to follow the doctor's—and Jack's—warnings and not go so full throttle, but he couldn't help himself today. Yes, he had pushed his body to the limits, but it felt great to do so without restrictions.

I feel free, he thought, a memory of his afternoon conversation with Lucy floating through his mind as he opened the door. He realized too late that he probably should have tossed on a shirt at least. He had pulled on some low-slung sweats, and he was currently dragging a towel across his head with his other hand in a quick effort to dry his hair.

"Well, would you look at that!" Dante hooted as he came bursting through the door. "The gun show's in town, boys!" Dante was followed closely by Santiago, Mick, Jorge, and Conner—all fellow teammates and friends. He had other buddies he considered close as well, some of whom were still in the minors and others who'd been traded along the way. But coming up together through the fire of trying to make it in the big leagues tended to cement lifelong friendships fairly quickly. He considered each and every one of them his brothers.

But still…why are they here?

Tommy laughed as each one stopped to clap him on the back. He hadn't seen any of them since he got injured. "So, to what do I owe this honor? Miss me?"

"You know we do," Jorge said. "There's no better wingman out there, my man."

"Yup, he's not lying," Conner added even as Santiago was nodding, and Mick was heading into the kitchen. Mick started rummaging around in the cabinets, no doubt in search of a snack. He ate constantly. It was a complete mystery as to how he was able to stay in game shape with all the calories he was constantly consuming. Tommy watched in astonishment as Mick found a box of protein bars and eyed them dubiously. "Damnit, T, where's the chocolate?"

"You think T got all jacked up like this eating chocolate?" Santiago asked. "Takes hard work and dedication to be such a pretty boy."

"Hey, show some respect. It's 'pretty *man*'," Thomas said with a chuckle, grabbing a hoodie hanging near the door and pulling it on. "Seriously, everyone make yourselves as comfortable as Mick over there did."

"We don't want to get *too* comfy," Dante replied, even as he was flopping his large frame into the recliner and popping up the footrest. "We've got a hard night of partying and celebrating ahead of us."

"What? Nope, no way," Thomas told him, sitting in the middle of the couch between Conner and Jorge. Santiago, meanwhile, had joined Mick on his quest to pull the kitchen apart in search of empty calories. "I told you on the phone, D. I promised coach I'm staying on the straight and narrow until spring training. That means no partying."

"One little night of drinking and finding some honeys ain't gonna hurt you one bit," Dante said from his perch on the recliner. "It's our job as teammates to welcome you back properly. You didn't want to come to the party, so I brought the party to you."

"You guys, I love that you took the time to come see me, really I do. But I'm serious. I can't do this. One, because of my promise to Jack. And two, well, I've kinda found someone." Tommy wasn't really ready to talk with them about Lucy, yet he was desperate to make them understand why there was no way he was going to continue with them where he'd left off. Things had changed too much during his recovery, and he was no longer the guy who didn't have a care in the world. He had a lot to prove to his coach and his team, plus he had that connection with Lucy. He was well on his way to falling in love with her, he was sure of it. What they had wasn't exactly conventional, he knew. But it felt more real to him than anything he'd ever found with anyone else. By *miles*. She was it for him, and there was no way he would disrespect her by going out and partying to find a bunch of hook-ups. No way.

"Don't listen to him, boys," Dante was saying. "He doesn't even know her name."

Tommy winced at the looks on his buddies' faces, which ran the gamut from amused and confused to outright horrified.

"It's not like it sounds," he insisted. "We're just…taking things slowly while she works through some problems. Her mom has dementia, so she spends most of her time being a caregiver. She doesn't want to mess things up by starting something with me when she's down this low, you know what I mean?"

"All I heard is that you guys haven't started anything yet," Mick called out from the kitchen. "So Tommy's in!"

"Great!" Dante said as though he hadn't heard Tommy plead his case mere moments earlier. "Get dressed. Those beers ain't drinking themselves, my boy!"

"I told you guys, I can't," Tommy said again as he stood up and walked toward the door. "You're not hearing me."

"I got this," Dante said, snapping the footrest down and jumping up out of the chair. He walked over to Tommy, opened the front door, and all but shoved him out in the hallway. Then he shut the door again, so it was only the two of them.

"What the hell, D?" Tommy snapped, his frustration starting to boil now.

"I know where you're coming from," Dante said. "I do. I hear you about your mystery lady and your promise to Jack. But stop right there for just a minute and put yourself in our shoes. I know you went through hell and a lot of pain after that accident. But your boys in there went through something, too. Do you know how hard it was for us to see that pitch take you out? To know you could have *died?* It's a risk we take all the time when we put ourselves at home plate and wait for those laser pitches to come flying at us, and then suddenly all our own personal worst fears happened to you right in front of our eyes. We thought we'd *lost you,* man. Now we come here and find you looking all tan and healthy and fresh-faced like a baby and—so sue us—but we want to celebrate that. Don't take it away from us. Don't blow off what you mean to all your boys in there."

Tommy sighed in frustration and ran his fingers through his hair. "Okay, okay, I hear you. You're right, I didn't think about it from the team's perspective."

"It's cool, man, don't worry about it. So, we got a party on our hands, or what?" Dante asked again as he clapped Tommy on the shoulder.

"Yeah, okay," Tommy agreed half-heartedly, even as a sliver of regret—or was it apprehension?—snaked through him. "One party coming up." He followed Dante back into the apartment, as he tried to shake off his doubts.

I guess this is happening.

Chapter 26

BEFORE HE KNEW IT, they were at a steakhouse diving into deliciously rich meals.

He hadn't eaten like this in forever—probably since the last time he'd been with the guys, he guessed. Their stories about the end of the season that he'd missed, along with funny tales about locker room pranks and parties in various towns while they were on the road, made him glad he'd finally agreed to go out with all of them. This feeling, this intense camaraderie, was exactly what being on a team was all about. He loved these guys, and he'd do just about anything for them, including forgetting his worries and surrendering himself to the evening they'd planned.

They finished their meals with some drinks and then took an Uber to a local dance club. The music was pulsing fiercely as they made their way into the throng. Being as tall as he was had always been helpful in situations like this. He mostly could see right over the top of everyone's head. He used that advantage to survey the room as they first went to the bar, then found a table they could all fit around. They drank for a while before, one by one, they started drifting away. Santiago and Mick wandered onto the dance floor to join a group of women. Jorge and Conner spotted another group of ladies at a different table. They looked at each other, then stood up and walked wordlessly away, moving in sync as though they'd practiced the move a hundred times.

Hell, they probably have, Tommy thought with a smirk as he lifted his beer back to his mouth for another sip, hoping it might do something to ease the small headache starting to blossom somewhere behind his right eye.

"How about you?" Dante asked, assessing Tommy now with a knowing look. "See any lovelies you'd like to meet? Or are you still up in your head about that woman who's stringing you along?"

"She's not string—listen, D, I know it's hard to understand. I do." Tommy put the bottle back down on the table a little harder than he'd intended. *How much have I had to drink?* he wondered at that moment. "I know I wasn't sure about her or her motives at first. But I've spent a lot of time with her at this point, and I *know* her. Yeah, she's still holding a lot back. But we've connected in ways I've never known before. Someday she's gonna be mine. And I know this sounds sappy as all hell, but it'll be forever. We just have to…well, our forever is going to take a while to find, that's all."

"Okay, okay. I can accept that, I guess," Dante said, still looking thoughtful. "And you have to know that if you're happy, I'm happy. So where is she this fine evening, T?"

"Where she always is, man," Tommy said, feeling guilty now that he was out having a good time while Lucy sat home caring for her mother. "I told you, she's on 24/7 lockdown with her sick mom."

"Well, I'm sorry to hear about that, I really am," Dante replied. Then he stood as if he'd made some sort of decision. "But you're not doing your girl any favors by sitting here getting drunk and not having any real fun. Get up and let's dance off those steaks. There are some gorgeous ladies here just dying for someone to get them out on the floor."

Tommy took one final long drink, set the glass down, then followed his best friend to the dance floor. Dante was right that he wasn't doing Lucy any favors by just sitting there, although his growing headache was telling him he couldn't humor the boys for too much longer.

They wound their way through the dense crush of bodies until Dante stopped short suddenly and reached back, grabbing his arm and leaning in to almost shout into Tommy's ear, "My heart just stopped. Check out the smoke show in the red dress!"

Tommy looked over and spotted the woman Dante was pointing out. The red dress was a barely-there thing of beauty, hugging her gorgeous curves as she twisted and gyrated, her graceful moves both sexy and captivating. The lucky guy she was with leaned over to say something in her ear, causing her to laugh. Tommy found himself wishing he was closer so he could have heard that laugh. As he stared at her closer, though, he realized there was something vaguely familiar about her. The brown hair, the blue glasses…. *Blue glasses?* Even as he noticed them, she turned fully in his direction, and Tommy felt as if he'd just been struck by that curveball to the temple all over again. That beautiful, carefree woman dancing and laughing her evening away with some other guy was Lucy.

Tommy took a step back as shock flooded through him. *This can't be happening…no.* He could feel the throbbing pain in his head turn to more of a pounding now, and it seemed as though he couldn't get a deep enough breath to fill his lungs. He saw Dante turn and look at him—first in confusion, then concern—as he took another step back. *She wasn't stuck at home and caring for a sick parent. She didn't have a boatload of responsibilities and troubles tying her down and preventing her from taking a single moment away from them. No, she was out dancing and having the time of her life. Is this how she spent all her evenings? She sure looked comfortable out there....*

He saw her laugh again, tossing her head back, the very picture of someone who didn't have any burdens at all. The vision sliced into him like a knife.

Lies—it had all been nothing but a huge pack of lies.

Yes, a part of him had been a little suspicious. A lot suspicious at first. But he'd fought those worries away. Over time, he'd come to believe everything she'd ever told him. In the end, he had trusted her completely. And she had him wrapped tightly around her finger. He'd wanted it all with her, but that future he'd envisioned—the one he'd told Dante about only moments ago—turned out to be pure fiction, based on nothing but his own imagination. The woman he believed to be quiet, studious, driven, and always just a little bit sad was, in fact, a stunningly confident and alluring goddess who apparently couldn't stop laughing.

How can this even be the same person?

As the shock receded, anger raced through him and took its place. He wished he hadn't had anything to drink. The anger and the alcohol were spinning together wildly inside him, and his headache was quickly escalating into a blinding agony, spurred along by the thumping beat of the booming dance music pulsing through the club.

Have to get out of here....

Just as he had that thought, though, Lucy's eyes settled on his, their gazes locking. The shock of recognition flickered in her eyes. Her face lit with a smile, then, and she quickly began to make her way through the crowd toward him.

"Oh, hell no," he muttered to himself, turning toward the door.

"Tommy, what's up?" he heard Dante call out as he moved away, pushing through the crowd as quickly as he could.

Then he felt Dante's hand on his arm. "T, talk to me," he said.

"Lucy…she's…," Tommy said, stopping as he realized she'd followed them.

"Thomas! Why are you leaving?" Lucy asked, an uncertain smile on her face. The anger was still rolling off him, and her sunny expression quickly disappeared. "Thomas?"

Dante figured it out quickly enough, Tommy knew. "I'll be right over there if you need me, man," he said, shooting Lucy a look that could kill as he gave Tommy a supportive pat on the shoulder.

"I'm so happy to see you!" Lucy said, clearly shrugging off Dante's icy look and trying to speak to him again. "But…what's going on?"

"What's going on?" Tommy repeated, incredulity punctuating his words. "*What's going on?*"

Was she for real? The pain in his head was getting more intense by the second. It reminded him of how he felt when he first was injured, when even talking or trying to turn his head nearly made him pass out. The pain, along with the alcohol, shock, and anger, were stealing his ability to think clearly or answer her questions coherently.

Still, he tried his hardest to turn his churning thoughts into words, especially since she was trying to pretend she didn't know precisely what was wrong.

"You played me. This was all just some huge joke to you, wasn't it?"

"What? Played you? Come on! What are you talking about? I didn't play you! I don't play games, Thomas. Wait, is this because I was dancing with some guy? You're actually jealous?" she asked, looking shocked. "Come on, I'm just out with some friends and dancing with whoever. I don't even know that guy's name!"

"That's funny, you don't know *mine* either!" he fired back, his cutting tone emphasizing each word clearly despite the noise of the club.

"Oh, come on. I guess this looks bad, but Mona…."

"No," he said, not wanting to hear any more. He started to shake his head, then stopped when the motion made him feel nauseous. "I don't want to hear it. I don't want to hear any more lies. Not from you. Never again."

"Thomas! Just let me explain! I haven't been lying about anything!" Lucy reached out for his arm, but he stepped back again, the thundering pain causing her words to sound like they were coming from a distance.

"All I wanted was some more of your time. To see you. To have dinner. To hang out with you and eat a pizza or watch a show. Just…be with you," Tommy said, his vision tunneling now. "But you gave me excuse after excuse, and I just bought it…I believed all of it. I was such an easy mark, wasn't I?"

"Thomas, please just let me explain to you about tonight!" Lucy said, tears now streaming down her beautiful face. "You're overreacting. It's one night out, that's all. My first in forever. Mona and Tania forced me!"

The pain was unbearable now. He could see her lips moving, but he couldn't distinguish her words clearly anymore. He had to get out of there; he wasn't sure how much longer he could even stay on his feet.

He took one last look at her. Her pleading eyes met his in a heated gaze. Their time together flashed through his mind, then he shoved those thoughts aside.

"A spot just opened up on your bench, angel," he shot out before he turned and walked away.

He moved through the crowd toward the door, the pain in his head reaching a crescendo as he walked out into the cool air of the evening. He tried to take a deep breath, but the pain was too sharp and intense.

He took his head in both hands, trying desperately to find some relief. But darkness finally overtook him, and he didn't even feel it when he hit the sidewalk.

Chapter 27

She told him she wasn't lying, and yet he just walked away.

Lucy was stunned. Also paralyzed with shock and worry and indecision. Should she run after him? Plead with him to give her a chance to better explain what happened? Then again, she honestly wasn't sure if that would help the situation or make it worse. Thomas had looked devastated and furious and...well, it also looked like he was in pain. Maybe he was having one of his headaches? Or had she caused him that much emotional turmoil that quickly...?

She glanced up then and saw the man Thomas had been speaking to earlier. He was talking with a few other guys. They were taking turns shooting angry looks at her. Clearly, they were a group of his friends, and she was glad in that moment he had that kind of support—friends so loyal they hated her guts on sight without even knowing what had transpired. If she could get at least one of them to listen to her side of the story, he could let Thomas know.

She took a deep breath, straightened her shoulders, and tried to exude confidence as she made her way over to the group.

"Hello, I'm Lucy," she started, then the one she'd seen Thomas speaking with earlier cut her off with a raised hand.

"Know exactly who—and what—you are," he said fiercely, his eyes narrowing as his features hardened into a menacing scowl.

Lucy gulped. If she wasn't so desperate to convey the truth, the look on this man's face would send her racing in the other direction. She tried to take another deep breath and start again.

"No, honestly, this is all just a misunderstanding," she said, trying unsuccessfully to find a sympathetic expression in their group. "Please let me explain it to you!"

The scowling man tilted his head toward the door where Thomas had disappeared and spoke to the others. "Go find our boy. I'll deal with this."

The four others walked away then.

"Okay, Little Miss 'I'm Lucy'," the man said. "Let's hear it. And this better be good, because I got to tell you, I love that man like a brother. Not looking to listen to a pack of lies about him."

"I'm not lying…what's your name, if you don't mind my asking?"

"Dante."

"Dante, I swear to you that I'm not lying, and I never lied to Thomas. Not once." She wished she could simmer the panic that was boiling inside so she could organize her thoughts better. She could tell Dante's patience with her was thin; she clearly had only this one small opportunity to get her story out.

"I am who I always said I was: a woman who's down on her luck," she began. "A woman caring for her sick mother. A woman who, until recently, had almost no one in the world in her corner."

"Okay, then why's my boy T so mad?" Dante asked.

"He wanted me to move our relationship out of casual chats in the park and into, well, an actual relationship, but I…you have to understand that I can't leave my mom."

"That's funny, 'cause unless you brought your sick mama out clubbin', you seem to have left her tonight," Dante countered.

"Right, that explanation is what Thomas didn't want to hear. My new friends and co-workers, Mona and Tania, showed up tonight completely out of the blue, gave me an elaborate makeover like Cinderella without the pumpkin, and shoved me out the door," Lucy said, thrilled at this point simply that Dante was still listening. "Mona insisted on staying with my mom so I could go out, but…I kept thinking that if I was going to go out for the first time in ages, I'd rather it be with Thomas, and not to some stupid club."

"And yet here you are," Dante said, eyeing her carefully.

"They told me I wasn't doing him any favors by sulking on my only night out, so, I…I guess I decided that I should accept their gift for what it was. They were simply trying to be kind to me. That's it. After months and months of drudgery and sadness, I got one completely unexpected gift of a single night of drinking and dancing with friends. And yet I was still missing Thomas but then…there he was! Like I'd conjured him up in a dream!"

"And then that dream became a nightmare, huh?" Dante said, and she nodded in reply. "Well, I have to say I think I might actually believe you. I don't know why, exactly. Just a feeling, I guess. But my feelings are usually on the mark. So…okay, when T's ready to hear it, I'll tell him what you told me. I'm not making any promises that he's ever going to want to see you again afterward, though. This whole thing has seemed crazy to me from the very start. But, well, T saw it differently. Thinking you lied to him this whole time…I think that's gonna really mess my boy up. But…maybe he'll see this clearly again at some point."

"That's all I want—for him to have all the facts when he makes his decision," Lucy said, feeling the first flutters of optimism since Thomas had left. "Thank you for listening and being willing to help."

"Don't thank me yet…." Dante's words trailed off as he looked down at his phone, which was lit up with a text. A horrified expression of shock registered on his face, then he looked up at Lucy. He opened his mouth, then shook his head, slid his phone in his pocket, gave her one last steely gaze, and rushed away.

What in the world was in that text? she wondered as she watched him move through the crowd and out of sight.

*   *   *

"There you are!" Tania said, suddenly appearing from the same area into which Dante had just vanished. "Where'd you go? I've been searching for y—wait, have you been crying?"

"I just…yes…it's a long story. Are you guys about ready to go?" Lucy asked with a hopeful tone. She was exhausted and terrified and wanted nothing more than to go home, take a hot shower, and try to pretend this night never happened.

"Eh, sorry, but we can't leave too quickly," Tania replied, tugging her arm and trying to move back toward the dance floor. "Some drunk guy passed out on the sidewalk, and the ambulance just got here. Let's wait until all that clears out."

Great, she thought listlessly as she let Tania propel her back into the throng. Any small pieces of happiness or enjoyment that she'd been able to wring out of the evening were long gone, and the whole thing was starting to feel like an endurance test. She ended up sitting at a table and numbly watching the others, her mind a tangle of regret and fear.

Why had she held herself back from him for so long? The girls had very easily proven tonight that getting out of the house was, in fact, possible. But she hadn't even really needed that because Thomas had offered to come over and hang out with her. She never actually required an elaborate solution—she just needed to trust that together they could have found a way to work it all out...had she only been willing to try. Which forced her to ask the obvious question—*Isn't that what being a couple is all about?* Working as a team toward the common goal of mutual happiness? Heaven knows Thomas would have been patient with her about it.

His words from earlier floated back through her mind: *"All I wanted was some more of your time. To see you. To have dinner. To hang out with you and eat a pizza or watch a show. Just...be with you."*

She'd been so wrapped up in her own woes that she hadn't been able to open herself up to him, despite the fact that the part of her life he had been asking for was extremely small. He hadn't pushed her to move in together or shove her mom into assisted living. He just wanted to be with her, no matter what form that took. And yet she'd shut him down over and over. She had insisted on keeping their time together limited to the park and never fully letting him into her life or her heart.

But somehow, despite all of the obstacles I put up, he

managed to get into my heart anyway, all on his own.

This thought struck her like a thunderbolt, followed by another that was even more powerful....

I love him.

She understood this with the kind of growing clarity that made it undeniable, and her eyes pooled with tears again as the final realization landed with devastating power.

I might never get the chance to tell him....

Chapter 28

BY THE TIME Tania and the others were ready to go, Lucy was practically catatonic. The late hour, the alcohol, the tears, the stress…all of it was stirring a toxic brew of depression inside her. When the Uber dropped her off, it only took one questioning look from Mona to cause the entire story to come spilling out. They sat together on the couch as Lucy sullenly described her evening and what happened when Thomas saw her dancing with another man.

"Girl, I'm not the type to want to be right all the time or take pleasure in it, but you know I was right about this," Mona said with a shake of the head. "I told you that you were making this situation too complicated. Now I'm going to repeat myself here: You have to snatch happiness when you see it. I speak from experience here."

"What experience?" Lucy asked, reaching over to grab a tissue from the box on the table next to the couch. "What happened to y—or, wait, is that too personal a question?"

"No, it's okay, I can tell you. Mostly because I think it'll do you some good to hear it. Maybe you'll understand why I've started to stick my nose into your life. You remind me of my daughter."

"I didn't know you have a daughter," Lucy said through a round of fresh sniffles and tears that she wished would subside. "Where is she?"

"She's anywhere but where I am," Mona said with a shrug, the regret thick in her voice. "We're estranged. She won't talk to me, and she hasn't for years. I think I've got grandbabies out there I'm never even going to get to meet."

"What?!" Lucy asked. Mona had done everything possible to be kind to her after that initial confrontation. She couldn't imagine anyone barring Mona from their life. "What happened?"

"Well, you know that I can be a little…let's call it opinionated and rough around the edges…right?"

Lucy shrugged and then put her pointer finger and thumb together in a "just a little bit" gesture with an apologetic wince.

"You don't have to sugarcoat it, because I never do," Mona said. "And, actually, the woman you're looking at today has gotten soft in her old age. I used to be pretty harsh in everything I did and said. Whether you wanted my honest opinion or not, you were going to get it. My daughter…she got tired of it, tired of me trying to run her life and tell her just what I thought no matter what kind of feelings might be getting stomped on in the process. One day she just had enough."

"She…left?" Lucy asked gently.

"Oh, she left all right," Mona said. "But not before telling me that as far as she was concerned, she didn't have a mother. Said she never wanted to see my face again."

"Oh Mona, I'm so sorry," Lucy said, feeling tears forming yet again.

"I had a beautiful family at one point, Lucy. But my husband has since died, and my daughter's gone, and, well…." Mona's voice trailed off as a faraway look crossed her face. Lucy could tell she was lost in the memories. "When I tell you that you need to learn to spot happiness when you see it and grab it with both hands, I know what I'm talking about."

"Do you think your daughter will ever come back?"

"No, I don't," Mona said softly. "Sometimes we only get one chance to get it right."

"I'm afraid that's what's going to happen in my situation, too," Lucy confessed. "What if Thomas never comes back either?"

"Well, now, you might be right. He might never want to see you again. But let's say he did show up one day. Just what would you do differently if he did?"

"I would invite him into my life this time, even though that's roughly equivalent to inviting someone to join me in a burning car wreck." She laughed sardonically in spite of herself. "I told him my life wasn't such a great place to be, but, well, I think he wanted to join me all the same."

"Okay, so while your man does his soul-searching, why don't we see about cleaning up your car wreck?" Mona asked.

"What do you mean?"

"You don't know if or when he'll show up again, right?" Mona asked.

"Unfortunately, no. You didn't see how mad and hurt he was."

"But what you do know is that all your worries are what held you back from him from the start, right?" Lucy nodded in agreement, and Mona nodded with her. "Okay, so what's your biggest hurdle now? What's standing in your way of you turning your life around, with or without your man?"

"I guess…it's time," Lucy replied, wondering

where Mona was going with her line of questioning. "I need time to study for the bar, but I don't have any because of the requirements of my mom's care. And I can't afford to pay for a health aide beyond what I already do."

"Okay. So, each afternoon, I go home and sit on my couch and watch TV, and you come here and stay with your mother. Does that sound about right?"

"Yeah, I guess so."

"So, what if we start switching places? I sit on this couch and watch this TV, and you go to my place and do a couple of hours of study? How would that change things for you?"

"Oh…Mona!" Lucy said, staring in absolute wonder. "I…I couldn't possibly ask you to do that!"

"You're not asking, I'm offering," Mona replied. "Now you listen up. I don't get any more chances with my daughter. That door is closed. But you, you remind me of her. I see you, and I see my second chance, Lucy. Don't you understand? You're doing *me* a favor right back by letting me help you in this way. I'm helping you, but you're helping me too. So come on, what do you say?"

"I guess…I guess I have to say yes, don't I?" Lucy said, a radiant smile on her face. "A wise woman once told me that I needed to spot times when happiness is within my reach and then grab hold of it. I think this is one of those times."

"I think you might be right," Mona said, standing up. "Okay, your mom's been sleeping for a couple hours now. Go check on her, then get some sleep yourself. You're going to need as much as you can get so all that studying can soak into your brain properly."

Lucy stood then also, took a hesitant step toward

Mona, then abandoned all shyness and flew into the older woman's arms for a hug.

"Oh, get on out of here with all this," Mona said sternly, even as she squeezed Lucy back. "You're going to be okay, girl, no matter what that boy decides."

Lucy squeezed Mona once more before reluctantly drawing back and wiping her eyes.

"Thank you, Mona. For tonight, for all the kind words and great advice *before* tonight, and...well, for everything."

Mona merely nodded and said, "See you at the diner bright and early," as she went to the door. A moment later she was gone.

*   *   *

Lucy leaned against the door and closed her eyes as the events of the evening swirled through her mind. The makeover with Tania. The moments she'd spent actually letting herself go and simply enjoying being alive as she danced. The surge of joy she'd felt when she spotted Thomas's face in the crowd. Then the plunging dread when she realized how upset he was. She squeezed her eyes shut, trying to fight back the vision of him looking at her with such thundering expressions of betrayal and disdain.

She shook her head sadly and doublechecked that the door was locked. Then she walked quietly down the hall to peek in at her mother, who, she was surprised to see, was sitting up in bed, looking particularly panicked.

"What's wrong, Marie?" she asked.

"Where's Lucy?" she cried, her arms flailing as she dug around in the bed linens. "Where's my baby? I can't find her!"

"Shhh," Lucy crooned softly as she came forward. "Lay back down and go to sleep. Lucy's safe and perfectly happy, I promise."

Eventually her mother lay back again, her energy expended. Lucy patted her arm and smoothed the hair from her eyes. Then an odd thought came to her mind—had she just lied?

Lucy's safe and perfectly happy.

But was this true? And would it *ever* be? Would she be able to find happiness at some point? Real, honest, deep-in-her-soul happiness?

Or had Thomas taken the chance of that happening with him when he left...?

Chapter 29

LUCY WAS THERE, just ahead of him. He could see her long hair flying around her head, the stormy winds twisting and tangling it. How could it be so foggy at the same time? he wondered as he tried to move closer to her. But no matter how hard he tried, she remained just out of reach.

"Lucy!" he called, but she only smiled back. Then she started floating until, finally, she disappeared. "Lucy!" he screamed again, but she was gone.

"Darling, please wake up now," he heard his mother say gently. Then, in the background, his father yelled, "Who the hell is Lucy?!"

Tommy opened his eyes then, looking frantically around the room.

"Lucy? Where...?"

His voice was a scratchy growl. His mother, seated beside the bed, reached over and smoothed back his hair.

"You're in the hospital, honey," she said softly. "You have a concussion."

A concussion?!

Wait...was he *still* in the hospital? After all this time? Were Lucy and those amazing hours they'd spent in the park nothing more than a dream?!

He looked around wildly, as though he could find the answers if he searched the room thoroughly enough. His heart monitor began beeping furiously as his pulse skyrocketed.

"Whoa, T, chill out!" Jenna said then from the other side of the bed, stepping forward and grabbing his right hand. "As much as I normally enjoy teasing you, I'm not kidding now, so listen to me, okay?"

He allowed himself to calm down a little and met her eyes, then he nodded mutely. He could still feel his heart hammering in his chest.

"This is a *new* concussion," she explained slowly. "Not the original one, courtesy of Zach Hiller. This one was courtesy of Jack Daniels and your own stupidity, got it?"

"Yeah," he breathed out, closing his eyes in relief. Then he felt Jenna lean down to whisper in his ear, her hair tickling his neck.

"She's real, T. Not a dream."

He opened his eyes and nodded again. "Thanks, Jen."

"So now that we've got that cleared up," his father boomed from his seat in the corner, "you gonna tell us why you're collecting concussions like it's your job?"

"I'd like to hear this answer, too," Dr. Singh said then as he breezed into the room to assess Tommy. "Mr. Layton, was it only a day or two ago that I was signing off on your recovery? I believe I congratulated you on taking the healing process seriously. What happened to the young athlete who was ready to do everything necessary to rejoin his team?"

Tommy closed his eyes and thought about this question as well as Jenna's assurances that Lucy was, in fact, part of his reality. *That meant...oh no....* It meant the events of the previous evening—which came flooding back to him in that moment—were also real. The dinner. The drinks. The horrifying way his hopes of a future with Lucy had come crashing down. And the pain that followed....

"Um...what was the question again?" he asked lamely.

"What happened to the guy who was serious about his recovery?" Dr. Singh repeated patiently while his dad shook his head, the exasperation and disappointment as clear as a billboard flashing in Times Square.

"Uh, well, his teammates showed up in town ready to celebrate, I guess," Tommy admitted, noticing from the corner of his eye that the thunderous expression on his dad's face was getting darker by the second. "I had some drinks, I'll admit that. I definitely had too many to even think about driving. But I wasn't falling-down-sloppy drunk, I swear."

"Okay, start from the beginning," Singh requested.

"Well, it was just like I said: My friends showed up in town and took me out to celebrate my recovery. We had a huge meal and drinks, and then we went to a club. I had a beer or two there...." Tommy paused, absolutely dreading the thought of recounting what happened next. "Then, uh...something stressful happened."

"Stressful?" Dr. Singh prodded.

"I, kind of, found out that my...girlfriend?...uh, she wasn't what she seemed," Tommy said.

"You have a girlfriend?" his mom and dad shrieked in unison even as Jenna was saying, "Oh Tommy, no! I'm so sorry."

"Yeah, well, I'd had the start of a headache before I saw her," Tommy went on, wishing he could go back to sleep. "But when she and I were talking—and I was getting increasingly upset—the headache was building and building. It got to the point that I felt like the top of my head might blow off. And part of me was sort of wishing it would, just to relieve the pressure."

"That actually makes sense," Dr. Singh said, looking at the tablet he held in his hands. "The EMTs noted your blood pressure and pulse were both tremendously elevated at the scene. So, then what happened?"

"I left, walked outside, and…woke up here, I guess," Tommy said with a shrug.

"What had you done earlier that day, before your friends arrived?" Singh asked.

"Uh, well, actually, I went for a long run in the morning, and I worked out all afternoon," he confessed with a wince. "I overdid it, didn't I?"

"We did tests while you were unconscious," Singh replied. "They show a new concussion, though it's quite mild. Nothing like your original injury. I think, based on what you've just told me, that you pushed yourself too hard all day, stirred in some alcohol and stress, and apparently passed out. Your body couldn't take anymore. The new concussion was simply courtesy of landing on the sidewalk. We're going to need to discuss the seriousness of the long-term effects of cumulative brain injuries and CTE, but not now. I need you to rest now, although we do have a waiting room filled with people who want to at least see for themselves that you're alive. I think you gave your friends quite a scare."

Dr. Singh left then, cautioning Tommy to keep the visitation times limited.

"Look, I know you guys have a million questions," he started to his parents and sister before they could interrogate him further, "but I don't really have anything else to add. I messed up. I pushed too hard, too quickly. That's it."

"And this girlfriend?" his dad inquired, moving from his perch in the corner and joining his wife at Tommy's bedside. "Lucy, I presume?"

"Yeah, Lucy. I thought…well, it doesn't even matter what I thought," Tommy said. "I don't really want to talk about her, other than to say it's over. Before it ever began, really."

"Okay, son, we'll take that at face value then," his dad said, his features softening at last. "Can't say I'm happy about any of this, but you look like you already regret it enough without me piling on." He took a deep breath, then continued with, "Well, we'll let your teammates have some time with you now. They were all pretty torn up. I think they feel guilty about what happened."

"Can you let me be the one to get them?" Jenna asked. "I just want a minute alone to yell at my idiot brother first."

"Don't yell too loudly, Jen," his mother said, with a wink. "He's got a headache, remember."

Tommy watched silently as his parents left the room, wishing Jenna would go with them. As he drew in a shaky breath, he thought about how he owed her the rest of the story, unfortunately. He deeply regretted having told Jenna anything, and he was dreading the inquisition he was about to face. He didn't ever want to think about what had happened again, and he certainly didn't want to talk about it. And, even worse, it was embarrassing to admit to his little sister how expertly he'd been played. He was going to be forced to give voice to what he knew now to be the truth: The entire "relationship" had been nothing but lies.

Chapter 30

AS SOON AS the door closed, Jenna sat on the bed and turned to face him.

"What happened?" she asked softly.

"What?" Tommy teased. "Thought you were going to yell at me. This is so weak."

"Come on, stop joking. You confided in me about Lucy from the start," Jenna reminded him. "I know the whole story. Let some of that stress out in a way that doesn't involve a sidewalk and EMTs."

"Jen, I…I just can't believe how wrong I was about her." He was mad at himself for believing the lies. He was also mad at Lucy for not being who she claimed to be. But he couldn't avoid admitting he missed that person. Okay, so it was an imaginary figure that he'd been slowly falling for over the last few months. But he wished that person—*that* Lucy—was here right now, sitting on his bed, consoling him. But that was impossible, wasn't it?

Because that person doesn't exist….

"Wrong…how?" Jenna nudged.

"You know the basics of what she told me about herself, right? That she had a sick mom, and she was the primary caregiver. Plus other unnamed problems that she never got around to divulging…or inventing, I guess. So, I kept reassuring her that I didn't need extravagant dates or huge time commitments. I would have been happy to just sit on the couch and help her watch her mom. Seriously, Jen, I was *that* far gone about her."

"I know," Jenna replied gently.

"She kept telling me no, that she wanted to solve her problems alone. That she had no time and no headspace to give me. Just the hour each day in the park. So, I took those hours from her like the gift I thought they were. I looked forward to sitting next to her every single day. She gave me so little, and I just lapped it up like a dog."

"Oh Tommy, you're breaking my heart," Jenna said, her eyes starting to sparkle with unshed tears. "So what, exactly, happened last night?"

"We walked into the club, and Dante pointed out a beautiful woman in a tight red dress dancing and laughing with some guy out on the floor, like she didn't have a single care in the world."

"Oh no," Jenna said as a tear broke free and trickled down her face.

"Yeah," Tommy said, "it was Lucy. She sure didn't look like a woman who couldn't give me even one extra minute of her time. I saw her dancing and laughing and...Jenna, I got so furious. I felt embarrassed and so played and...annihilated inside."

Jenna nodded empathetically. "So, what did she say about it?"

"Actually, T wouldn't let her explain," Dante said, slipping in the door then. "Hey there, gorgeous, good to see you again."

"Thanks," Tommy teased, trying to dispel some of the tension in the room as Jenna laughed.

"I think he meant me, dork," Jenna said. "Good to see you, too, Dante. What do you mean, he wouldn't let her explain?"

"He got so mad that he didn't hear a word of what she was trying to tell him. But I listened to her after he took off and pulled his fainting goat act out front." Dante turned to Tommy. "I want to talk to you about that now, T."

"Listen, Dante, I appreciate that you're trying to clean up my messes, but I think what I saw was pretty clear," he said. "I don't need to hear her excuses."

"What if they're reasons and not excuses?" Dante countered.

"I…I mean, I guess? I don't know…I…wait, is that my phone?" Tommy asked. He could hear the ringtone, but he couldn't tell where it was coming from. Jenna stood up, walked over to the small closet, pulled his phone out of his bag, and handed it to him. When he saw Jack's name on the screen, he shook his head. *Oh great*, he thought as he answered it.

"I hear you're one concussion away from a tic-tac-toe win," Jack snapped through the speaker with no preamble. It was clear from his tone that he wasn't in the mood for excuses or arguments.

"I…yeah."

"So, let me just make sure I have all the facts here," Jack rolled on as though Tommy hadn't spoken. "You swear to me that you're going to take it easy. I tell you that as far as I'm concerned, you're still under protocols. Then, not twenty-four hours later, I'm getting a phone call telling me that EMTs had to scrape you off the sidewalk with a spatula. Have I misrepresented any of the facts?"

"It was a combination of too much exercise earlier in the day, a few drinks with the boys who came to see me, and a stressful breakup," Tommy said. "It was basically too much, too soon."

"Well, I can see now that your recovery is something that we can't rush or trust you to handle properly, now can we? The minute they release you from the hospital, I want your ass on a plane. Then I want you to go straight to the training facility and report. You're going to be supervised in your recovery by the team around the clock. If the doctors and trainers allow you to participate fully in spring training, then fine, I'll allow it. But when that's over and the team doctors sign off, you're to report to the Delmarva Shorebirds."

"Coach, no! Single A?" Tommy asked, shocked.

"Yeah, that's right. You're starting over," Jack said. "You told me you were afraid of getting Pipped. But son, Wally Pipp didn't do anything wrong except to have the misfortune of getting replaced by a legend like Lou Gehrig. You on the other hand? You did this to *yourself.*"

Jack disconnected the call before Tommy could respond further.

*   *   *

His career was over.

It was now sitting on top of a Single-A scrap pile. He was going to have to start from the beginning, putting in long hours and grueling work in an attempt to catch the team's eye again. And this time, they'd be cautious and dubious about him. They thought he was a screw-up. *They're right,* he thought miserably. *I've screwed up my whole life.*

He looked at Dante and Jenna, who were wearing matching expressions of horror combined with pity.

"Tommy, I'm so sorry," Jenna said.

"Yeah, listen, I just need to sleep. I'm exhausted, and I feel like hell," Tommy said. "D, can you tell the boys I'm fine, and I don't blame anyone? It was my own damn fault."

"Sure T, thanks. They'll be glad to hear you don't blame us. We really are sorry, though. You know we just wanted to have some fun and see you again. We never would have wanted to hurt you."

"I know that," Tommy said, looking him in the eye. "Seriously."

"Thanks, man. But before I go, can we just finish the conversation we started before?"

"About Lucy, you mean?" Tommy asked.

"Yeah, about what she told me."

"No," Tommy said, closing his eyes. "I've got to take a page out of her playbook now and put my blinders on. I can't afford to think about anything other than trying to salvage my career. I don't care what she had to say. Doesn't matter anymore."

"Okay, T," Dante said with an affectionate squeeze of Tommy's shoulder. "I know you're feeling a way about things right now. But when you're back with the team—and yeah you heard me say *when* and not if—you and I *will* have this talk. Do you hear me?"

"Yeah, fine, okay. If I'm back in Camden Yards again someday, and not as a fan in the stands, I'll listen to whatever you want to tell me."

"Make that 'anywhere in the Majors with any team,' and you got yourself a deal, my boy," Dante said, winking at Jenna as he turned to leave, then he slipped quietly from the room.

"I wish you'd let him talk," Jenna said, studying him closely now. "What would it hurt to simply hear her side?"

"Jen…I just can't, okay?" Tommy replied, his chest tight with worry and stress. "I just…can I have some time alone, please?"

"Sure. I get it, Tommy. You've been through a lot, and I know you've got a lot to think about." She rose to leave, turning toward the door before stopping to add, "But Dante's right. You will be back on the team. I think Jack's just making you jump through hoops to prove a point."

"Yeah, maybe," he said, only half meaning it and half caring by that point. He gave her a small wave as she left.

He hoped she *was* right, of course. Dante, too. But he couldn't afford to rely only on hope. Baseball was his life. He needed to focus all of his energy and time on getting back to the highest level of the game he loved so much.

Everything—and everyone—else just didn't matter anymore.

Chapter 31

LUCY AWOKE in a daze. She'd barely slept all night, and the few paltry hours of rest she'd managed to get hadn't been all that restful.

She'd been haunted by uneasy visions of Thomas. She could barely remember, as her eyes slowly opened, what precisely had happened in those dreams, but the memories left her with a deeply unsettling dread. It was as though Thomas was so far away that she could never bridge the divide between them. She felt more alone than she'd ever felt before, even in her darkest hours of misery following her father's death. At least back then she'd had her mother, who still knew and recognized her then. Not anymore, though. Lucy couldn't even recall the last time her mother had looked at her with recognition and clarity.

Lucy sat up, working to shake off the wisps that still remained of the dreams—or had they been nightmares?—and start her day. She was eager to get to it, in a way. Despite the heaviness of the dread, she wasn't ready to give up on Thomas or on what they might build one day. If only life would give her one more chance to get it right. She'd meant the things she'd said to Mona the night before. She would do things differently this time. Unfortunately, it had taken a swift kick in the head for her to see how much of a mess she'd made. But wow did she see things clearly now.

She'd tempted fate one too many times. For example, by repeatedly refusing to exchange contact information with Thomas. That had been foolish. He'd seen how precarious their ties were, and he had offered to simply exchange phone numbers to ensure something like this would never happen. She also kept relying on the thought that they would have a final farewell before he left town, a time to truly say goodbye to their magical time together in the park and move on to a more concrete—albeit long-distance—relationship. She'd never even let herself imagine a scenario where he'd simply disappear. She knew now, without any doubt, that she wanted that something more with him. Would he ever know this, though? Would his friend Dante really plead her case? And even if he did, would Thomas care?

She shook off all these questions since none would have any answers until she found him. Then she threw back the blankets so she could get moving.

She stood with a sigh and went to the bathroom, taking extra time with her hair and gently brushing on some make-up, something she didn't typically do for a shift at the diner. She wanted to look especially pretty today when she went to the park, since hope still burned inside of her. Part of her was sure that if she showed at the bench like always, Thomas would be waiting and ready to at least have a rational conversation about what happened at the club. She needed the extra dash of confidence to face him again. It had been agonizing seeing him so mad and so devastated, knowing she'd put that look of shock and fury on his face. She never wanted to see him that way again. It had been paralyzing, a knife of agony straight through her heart.

Celia, the health aide, arrived a few minutes later. Lucy greeted her and helped to get her mother in the shower chair, then she left and went to the address Mona had provided the night before. They had agreed to meet there before their shifts began so Mona could give her a spare key and a quick walkthrough.

Mona opened the door, a soft look of concern filing away the jagged edges of her normally steely gaze.

"You can't possibly understand how much this means to me," Lucy said, skipping a proper greeting. Mona stood back and gestured for Lucy to walk inside her modest Cape Cod home, a style that dotted northern New Jersey. The house looked like a time capsule, the dated furniture and decorations screaming that they hadn't been updated since the '50s or '60s. Lucy's parents' own home was eerily similar. She'd bet a paycheck that Mona's bathrooms were still decorated with pink and black tile, as so many of them were.

"You don't have to thank me," Mona said. "It's definitely not much but, well, it's clean and quiet, and I got hooked up with fancy internet when they were upgrading the lines on this street. I figure you should be able to use it with no problems. I'm not that smart when it comes to computers, but I forced myself to learn in the hopes I might catch glimpses of my grandbabies online."

"And have you?" Lucy asked. "Caught sight of them, I mean."

"Sometimes, although my daughter has her accounts set on private," Mona replied with a resigned shrug. "And she's refused all my attempts at being friends or whatever you call it."

"I'm so sorry." Lucy knew her words could never take away the pain Mona must be feeling, but she wanted to try anyway. "And this is absolutely perfect—I already feel at home. Your house is a twin of my mom's."

Mona nodded. "Feel free to take over the dining room table with your books or whatever you'll need. I don't exactly entertain these days, and I eat all my meals in the kitchen. That empty dining room makes me feel…well, anyway, take it over. It's yours. No need to be dragging your supplies back and forth."

"Investigating what types of materials I'll need will be today's project," Lucy said. "My guess is that it's all available online, so I likely won't be taking up your space with physical books. But we'll see. When I graduated, my life was such a mess that I never looked into it."

"How are you going to pay for all these materials you need?" Mona asked. "That gonna be expensive?"

"Oh yes, every step of this journey will be ridiculously expensive, but hey, I'm already floating in an ocean of debt. What's a little more going to do to me?" Her breezy, unconcerned tone was just a cover for her fears, which were anything but an illusion. How *would* she pay for all of this? She still had no idea. And with only a couple hours a day to devote to studying, how long would it be until she could conceivably try taking the test? A year? Two years? She was still years away from finding a job that would ensure a large enough salary to start paying off her debt. But Mona didn't need to know all of that. It wasn't her burden, of course. But the same old questions and worries that had been haunting her for months—the same questions and worries that had kept her from opening herself up to Thomas and, in turn, led her to ruin her relationship with him—were all still right there.

What Mona was offering her was a small step forward, and Lucy was determined to make the most of it. Yes, it was a baby step; it was only the tiniest, shuffling bit of movement toward her goals. And it certainly wasn't a perfect solution. By the time she finished her shift at the diner each day and then spent an hour in the park, that would only leave her with about two hours before she had to relieve Mona from her voluntary shift with Lucy's mom. A truly ideal situation involved studying all day long. But, hey, forward movement, no matter how small, still meant she was heading in the right direction. Did it even matter at this point how long it took? What was that old saying? Wasn't it something about a journey of a thousand miles starting with one step? Well, today, thanks to Mona, she was finally about to take that step.

"Well, girl, like Pat's always telling you," Mona said, "those plates ain't serving themselves. Guess we better head on out so we're not late. Oh, and before I forget, here's the spare key."

Lucy took it from her solemnly, appreciating what an important gift it really was.

*   *   *

Her shift at the diner felt like it lasted forever. If clock-watching was an Olympic event, she'd definitely be standing on the winners' podium that day, clutching a gold medal while the National Anthem played.

Taking Mona's key that morning—and knowing she'd be spending her afternoon investigating and ordering her study materials—had Lucy wired with nervous, buzzing energy. Additionally, she wanted to get to the park as quickly as possible. She was desperate to share her news with Thomas. She yearned to invite him to walk into her life as openly as Mona had invited

Lucy into hers. If he would only show up, just one more time, she could make it all right. She knew she could.

When her shift finally—*finally!*—came to an end, she double-checked that Mona had everything she needed, then she raced off toward the park.

Please, please, please, please….

Her urgent pleas beat a rhythm in her head, and she hurried with determined focus down the pedestrian path, barely noticing the skaters, bikers, joggers, and parents and nannies pushing strollers. She slowed, though, when she neared the bench, taking a moment to slow her thrumming pulse and collect her thoughts.

What would she say when she saw him if, *please God*, he was waiting for her around this last turn? Would she explain precisely what had happened, and why she had been able to do something as frivolous as go to a dance club? And would he then fully accept her apologies? Would he maybe even tease her about finally sharing her cell number after all this time? Would the crackle of chemistry between them still be there? Or would he hold a grudge and never quite trust her again?

She quickly realized that she was wasting time with all this theorizing. She took a deep breath, gathered her courage, said yet another silent prayer, and started taking the final few steps that would bring the bench into view.

Her hesitantly hopeful movements carried her through the grass and trees until she stepped out into the opening, the color quickly draining out of her face as she realized what was in the park waiting for her, and that her myriad questions were answered at last.

It was disappointment that awaited her. Thomas's side of the bench was empty.

Chapter 32

WHEN DR. SINGH finally signed the discharge papers, Tommy went back to his apartment and started the process of walking away from his life in New Jersey.

It was stunningly easy to do. The apartment had come furnished; he essentially just needed to pack suitcases and empty out the refrigerator. He dumped off a box of food—okay, mostly condiments—at his parents' house. He also threw a bunch of money in Jenna's account and asked her to deal with having the apartment cleaned, and then either break the lease or pay off the remaining months. He didn't care how it wrapped up, as long as he didn't have to deal with it or think about it.

Actually, he didn't want to think about much of *anything* at the moment, because all trains of thought, no matter where they originated, eventually pulled into the station where his memories of Lucy dwelled. And the last thing in the world he wanted to do was think about the woman who'd taken a sledgehammer to his heart. So, he focused instead on the main task at hand: walking away.

Within two days of his release from the hospital, he had said goodbye to his family, tied up the loose ends on all practical matters, and gotten on a plane headed for Sarasota. Once there, he would meet up with the team trainers and doctors, all of whom would be taking over his life in the weeks to come.

When he arrived, he rented an SUV, then dropped his suitcases off at the hotel room he'd be calling home for the next several months. After that, he headed to the team facility. He updated everyone on how he was feeling…physically, anyway. He left out the parts of the story that involved…well, *her*. Instead, he approached the situation like he was a robot in the shop for a tune-up. He submitted to any and every test they suggested. He followed their rehabbing instructions to the letter. If they asked him to get on the bikes, he made sure he understood precisely how long and at what speeds and inclines. If they asked him to stretch or lift weights, he asked them specifically which muscles he should target and for how many reps. He didn't fight anything, didn't argue, and most of all, didn't think. He simply executed the tasks at hand. He didn't want anyone on the team to have a single reason to give a bad report to Jack or any of the other team brass, either the owners back in Baltimore or the managers who had already arrived in Florida to get ready for spring training, which would be starting soon.

When he got back to the hotel each evening, he ordered room service and shoveled healthy meals into his mouth, checked in with his family, showered, and went to bed early. He got really good at making sure he didn't let himself think, and he definitely didn't let himself feel. A robot. He turned himself into a rehabbing automaton, devoid of emotions or plans for the future that didn't involve trying to wow the Orioles with his drive and dedication.

In the quiet moments, when thoughts of Lucy would sneak past his defenses, he had to acknowledge that he now had a better understanding of how she had tried to handle her problems. And there was something to be said for the approach she had taken. He got it. That single-minded devotion to focusing on the issue at hand—to the exclusion of everything else—was coming in pretty handy, he admitted. He wondered if she'd appreciate the irony.

As it turned out, his subconscious wasn't at all interested in trying to eradicate her, however. His dreams were still filled with her every night. She was always the last thing he thought about before falling asleep and the first thing on his mind when he woke up. And if he was being one-hundred-percent honest with himself—which he mostly wasn't these days—he might even admit that those dreams of Lucy played a part in his sudden devotion to going to bed early. The sooner he fell asleep, the sooner his mind was free to dream of her again.

When the rest of the team started arriving—first the pitchers and catchers came, and a month later all the position players—Thomas found himself avoiding his friends. They were a painful reminder of what had happened. As much as he loved the guys, he couldn't afford to be distracted. He definitely couldn't risk any mistakes brought about by drinking or any of the other things he once found enjoyable. He also discovered that he really didn't want to join them when they went out to find women, something he used to do with them all the time. Even though there were always plenty of women in nearby bars who specifically wanted to spend the night with a professional athlete, Tommy found he just couldn't do it anymore. His days as a wingman were over.

He told himself it was because he couldn't afford the distractions. The eyes of the entire Oriole team management were focused on him, after all, intent on seeing if he could pull his career back together. But a quiet voice deep inside was saying it had something to do with Lucy. Even after everything that had happened, he wasn't ready to think about other women yet.

So, even though the whole team was back, and spring training was well under way just like it had been a year ago, everything felt different. The challenge of going through the fire with his buddies was gone. His confident swagger was gone, too. Tommy was as driven and focused as ever, but also still going through the motions like a robot, impersonal and detached.

Dante, of course, noticed all of this. Tommy could see his friend's looks, sense him constantly assessing, and feel him always worrying. He appreciated that Dante wasn't pushing him, but late one afternoon, after a grueling day of practice, the reprieve he'd been given was clearly over; Dante had had enough.

"Who you tryin' to punish, T?" Dante said as they walked out of the facility toward their cars in the players' lot. "Me? The boys? Yourself? Your lady? Who?"

"Dante, it's been a long day, and I'm tired," Tommy replied, popping open the hatch on his rental and tossing his bag inside. Then he closed it and turned to face his friend.

"I don't care, my boy," Dante pressed, looking mad now. "I've given you time to lick your wounds. I haven't said anything while you pushed Mick and Santi and the boys away, turning us down night after night. I know you're on edge, worried about your career and missing your girl, so I've given you your time and space."

"She's *not* my girl, and she doesn't have anything to do with me anymore," Tommy fired back, his clipped tone not masking his annoyance. "Regardless, I'm not trying to push you guys away. But you were there, D, and you know how much deep shit I'm in with Jack and the team. One wrong move and that's it, I'm out. And we both know there are no guarantees that any other organization is going to come looking for a washed-up charity case who couldn't handle the big time."

"What are you saying here?" Dante asked, the frustration washing off him in sheets now. "Who couldn't handle it? *You?* You still think that original hit from Hiller was your fault? Is that what you've got bouncing around in that thick skull of yours? I know your brain is all bruised up right now, along with your ego, but you listen to me, and get up close so you can hear real clear: That was an accident. An *accident!* Everybody knows that, the same way Jack and the team all know full well that your second concussion was just an unfortunate set of circumstances brought about by a guy so driven to get back here that he about made his brain explode by overdoing it. You think they don't find your drive to be a *good* thing? Don't kid yourself, T. Things are not as bad as you think they are. Jack's messing with you just to make sure you're okay. My guess is that your stunt at the club freaked him right out, and he was just doing whatever he could to put his golden boy in bubble wrap. Don't forget, T, less than a year ago you were being talked about for Rookie of the Year and even MVP. The Orioles are *not* going to forget that, believe me."

"Yeah, yeah, you might be right," Tommy said, running his hand through his hair. "Maybe they *are* just making me jump to keep me on my toes and safe. But Dante, it's still stressful as all hell. Baseball is all I've ever wanted to do. Spending this year out of the game…it's messed with me, man. I'm not the same guy I used to be."

"Yeah, you've changed, that's for sure. But I think it has more to do with Ms. Red Dress than you sittin' on the sidelines for a while."

Tommy shook his head. "Dante, I still don't want to talk about what happened, and I definitely don't want to talk about *her*. But…well, you're not wrong. She's a major part of why I'm not myself right now."

"I know, my man, I know," Dante said. "But don't you forget that deal you made with me. The minute you're back on the team, you and I *will* talk about her. It's gonna be a nice long conversation that will start with me telling you that you're an idiot, and it's gonna end with you agreeing with me. You got me?"

"Yeah, I got you," Tommy said, a swell of affection for his wonderful friend washing through him. Dante had proven himself time and again to be exactly who you'd want in your corner no matter how spectacularly your life was going off the rails. He'd always be there to pick up the pieces. "Thanks man, for everything."

"Of course, brother," Dante said.

"I'll work on getting over myself and lightening up a bit," Tommy told him. "Maybe I'll start by seeing if Jack will talk to me after practice one day. Maybe I can get an idea of where things stand."

"Good idea," Dante said. "And give some thought to spending time with your buddies once in a while. You know part of all our success is tied into the chemistry in the locker room. This ain't golf. You're on a team. Start acting like it again. It'll help you more than you think."

Dante turned then and made his way over to his

truck. Tommy watched him for a moment before climbing into the driver's seat of his rental. He let Dante's parting words roll through his mind. He'd lost sight of that team-sport fact for a while, but Dante was a thousand percent right about it. Team chemistry was as important to winning as individual hits and spectacular catches. *Maybe my detached, laser-focus approach isn't the right way to handle things after all.* He had credited Lucy with the idea, but it didn't seem like it was going to work for him any better than it seemed to have worked for her.

He found himself really thinking about her then, wondering what she was doing. How was her mother? Had she managed to solve any of her other problems? Or were all of those details part of her lies? Was she still going to their bench in the park?

He closed his eyes and leaned against the headrest, finally letting the emotions flood through him. The truth was that he missed her desperately, like a drowning man missed oxygen.

Maybe I will have that conversation with Dante once I'm back on the team, he thought. *Maybe I'll be ready to hear her point of view on what happened.*

But first he had a career to revive. Team sport or not, he still needed to limit his distractions and get himself back in that starting lineup.

He started the SUV, made his way out of the lot, and headed down the street toward his lonely hotel room.

Chapter 33

TWO WEEKS. Maybe three. Lucy knew he'd be leaving town after that, but she was convinced Thomas would never actually go without at least talking to her one more time. No way. Dante was going to tell him what a massive misunderstanding they'd had, and then he'd come back to their bench. Even if he didn't forgive her, surely he'd want to tell her off one last time? Make the break official? Good or bad, she'd see him at least once more, right?

So, her new normal became working at the diner each morning, walking to the bench with a sure sense that Thomas would reappear, then experiencing crushing devastation when she turned the corner and found the bench empty. After a week, she figured he just needed some time to cool off—not a big deal. When the second week passed, she decided he was probably busy packing and making travel arrangements. So, it was still going to be okay. After the third week, though, her fears were starting to build. *Why hasn't he come yet? Is he okay?* He'd never said when precisely he had to leave, but she knew it was soon. She kept holding onto hope, walking bravely into the park each day, and then leaving an hour later, crushed. Four weeks. Five. Eventually those weeks stacked into months, and still the bench remained empty. And every time, her heart broke a little more.

She knew she was torturing herself. But she still

wasn't ready to give up. Even though logically she knew it was time, she just…couldn't. It didn't matter that he was far away, likely on the set of some movie. He had probably returned to that life he'd described, the one filled with beautiful women throwing themselves at him. And why shouldn't they? He was gorgeous, kind, romantic…and single. She knew the day was coming that she should stop putting herself through the torture. Every day it was the same burst of hope as she rounded the final corner, followed by punishing devastation. It was taking its toll.

The other problem was that she knew she shouldn't be wasting that precious hour. If she instead went straight to Mona's from the diner, it would give her that much more time to study. It would push her closer to her goal of taking the bar exam, meaning the day she could break out of this pit she'd been living in would be that much closer, too.

"Mona…I…I think that maybe it's time that I stop going to the park for lunch," Lucy said hesitantly one morning as they gathered their bags following another shift at the diner. "I'm starting to…feel guilty about wasting the time you're giving me, for one thing."

"I didn't put a bunch of strings on that time," Mona pointed out as they walked out of the employee room, waved at Pat, and pushed the heavy front door open. "And I don't get there until after lunch anyway. So don't use me as an excuse."

"No…I'm not…." Lucy trailed off as they walked toward the employee lot. Was this really about the time and how she was choosing to spend it? Partly, at least, she admitted to herself. She wanted to do anything she could to push up the timeframe for taking the bar. Still…this likely had more to do with Thomas and not wanting to continue torturing herself with wasted hope. "I think it's time to admit to myself that he's never coming back. It's over, and I blew it."

"I'm sorry, hon," Mona said. "I know you loved that boy. It's tough to admit to ourselves when it's time to give up hope. Even after all these years, I'd be lying if I said there wasn't still a part of me that believes my daughter will be back someday."

"What's her name?" Lucy asked, something she'd never dared before. "You've never told me."

Mona blew out a long breath, eyed Lucy quietly for a moment, then seemed to reach a decision about whether or not she wanted to answer. "Meredith. I always called her Merry when she was little."

"Oh Mona, that's a beautiful name. And who knows, maybe Merry will come back someday. You never know."

"If that's how you feel, Luce, then maybe you're *not* ready to give up on your young man," Mona pointed out. They had reached her car, and Mona tossed her bag in the passenger seat before turning to Lucy again. "Take your time deciding, girl. You'll know when—or if—it's the right time to let go."

As Lucy watched Mona drive away, her mind was churning. Was it time? Was she being ridiculous holding onto the ghost of a relationship, one that had never actually *been* a real relationship in the first place? If only she hadn't fallen in love with him, this process of letting go would be so much easier. The old saying, "It's better to have loved and lost than never to have loved at all," came to her then. *What a crock....*

She made her way to the park and walked to the bench again. She didn't stop before the last turn and say a silent prayer like she usually did. No, she suddenly realized that she no longer believed that she'd find him sitting there, and she was right. The bench was empty, as usual. She simply trudged over to it, sat down, and let the memories assail her. She thought about the first time she saw him. Her teasing and saying he was a manbaby. Him nicknaming her his "angel." The first time he'd taken her hand in his. The day he'd playfully danced with her, spinning her to the beat of a song only he could hear.

She smiled at the memories, letting them swirl around. A tear made its way down her face. She swiped it away as she stood and pushed these thoughts away. Time to do what she did best: get laser-focused on her studying. No more park. No more remembering. No more useless hope. And no more tears.

She walked away from the bench without looking back.

Chapter 34

AFTER THAT LAST DAY in the park, time began to pass quickly, each day melting indistinguishably into the next.

Diner, Mona's house, and then home. She rotated through this process like a frustrated hamster on a wheel. She was constantly in motion but never seemed to get anywhere. Up close, the changes were imperceptible. But as the months joined together, she was able to get a better view of her life and begin to see that things *were* changing.

Some of the changes were bad. Her mother's health deteriorated to the point that Lucy had to put her in an assisted-living community. About a year later, a nurse called to tell her that her mom had passed away peacefully in her sleep.

But good change came as well. Once her mother's estate was settled, Lucy was able to significantly pay down her student debt. Her parents' house was paid off, and it was all hers now. Her money woes were no longer casting a dark shadow over her every decision.

She was also finally able to sit for the bar exam, passing it on her first attempt. She took her time researching local law firms, not feeling the need to jump into anything—and definitely not wanting to return to Stanley's firm. Eventually she identified one that seemed like a perfect fit for her: They were looking for a junior associate to specialize in immigration law.

The day she accepted the position, Tania and Mona asked if she wanted a little party to celebrate. She told them that she didn't need anything formal—their pride in her accomplishments was enough for her. But they clearly thought she was being ridiculous, because next thing she knew, a celebration was in the works. Tania and Mona—and even Pat—were meeting that night at a local restaurant.

"Thank you, guys," she said, hugging both Mona and Tania despite the former's gruff protests. "I couldn't have done any of this without you two. You're my family now and...well, I love you."

"We love you, too!" Tania sniffed, jumping in for another hug.

"Get on out of here with that," Mona said, but Lucy caught her wiping away a tear when she thought they weren't looking.

"Want to hang out this afternoon?" Tania asked. "You know, before your party and before you have to start your serious lawyer job?"

"Hah, well, my serious lawyer job doesn't start for a couple weeks," Lucy replied. "I told them I needed time to wrap things up here. But is it okay if I just meet you guys at the restaurant? I've got...well, plans today, sort of. There's one more person I want to share my news with."

This excuse was a bit of a stretch since she didn't actually have anyone else to tell. But something inside her was longing to go back to the bench one last time. She hadn't been back there in ages. *Has it really been two years already?* she wondered. *Or was it even longer than that...?* She'd moved on from that time in her life in so many ways, and all the problems that had held her back from being open with Thomas were gone now. It felt right then, somehow, to go back one more time. To let Thomas know—symbolically, anyway—that she had finally found the freedom they'd talked about so long ago. The girls had been bugging her about getting into the dating pool now that her life was finally on track. *Maybe saying a final farewell today will help make that feel right as well,* she thought.

Even though she hadn't been there in so long, the path was as familiar to her as walking through her own home. She remembered how she used to stop at the last turn and whisper a silent plea that she'd find him there again. She did it now just for the sake of maintaining the ritual, not because she actually thought he'd be there.

She took a deep breath and rounded the last corner. The bench was there to welcome her as it always had. It was so comforting to see it after all this time. She smiled affectionately as she paused to drink in the sight of it. It had the same wrought iron frame and wooden seat, although the wood looked more sun-bleached and worn than ever. She wondered if anyone else had discovered this oasis and used it as a way to find peace. She pulled out her phone and took a picture, envisioning framing it and hanging it in her bedroom. There was a time when that would have made her too sad. But…well, things had changed. She'd grown, and life had rolled on.

Then something else caught her eye; there was something new on the bench that she hadn't noticed initially. It was a plaque attached to the backrest. Leaning closer, she read the simple script: "Lucy's Bench—Where an Angel Came to Find Peace."

She gasped, her hand covering her mouth and her eyes widening with wonder. No one else knew the precise location of the bench. Certainly no one knew how *much* it had meant to her. And no one else called her *angel*....

Thomas!

It had to be Thomas. He'd done this. But how? And when? It hadn't been here last time, although that had been a really long time ago.

She looked around wildly, as though he'd come walking out of the trees like he had the day they met. But no one else was there.

So, what did it mean? And why would he do this? *Unless....*

Was it a message? Was he trying to tell her something? If so, what? She read the plaque over and over, then clicked a picture so she would have it with her always.

She sat down then in shocked silence as her thoughts cartwheeled through her mind. *He'd been here....* Or, more likely, he'd paid the city or the county or whoever to add this sign.

But why?

She closed her eyes and let the old memories flood back again. She didn't even have a picture of him, but she could still see his face so clearly in her mind. She thought about the good times they'd shared, and then she thought about the last time she saw him, that devastating night in the club.

Maybe he'd looked for her. Maybe she'd given up too soon. Regret twisted through her, even though she had needed to move on in order to survive and finally fix her myriad problems. She'd done the right thing for herself. But at the same time, she had ruined any chance they could have had to find each other. The message was probably his way of letting go and letting her know he'd forgiven her. Or perhaps that Dante had finally told him her side of the story, and he understood.

If only she could find him now. What would that search even look like? Where would she start? What did she know about him that she could tell a private investigator?

She rolled the idea around in her head for several long minutes. Well, she knew his approximate age. She had once guessed he worked as an actor, but he'd never confirmed that. He had a friend named Dante and a really beautiful sister named…was it Jessica? She couldn't remember for sure.

She shook her head in frustration. That was a really pathetic and inadequate number of clues. It would take quite the world-renowned investigator to find someone based on that microscopic pile of information. No wonder she never seriously pursued trying to find him before. It seemed almost impossible.

And yet, the more she thought about how wonderful it would be to find him, the more she wanted to at least try…and the more urgently she wanted to start immediately. So, what would she do? Call every Jessica in New Jersey until she found one who had a brother named Thomas? Talk about impossible, especially since she wasn't even sure she had his sister's name right anyway. Plus, who knew if his sister even lived here anymore?

She definitely remembered the name Dante, however. That desperate conversation she'd had with him would always be burned in her mind. But she had no idea if he was a friend from New Jersey or from wherever Thomas lived. After she thought about it a while, she decided that lead was also a dead end.

The only true lead, she decided, was that he was in

some sort of industry that would attract hangers-on. That maybe he was famous somehow. He'd been afraid of the bad press if she posted anything online about him that day they met. He traveled for his job extensively, and yet it wasn't for an office job. And whatever industry he was in, it attracted women who wanted to hang around, ostensibly just to sleep with him. Actor or stuntman had been her first guesses. He'd told her he wasn't a musician, so it wasn't that. Who else lived that kind of lifestyle? Reality stars? Athletes?

The good part was that if he was somehow famous, or at least working in that sort of world, then there might be evidence and information about him online.

She was going to ask her friends tonight if they had other ideas. Thomas had taken the effort to reach out to her with the message on the bench. Now it was her turn.

She was going to find him or die trying.

Chapter 35

DURING THE spring training before his rookie year, Tommy had dug deep inside himself, drawing on a strength he hadn't even realized he possessed. He had been utterly focused on his goal of breaking into the Majors, pushing himself to the brink in the hope of catching a coach or trainer's eye.

And here he was again—had it really only been a year ago?—and his commitment to proving himself now doubled in its intensity. He was running the bases like a demon was at his heels. He was diving to make spectacular catches in the outfield. And he was spending as much time in batting practice as he could. He'd been out of the game a long time during rehab. He had a bunch of kinks to work out and an endless list of things to prove, to the team and to himself. He knew he was putting on a show and matching or exceeding the skills of the other players, veterans as well as others in his position. Under normal circumstances, he was pretty sure there would be a spot on the team for him.

Unfortunately, these circumstances weren't normal. He'd let his manager down, and now the man was unlikely to walk back his threats. Tommy was pretty sure that no matter how many home runs he hit or diving catches he snagged, he was about to make the walk of shame right back down to Single A.

Jack hadn't said anything to him about it since Tommy reported to Florida. And although Tommy considered approaching him and begging for just one more chance at explaining himself, in the end he had decided not to push his luck. He'd kept his head down and his eyes on the prize, letting his performance and work ethic speak for themselves. He'd remembered what Dante had to say about the way team bonds and chemistry were just as important as on-field play. So, he started making time to get dinner with his boys when they offered. He stopped short at going out drinking in the local clubs, though. He told himself this was because he didn't want word to get back to Jack. But if he was being completely honest, he wasn't ready for that kind of thing just yet. The sting of everything that had happened with Lucy was still too fresh and painful.

On the last day of camp, before the rosters were to be announced, Jack called him to his office. Tommy tried to clear his mind of any expectations or excitement. This likely wouldn't be a congratulatory conversation and therefore wouldn't end well for him.

"Coach, you wanted to see me?" Tommy asked, knocking on the open door even as he stepped in. "What's up?"

"Close the door and have a seat, son," Jack said, not getting up from behind his desk. "How's the head?"

"I think my bell finally stopped ringing for good. I rarely get headaches these days."

"Good, good, glad to hear it," Jack said, leaning back in his chair now, his steely gaze not leaving Tommy's face as he quietly assessed him. "We've had a close eye on you, and I had everyone in the facility following your progress. Every single one of them had a glowing report, every single time. 'This kid's the real deal,' they said. 'The first part of his rookie year was no fluke,' they told me. 'You'd be crazy not to put him in your starting lineup,' or so I hear."

"They're right," Tommy said. "I'm ready, Coach, I am. I know you were furious with me after what happened at the club that night, and I totally get it. I *do*. But I swear to you that it only happened because I was so driven to get back in game shape that I exercised the whole day away. I did it because I was ready then, and I'm even more ready now, to prove to you what I can do. When I was working out that day, I had no idea the boys were coming to get me and take me out. I didn't plan on having a headache start up at the club. And I certainly didn't know I was going to get blindsided by a messy breakup with my girl. All those things came together in one night, and it was a disaster. And yes, I banged my head up pretty good when I passed out. But I wasn't falling-down drunk. I didn't do drugs or get a DUI or wrap my car around a telephone pole. I know you were disappointed in me, but Coach, I'm sorry. I made mistakes, and I'm ready to spend my career proving to you that you're not making a mistake today if you put me on the team. Or if you do it tomorrow, or in two weeks, or in two months. I can do this. I'm ready. Let me play."

"Thank you for owning up, kid," Jack said after pausing a moment to let Tommy's words settle in the room. "I see you, and I see the effort you've been making toward turning things around. I'll talk to the hitting coaches and the rest of the staff. You'll know our decision soon."

"Thanks, Coach," Tommy said, retreating quickly.

It felt like his whole career was teetering on the edge of a cliff, and although he'd tried his best, there was nothing more he could do to pull it back on solid ground. It was totally in Jack's hands now.

Chapter 36

THE NEXT DAY, the team started pulling guys in to let them know who had made the roster and who didn't. Tommy was on edge the entire time, but his agent called him early in the afternoon with the news: He'd done it. He was back in right field.

"Hey, you comin' out with us tonight to celebrate?" Mick asked as they were heading out that night. "There's about a fifty-course meal out there just callin' my name!"

"Of course there is," Tommy said with a chuckle as he promised to join them, thrilled they were his teammates once again.

Back at the hotel after dinner, Dante cornered him in the lobby with a laser stare.

"Let's have a seat," Dante said, tipping his head toward a quiet area tucked in the corner of the lobby. They sat across from each other, Tommy leaning back while Dante, pinging with energy, leaned forward, his arms resting on his knees.

"You're on the team, right?" Dante asked.

"Yep, you know I am," Tommy replied. He had a feeling he knew where Dante was going with this. "This is about Lucy, isn't it?"

"You promised me, T. You make the team, you make the time for this talk. So now that's what's happening—I'm collecting on our deal. But I'm doing the talking and you're doing the listening, you got me?"

"I got you," he agreed easily. He was feeling lighter about everything now that he'd managed to snatch his career out of the trash. For the first time, he felt ready for whatever Dante was about to hit him with. "What is it? What have you been burning to tell me?"

"You know you're my boy, right T? You know I've always got your back?"

Tommy nodded. "Yeah, man, of course."

"Then you have to know that I'm not playing you or lying to you now," Dante continued.

"I know, D."

"Tommy, she wasn't lying to you, either. Whatever you thought happened that night is *not* what happened. You with me so far? That girl swore to me that she was exactly who you thought she was: a beautiful lady caught in a really tough life. I'm a pretty good judge of character, and I believed her."

"Okay, so why was she dressed like she was on a date and dancing with some guy in a club?" Tommy demanded. "She told me she had absolutely no time to herself. It made no sense. It *still* doesn't."

"Shhh, I told you, Uncle Dante is talking, and you're listening. So, let's backtrack. What happened to you that night? Why were *you* in the club?"

"My friends showed up and took me out to celebrate my recovery," Tommy replied.

"Right, and did you particularly want to go, or did I all but kidnap you and guilt-trip you about how the boys needed to spend time with you?"

"Uh, well, yeah, you basically forced me," Tommy agreed. "I told you I couldn't go out because of my promise to Jack."

"Right, yet you went anyway. For us."

"Yes, but what does this have to do with Lucy?"

"Boy, are you *trying* to be dense here?" Dante roared, his tone causing a few startled hotel guests to look over at them. "The same exact thing happened to *her* that night! Her girl-pack showed up, totally surprised her, played pretty-princess dress-up on her, and shoved her out the door. Meanwhile, one of them stayed back with her mama. They guilted her just like we guilted you. She went for *them*, but she told me she spent the whole night wishing that all that effort went into getting dolled up for *you!*"

"She didn't look like someone who'd been dragged out of the house against her will," Tommy countered. "She was dancing with some guy and laughing like he was putting on a comedy show."

Dante shrugged and rolled his eyes. "Dude, she just surrendered to the whole thing. That poor girl decided to allow a single drop of fun to fall on her. Then, the minute she let herself smile, you came in and destroyed her. What, you only liked her if she was sad and miserable? Well congratulations, because I'll bet she still is."

Tommy stared, unseeing, as his mind worked to match his memories of that night with the things Dante had just told him. Making his way through the crowded dance floor, seeing her when Dante pointed her out, realizing it was Lucy, battling back the jealousy and shock when he realized she was with another man.... How had she reacted though when she saw him? Their eyes had locked and...had she smiled at him? Immediately started walking toward him, a happy look on her face? Is that how a woman would react if she'd been caught in a web of lies? *No...probably not*, he admitted within himself. Wouldn't a more natural reaction in that type of situation be a look of blazing guilt? Followed by an attempt to create a cover story?

Tommy rubbed his head; another headache was starting. But he tried to ignore it and concentrate on what Lucy's exact reaction had been. Did it line up with how he'd seen things, or was Dante's version of events starting to make more sense?

"You okay over there, T?" Dante asked.

"Give me a minute," Tommy replied. "Still trying to pair up what you said with what I thought I knew. I'm thinking that if she'd had something to hide, she would have come in hot with a cover story or at least *looked* guilty, huh?"

"You'd think so," Dante agreed, "especially if she'd supposedly spent months trying to reel you in like a fish she caught."

"I'm trying to remember her exact reaction to seeing me," Tommy continued. "You pointed her out, I recognized her, and a few seconds later she saw me, too. Then my memory kind of fades. I got mad in that moment, and I think my brain shut down. That's when the pain started spiking, too, by the way."

"A smile lit up her pretty little angel face," Dante said, "and she came running over to see you. She never even looked back or said a word to the guy that you believed she was with."

"I used to *call* her angel," Tommy said softly, almost to himself, as his chest was starting to tighten. Great, was a heart attack next?

"I can see why," Dante continued. "She tried to chase your dumb ass down, a sweet little smile on her face. I think she even said something about being so happy to see you. I didn't hear any excuses or see any guilt, T. I didn't. But like always, brother, I had your back. So, I shot her some looks that could melt paint off a wall and then stepped aside to give you two privacy. By the time you went storming off, the rest of the crew had joined me, and I'd filled them in. That girl was so desperate to tell her side of the story that she braved talking to a whole line of angry men. I sent the boys to find you, then I let her talk. She was only about a sentence or two into her story when I started believing her."

Tommy leaned forward to rest his elbows on his knees, his head gripped miserably between his hands. "No, no, no...I messed up so badly. Why wouldn't I let her talk? Why wouldn't I listen?"

"I don't know, man," Dante replied with a shrug. "But you were right about one thing."

"What's that?" Tommy asked, almost afraid to hear the reply.

"Your girl *is* an angel."

"Yeah, I know," Tommy said with a nod. "I was falling in love with her, man. Or maybe I *already* loved her. How did I do something like that to the woman I loved?"

"Stubbornness? IQ of a turnip?"

"Yeah, both I guess."

"Fine. So, what are you going to do about it?"

"I need to get back to New Jersey," Tommy told him. "Do you think I could stack enough hours together to fly home?"

"Nah, man, you crazy?" Dante said, a look of incredulity on his face. "You just made the team! You can't go pulling some crazy stunt now. Come on, you know we play the Yankees about a million times during the season. Just go find her after our first road game with them."

"Yeah, okay, that sounds good," Tommy agreed.

"I'll go pull up the schedule and see when we have our first series with them."

Dante pointed. "*Now* you're thinking."

"Thanks, man." Tommy stood up, fighting back the urge to pull up the schedule immediately. "Seriously, next time you see me throwing my life away, have the boys sit on me until I listen to you, okay?"

"You got it." Dante stood and smiled, clapping Tommy on the shoulder. "You'll figure this out, T. I'm sure it's not too late. I saw the look in her eyes. She loves you too, man."

Does she? Tommy couldn't help but wonder.

Chapter 37

HE WALKED BACK to his room as the regrets pummeled him. He'd been so ready to think the worst of her. Why? Why wouldn't he let her speak? Did he even deserve a second chance? *Probably not*, he thought as he swiped the key card on his room door and pushed inside. But second chance or not, he had to at least find a way to apologize to her. She deserved that much.

He kicked off his shoes, sat down on the bed, and pulled up the Orioles' schedule on his phone. They had a home series with the Yankees early in the season. But they'd be in New York a few weeks after that. As teams in the same division, they met up frequently each year.

That's what I'll do then, he thought. When they were in New York for that first road series, he'd find a way to get to their park.

But wait, if I go to the park at the usual time, will I have enough time to say everything I want to say and still make it back to Yankee Stadium for the report time before a night game?

He did the math in his head…*no, probably not.* Especially when he factored in the infamous New York and New Jersey traffic. It wasn't going to work. He needed a series with New York that was bookended by a day off, followed by a home series. Baltimore was only three or so hours from New York.

Maybe I could miss the team flight and drive a rental back in plenty of time.

He scanned the schedule again, looking for days

off next to away games with the Yankees. There was one that matched up perfectly, but it wasn't for months.

Months?!

Maybe he could make a quick flight on an off-day? He'd be taking a lot of chances by doing that, but...*maybe?* Or there was always a chance he might luck out and a game would get postponed for rain when they were there, since Yankee Stadium didn't have a retractable roof. Perhaps they had some games with the Mets or the Phillies? He'd have to pull the whole schedule apart and try to figure something out. Either way, he *had* to find a way to reach out to her. To tell her how very sorry he was for being a stubborn jerk. *And to just...see her again.*

But the schedule didn't give him any chances to sneak away and see her for months. He tried calling Jenna to see if she could go for him, but her schedule wouldn't allow it, either. He was soon miserable, knowing Lucy was out there somewhere, still dealing with her problems alone, and now likely hating him on top of everything else. *Did* she hate him? Or maybe she just missed him...? He wondered if he'd ever actually see her again. By the time he got there, would she still be making her daily trip to the bench? Or had he managed to steal that small bit of comfort from her?

He eventually had to push those worries aside, though, for the sake of his career. So, he copied her approach for the second time and put his entire self into focusing on the game. He worked on his hitting endlessly, looking for ways to switch things up once pitchers thought they had him figured out. He wanted to show the world that he still had it, and that his success in the early days of his career hadn't been a fluke. He threw himself into his fielding, making amazing catches with no thought to the effects on his tired, bruised body. Soon his hard work was paying off, and he had amassed the homeruns and RBIs to prove it. Everything was finally falling into place for him. Now he just had to make it to that series with the Yankees that bordered a day off.

He had to find her.

*   *   *

When the New York series in question finally arrived, Thomas was a jumpy bundle of nerves. His mind was already on that park bench in New Jersey, and his playing showed it. His focus was off, and he couldn't have hit a beach ball if he'd tried, let alone a big-league fastball.

By the third game, his coaches had figured out that something was off. Jack benched him then, telling Tommy he clearly needed a few days off. Tommy was so distracted he didn't even argue, opting instead to take the time in the dugout to let his mind swirl with the possibilities of what might happen in the park. He was grateful for the reprieve from playing, too. He needed to sit this game out. With his luck and current level of distraction, he might end up taking another pitch to the head.

He let the coaching staff know he was staying back and would catch up to the team in Baltimore. Then he secured another night in the hotel while the rest of the team went to the airport. He needn't have bothered, though, as he barely could sleep. The thoughts and worries about what might happen slammed through his head all night.

He took a long and ridiculously expensive Uber ride to the park and jogged the familiar route toward the bench. This was going to be it for a while, he knew—his only chance to reach out to her until, at the very least, the All-Star Break in July.

Please let her be here, he thought. *Please, please, please....*

He waited for hours, but she never showed. He spent so long waiting, in fact, that he ended up having to take a last-minute commercial flight so he could make it back to Baltimore without having to drive through the night.

As he sat on the small commuter plane, he wondered what he could possibly do to find her now. How could he get a message to her? Basically, all he knew was that she loved that bench. That seemed to be the most direct route to her. Even if he took a billboard out somewhere, there were no guarantees she'd ever see it.

In the end, he asked Jenna to help. She contacted the county parks department and made a generous donation in exchange for a simple plaque. Tommy contemplated what he should put in the message for days. It had to be something the parks department would approve, yet his angel would understand. It couldn't be a long apology that ended with him giving her his number or anything equally direct. He finally settled on a simple dedication, hoping maybe one day she'd see it. And hopefully she'd understand that he was sorry, too.

Maybe she'd even feel, somehow through his simple words, that he had loved her.

Chapter 38

"SO, WHAT are your plans now?" Tania asked at the small gathering they'd planned for Lucy. The group had picked an informal sports restaurant and bar, and they were currently perched at a pub table, eating and drinking in celebration of her happy news. Televisions circled the bar, each featuring a different channel. The atmosphere was casual, happy, and relaxed...whereas Lucy was feeling anything but.

She knew they were all there to celebrate her achievements and lovingly launch her into this next stage of her life. But she couldn't focus on any of that or even be mentally in the moment. Her every thought was about Thomas.

How can I find him?!

"Uh...what were you saying?" she asked when she realized all eyes were looking at her expectantly.

"Where are you tonight?" Tania asked with a laugh. "Already mentally decorating your fancy new office?"

"Oh, no, nothing like that," she said with a small laugh. "Actually...well, something kind of strange happened to me today. I think I need some advice. Maybe one of you will have the perfect idea for what I should do."

"Oh great, girl talk," Pat groused, shaking his head. "I'm so excited."

"Shut your trap, old man," Mona snapped. "What's on your mind, girl? What happened today?"

"Well, I…uh, do you guys remember me talking about Thomas?" she started cautiously. "The guy I met in the park?"

"Remember him?" Mona said with a sharp chuckle. "You mooned about that boy forever. Hell, you're *still* mooning over him."

Tania gave Mona an obvious kick under the table then, causing Mona to look back wide-eyed. Then Mona shrugged a defensive, "What?" posture while Tania chimed in, "Yes, of course we remember. You confessed that he's the gorgeous guy I served at the diner that day. I'm still hot and bothered just thinking about that chiseled face of his. So, yeah, short answer: of course we all remember."

"*I* don't remember," Pat bit out grumpily as he took another drink of his beer.

"Okay, good," Lucy continued as though Pat hadn't spoken. "Do you also remember how that…uh…relationship ended?"

"The big break-up that Mona and I kind of had a hand in," Tania said. "I'm still so sorry about dragging you out that night."

"No, it wasn't your fault," Lucy reassured before continuing. "Well, okay, then I guess you're all up to speed. He and I had that terrible argument in the club, and I haven't seen him since. I looked for him at the park for a long time, but eventually I stopped going. It was just too hard, plus I needed to study."

"Did you find him today?" Mona asked. "Is that where this is headed?"

Tania gasped in delight at the thought.

"Oh, no, I wish!" Lucy replied. "Unfortunately, it's not as good a story as that would be. But I did go back to the bench where we met for the first time in a long time. I suppose I wanted to…maybe visit that small part of my life once more before finally closing the book."

"Makes sense," Tania said.

"Still don't know what we're talking about," Pat said to no one in particular.

"She got separated from the man she loved," Mona snapped. "Keep up!"

"Why doesn't she just call him?" Pat asked, looking progressively more confused.

"We didn't have contact information for each other," Lucy said. "And that was my fault. I made losing track of each other stunningly easy to accomplish."

"Well, that was stupid," Pat offered.

Lucy laughed then. She couldn't help it. This ragtag group—this family she'd managed to find—was such a funny mix of wildly differing personalities. "Yes, it was stupid," she agreed. "*I* was incredibly stupid."

"Get back to today!" Tania insisted. "You're killing me with the suspense!"

"Sorry. Okay, so…" Lucy began, a smile dawning on her face, "I got to the bench where we used to meet, and I found a message from him—he had a plaque placed on the bench with a dedication to me, but he chose words that I know only he would use. Like, he called me *angel,* which was his nickname for me. He has to be the one who left it. It couldn't have been anyone else."

"Oh, how romantic!" Tania said, delight sparkling in her eyes.

"Yes, it was a beautiful and romantic gesture," Lucy agreed, "and I think it means…well, I think it means he forgives me for what happened. But I still don't know how to *find* him. It's not like his phone number was etched into the plaque, too."

"Oh," Tania said, looking crestfallen now. "That's so sad."

"Yeah," Pat added dryly. "A real emotional roller coaster."

"So help me, old man…," Mona said, menacingly.

"So, this is the part where I need everyone's help," Lucy explained. "I know very little about him, so hiring a private investigator would be…well, probably it would be just as effective to set the money on fire. But some things he said and some clues I put together…well, they made me think that maybe he's famous. It's not much to go on, I know. I can't prove that, and I don't even know what kind of famous I'm talking about, other than to say I know for certain he isn't a musician."

"Okay, so what *are* we talking, here?" Mona asked. "Heir to the crown of some country…that kind of famous?"

Lucy pondered Mona's guess for a moment. "Well, no, I hadn't thought of that, but I don't think that quite fits with what I know. More like Hollywood actor, stuntman, producer, or director, maybe. Something along those lines."

"So, definitely Hollywood?" Tania asked.

"No, I can't really say anything *definitely*. And that's a big part of my problem. Reality star, perhaps? I don't think dancer fits him. Maybe professional athlete…or maybe he's an Olympian? Something along those lines might work with what I know, too."

"Okay, so what do you think we can do to help?" Mona asked. "I don't exactly have a lot of pull in Hollywood circles."

"No, me neither, of course," Lucy said, feeling a bit more dejected now. Honestly, what *could* any of them do to help? "I guess…well, I guess I thought it might help to brainstorm ideas for what to do with this tiny drop of information I have."

"I suppose we could look for people named Thomas on the *IMDb* website," Tania offered.

"He said people in his life call him 'Tommy' or 'T,' so maybe we could look for those names too," Lucy said, liking the idea. At least it was a start.

"And maybe Wikipedia too," Tania continued. "Not sure how far we'd get on social media with just a first name, but we could probably poke around a few sites as well."

"Well, I'm out," Pat said. "I can barely operate my phone."

"Yeah, I'm not going to be much help either, I'm afraid," Mona said, giving Lucy a knowing look. "You know how little luck I've had tracking people down on the Internet."

"Wait! Do you have a picture of him?" Tania asked, excitedly. "I think there are ways to try to face-match pictures!"

"No, this goes back to Pat's 'Lucy's an idiot' stance. But I never even got a picture of him."

"You sure this guy actually exists?" Pat asked, a dubious look on his face now. "I need another beer if we're going to be ghost-hunting. Anyone else?"

"I'll go with you," Tania offered, sliding off her chair and walking toward the bar with Pat before stopping short, her eyes wide. "Umm…Lucy? I think you need to see this."

Lucy slid off her seat and followed Tania toward the bar.

"What?" she asked. "What are you pointing at?"

"That television," Tania said, looking utterly astonished. "The one in the middle. It's the craziest thing, and I know it's been years since I saw him, but wow—that guy on the TV sure looks like the guy I was drooling over in the diner that day."

Lucy stared at Tania as her mind slowly processed what she'd just heard. Afraid to allow Tania's words to ignite hope in her chest, she finally had to force herself to break free from Tania's gaze and look in the direction she'd indicated.

Once again, Lucy found herself mentally praying that familiar pleading refrain that she would see him again.

Please let Tania be right. Please let it be him....

Chapter 39

LUCY'S EYES skirted across the screens until they landed on the person Tania was indicating. She blinked a few times and then walked trancelike until she was at the bar and could go no further.

Tania was right, and her prayer had been answered—it was Thomas, and he was on television! There was no doubt about it.

I've found him....

"Can you turn the volume up on this one?" Lucy asked after seeing a logo on the screen. "It's the MLB Network."

"Oh, no, I'm sorry, we usually just keep the closed captioning on," the bartender replied. "Is it not on? And did you need another drink?"

"Who is that?" Lucy went on, pointing. "Do you know his name?"

"Well, I can't see it from here, but MLB Network, you said?" the bartender asked as he handed a couple beers to another customer. "The top story that's been scrolling all day long is about Hiller and Layton finally meeting up again. My guess is that whatever you're seeing has something to do with that."

"Hiller? Layton?" Lucy asked in rapid response. She wanted to reach across the bar and wring the story out of this idiot. "Can you give me the basics?"

"Pretty much everyone has heard at least some part of this story if they follow sports at all. Um…when was it? Three or four years ago maybe? Zach Hiller, a big-time pitching ace for the Yankees, knocked Tommy Layton's lights out with a wild throw. Poor guy missed the rest of his rookie season rehabbing."

"Tommy? Layton?" she asked, repeating his words like a parrot as the excitement bubbled inside her. "What team does he play for, do you know?"

"Oh yeah, Baltimore Orioles," the bartender said. "I think he's been back with the team for a while. Well, you know, once he recovered from that head injury. Guess it all turned out okay."

"Then why is he being interviewed now?" Lucy asked, suddenly nervous. Had Thomas gotten hurt again?

"Well, after the pitch took Layton out, Hiller lost his mind or something and disappeared for a while. I don't know anything more about that, except that suddenly he's back with the Yankees. Tomorrow is the big matchup in the Bronx. Hiller's pitching, so it'll be his first time facing Layton since he about killed both their careers."

"Tomorrow," she repeated, feeling dazed now. "In the Bronx...."

"Uh, yeah...hey, are you okay?" the bartender asked, looking at her more closely. "Should I call you a cab?"

"Oh...no, sorry," Lucy replied, reaching into her purse and pulling out a few bills as a tip. He'd certainly been more than helpful. "I just...I thought I recognized...anyway, thank you so much for taking the time to fill me in on that story."

"Sure, no problem—and thanks," he said, accepting the tip and then turning away to help another customer.

*   *   *

Lucy swung around to find Tania still there, wide-eyed with shock.

"You heard all of that?" Lucy asked. "Oh my gosh, Tania! You found him!"

"Come back to the table," Tania said. "You've *got* to tell Mona and Pat!"

"Yeah, okay...sure...."

Lucy ended up in too much of a daze to say much, though, so Tania proceeded to give Pat and Mona all the incredible details.

"Baseball!" Pat said, a gleam in his eye at last. "*Now* I'm interested!"

Lucy's mind spun wildly as she tried to match up the story the bartender had told her with what she already knew. His name was Tommy Layton. He was a professional baseball player. That injury—the one she could still remember him wincing from—had been caused by a baseball to the head. And the traveling he said he had to do...that all fit, too. She didn't know much about sports, but she knew they had to fly around the country for their games. And the lifestyle of a professional athlete also fit the one he described.

She found him. She *actually* found him.

She closed her eyes and let the happiness that this newfound knowledge brought wash through her.

"Lucy, girl, you alright over there?" Mona asked. "I assume you're scheming up a way to go see him now. I mean, you do have a little time before your new job starts. You may as well take this opportunity to track him down."

"Yes, of course," Lucy agreed...until a new thought shocked her back to reality. "But wait—how will I even contact him? It's not like I can walk into the stadium and ask to see him. I'll never get past security, I'm sure."

"He's playing tomorrow, right?" Tania asked. "Oh Lucy, you *have* to go to the game!"

"Yeah, sure," Lucy said, her mind churning, "but how in the world will I get his attention? I'm sure regular fans can't just chat with the players whenever they please."

"Maybe try to sit near the field?" Tania suggested. "Find out what position he plays and get a seat close to that area so you can wave him down?"

"This game is all over the news, though," Pat pointed out. "You'd be lucky to even get a ticket in the first place, let alone one close to the field."

"Maybe you could drop off a note at the ticket window or at customer service?" Mona offered.

"I doubt they'd pass along a message from a random fan to a player," Lucy said, feeling discouraged now. "Maybe I could try standing outside after the game is over? Maybe he'd drive by?"

"Wow, I don't know Lucy," Tania said, shaking her head. "That doesn't seem very likely."

"What about a sign?" Pat asked. "He sent you a message, now you can send him one back."

"A sign?" Lucy asked, confused. "What do you mean?"

"Sometimes fans carry signs—like on big poster boards—to root for their favorite players," Pat said, clearly happy to be the baseball expert in the group. "Get a ticket as close as possible to the field, then hold that sign up during the game. The cameras might even pick you up if you do it right."

"A sign!" Lucy repeated, thrilled with this suggestion. "That's it! That's *perfect!*"

Ideas for messages were already whirling through her mind.

*　　　*　　　*

She stopped at a drugstore on the way home to pick up a poster board and some markers. Then, sitting in her living room with her laptop, she launched herself into finding and reading every article she possibly could about Thomas.

The pictures confirmed it: Tommy Layton, jersey number 67, right fielder for the Baltimore Orioles, was her Thomas. She looked to see if she could find any mention of him having a wife or girlfriend, but there was very little personal information about him. The stories were all about his great rookie year, his devastating injury, and now about this rematch with Zach Hiller.

She looked for information on his teammates and discovered a player named Dante Jackson, the centerfielder. The picture matched her memory of the man she'd seen that night at the club. It all fit together. The tiny shreds of information she'd had about him easily wove together now to create a fuller idea of who he was, of why he'd had so much time to spend with her, and why he had disappeared so thoroughly at the end.

She went to an online ticket site and bought a seat for the game. She took Pat's advice and got as close a seat as she could and still afford. She'd be in the second tier; not ideal, but it would have to do.

Now she had to decide what message to put on the poster. She realized she had to do the same thing he had done: send a message that he'd know, one-hundred percent, was from her. She tried and discarded numerous drafts of different messages on scrap paper, working late into the night until she was finally satisfied that she'd gotten it right.

Wow, she thought, *maybe this will actually work....*

Maybe she'd get a chance to talk to him again. Maybe he'd finally let her explain her side of things. How would it feel to be with him again? Would their old chemistry still be there? Or would he be more like a stranger, detached and distant? Maybe polite and kind but uninterested in anything more. Maybe he'd introduce her to his wife and kids. *And maybe he won't talk to me at all....*

She pushed all these fears aside, because no matter which scenario played out, this was something she had to do. Thomas had sent her a beautiful message.

Now it was time to send one back.

Chapter 40

AFTER TOMMY was sure the plaque had been placed on the bench in the park, he wondered if he'd maybe feel a sense of closure. A readiness to move on since he hadn't been able to find her. But that feeling eluded him. The baseball season continued to churn along, and the anniversary of his injury came and went. So did the anniversary of the day he and Lucy had met. Time was passing, but it wasn't providing a feeling of resolution.

He found himself excited for the off-season so he could look for her again. But when that time came, after a few weeks of checking the bench and not finding her, he stopped trying. It seemed like he was just torturing himself. He wondered, then, if cutting off that daily burst of hope would help drive out the feelings of longing and emptiness. But that didn't happen, either. He still looked for her face in every crowd, no matter where he was.

The next baseball season came and went, and again he hoped he could move on and find peace. His family and teammates all began urging him to put himself out there again, sometimes even going so far as trying to set him up on dates. But he just couldn't enjoy them or find ways to connect with any of the women he met. Soon he started refusing these efforts altogether. As long as he knew Lucy was still out there somewhere, and likely still stuck in that tidal wave of problems she had once described to him....

They had never really put a proper end to things between them and, because of that, he just couldn't let her go. Theirs had been a very untraditional love story, certainly. Neither of them had fallen for someone else or decided there wasn't a strong enough foundation for them to build their lives together. Their relationship hadn't really even started, and it didn't really end, either. So, in his mind, it was like being frozen in time. It was her fault for refusing to exchange numbers or personal details, and it was his for storming away that night at the club. So, as long as she was still out there and out of his reach, and as long as their story remained unfinished, he just didn't want to move on. It was like a wound that wouldn't heal.

Then there was his strong sense that they'd find each other again. That seemed fairly illogical, of course, since both of them had stopped going to the park. How would it even happen? He figured that the only chance they had would be if Lucy recognized him in a baseball game. But he doubted she'd ever even seen any professional sports before. So, unless she suddenly became a fan, it was doubtful someone living in northern New Jersey would just happen to take particular notice of the Orioles' right fielder one day. Even though he'd made the All-Star team the last season, he wasn't exactly a huge star. And he definitely wasn't a household name.

He got a lot closer, however, when Zach Hiller returned to baseball. He'd vanished from the game after the pitch that put Tommy on the injured list. And no one thought he'd come back after he broke his contract with the Yankees. Then the whispers started that he might return the previous season, and soon the media was covering his starts in Japan for the Yomiuri Giants with a zeal that bordered obsession. That's when the momentum really started building, followed by the buzz of speculation about what it all meant. The speculation finally ended that spring when the Yankees welcomed him back with a multimillion-dollar, multiyear deal. It was official: Zach Hiller was a pro ballplayer again.

When Hiller officially signed, that's when Tommy found himself once again propelled into the spotlight. He knew his name had been all over the headlines after his injury, of course. But he'd been in so much pain and misery that he barely noticed. Now that he was back on the Orioles, though, there was no avoiding it. Every move he made and word he said was analyzed against the backdrop of this enormously anticipated matchup between Hiller and himself: the first time he took a turn at bat with Zach on the mound since both their worlds had exploded so spectacularly.

In a way, he was mortified by the attention. He wanted to be known for his strong offense and his work in the field, and not for being too slow to get out of the way of a missile off the fingertips of a legend. A big part of him wanted to avoid the interviews and the chatter and the nonsense and just keep his head down. He wanted to play the game he loved, not become talk-radio fodder.

But there was another side of him that was thrilled at the idea of all the press coverage—because the more his face got out there, the greater the chance that Lucy could see him on television, hear him on the radio, or find his picture online. That part of him won out in the end. So, as the Orioles' first series with New York drew closer and the chatter became louder, he agreed to go on local radio shows both in Baltimore and New York.

He gave time to the print media. He flew to Bristol, Connecticut, on an off-day and did the rounds of the ESPN programs—affectionately called the "car wash" by anyone who'd ever donned a suit and bounced from show to show in a day packed with interviews.

He basically said the same things to everyone who asked. He walked through what he remembered of that fateful game, and he gave a quick summary of his rehab, which had stretched longer than anticipated because of the ongoing headaches. He made sure to say each time that he had never, not once, blamed Zach, adding that he'd felt a tremendous amount of guilt when he heard that Zach had left the game. Tommy told them that he was thrilled for the opportunity to face this legendary pitcher again and happy that they were both back to playing the game they loved.

Before he knew it, they were in New York for the series, and the media blitz was a full-blown furor. It was time to get this big moment behind them. The whole experience had left Tommy exhausted. And deep in his heart, despite everything, he didn't actually believe Lucy would show up. Even if she did, would she want to see him again anyway? After everything that had happened?

At least, he told himself, he'd done everything he could to land in as many headlines and social-media posts as possible. Now he needed to keep his head in the game and focus. It was like he knew that if she didn't see him now, she never would. But maybe that was a good thing, right? Who knew, maybe this matchup with Hiller was what he needed to find the closure he'd been seeking so long?

Maybe he could finally seal all of it in the past.

Chapter 41

AS THE SERIES with the Yankees began, Dante was, as usual, looking out for him. He'd become skeptical about why Tommy bothered to put himself out there in the media the way he had. They knew each other like brothers, and Tommy was fully aware that Dante would find it out of character for him to submit to the spotlight the way he had.

"I couldn't figure it out," Dante said after the first game of the series was behind them. Hiller had been announced as the pitcher for game three, so a few reporters had used that as a talking point with Tommy after the game. "I was watching you, T, doing all these fool interviews. One or two, sure, I get it. But I just couldn't figure out why you'd done so many others."

"Oh, yeah?" Tommy asked, his tone teasing. "Maybe I just like being a superstar."

"Nah, I know you man. That's not your style." Dante gathered the last of his things and closed the locker he was using at Yankee Stadium. It was time to go catch the bus to the hotel, grab a late dinner, and bask in their game-one win. "But I think I might have finally figured you out."

"Oh, this I have to hear," Tommy said, picking up his bag as they started to walk toward the exit. "Hit me: What's your theory?"

"Can't say it's a great one," Dante pointed out, clearly hedging now. "I mean, I don't know. I still wonder if I'm missing something here. But, well, maybe you think you've got some kind of penance to pay. Z's the one who threw that pitch. He felt so guilty that he dropped off the planet for a few years. He did his time feeling bad about what happened. But you, on the other hand? I don't know. I think there was a big part of you that felt guilty for not getting your fat head out of the way. So, it's like you think you owe this whole time in the spotlight as a way to say sorry for all of it."

"Huh," Tommy said, thoughtful now.

"How'd I do?" Dante asked as they climbed aboard the bus.

"You know, I hadn't thought about it that way, I guess." Tommy slid into an open seat and waited for Dante to take the one next to him. "But I suppose there might be a pinch of truth in there somewhere. I don't know if you remember, but you were the one who broke the news to me that Z had ended his contract and left the game. Man, I felt so guilty when I heard that. I *did* think I should have been able to get out of the way of that pitch, you're right about that. Ask Jack, but I was worried in a big way that I'd get Pipped because of that injury. So, I was worried about *my* career already, and then suddenly I felt like the responsibility of Z's career was on me, too. You know, I never had a chance to talk to him about any of that. I think I'm going to put the word out to the staff and send a message to him. Maybe see if he'd be willing to talk after game three."

"Good idea," Dante said, nodding. "But I suppose that means I guessed wrong about your motivations in all of this. If all you're admitting to me here is that there might be a little truth to what I said, then that means it's not the *full* reason. Something else on your mind, brother? Something eating at you and making you put yourself through all of that media frenzy? If you needed to get something off your chest, you could have just written a piece for *The Players' Tribune*, you know. You didn't have to go through all of those interviews."

"I know," Tommy replied. "And you know me so well after all these years together. You were right that I didn't actually want any of this notoriety and press."

"Then why?" Dante asked with a concerned look on his face.

"You're not going to want to hear it, I'm sure...but it's because of Lucy."

"*Lucy?*" Dante said, looking surprised. "What does she have to do with this? And why are you still thinking about a woman you haven't seen in years?"

"I know you've told me a million times that I needed to move on," Tommy reminded him, "and I'm sure that's true. But I figured this was probably my one chance to get myself out there in a big way. I don't think she's a sports fan, so I figured this was it: my last chance to reconnect with her. The more media I did, the greater the shot I had of her noticing me."

Dante was nodding again, slowly this time. "I know you feel a lot of guilt about the way that all went down. I had a front-row seat to the whole thing, so you know I get it. But I don't think it's healthy for you to keep carrying this around, just like I don't think it was healthy for you to worry about Z's career. You can't be responsible for *everything*, T. Hiller's back in the game, and I'm sure Lucy is back in her groove, too. Time has moved on, so you need to do the same thing. So, okay—if she doesn't see you after all the press you did, then it's obviously never happening. Promise me you'll work to let her go after this, T. It's time."

"I've tried to let go before," Tommy said. "I really have. But I couldn't do it. I…well, I guess I'm hoping that after all these interviews and articles and pictures…well, I'm just hoping it'll feel like I did enough, you know? So, yeah…maybe I *will* be able to finally move on now."

Dante gave him a pat on the back, and Tommy returned the gesture with a half-smile. Deep down, Tommy told himself that Dante was right—he'd done everything he could. Everything that anyone could reasonably expect him to do under the circumstances and more.

Now he had to find a way to let her go.

Chapter 42

LUCY BARELY SLEPT at all after making her sign. She used her nervous energy to research everything she could about her trip to the stadium: parking, bag policies, and, of course, rules about fans bringing in signs. By the time she arrived at the diner the next morning, she was running on coffee and sheer stubbornness. Mona took one look at her and shook her head.

"You didn't sleep one wink last night, did you?" she said with a sigh. "Help me get through the first big rush, and then get on home and go to bed. You're going to drive straight into a ditch on your trip into the city if you don't."

"Thanks," Lucy agreed as she stifled another yawn. "I hate to dump the whole shift on you, but I think you might be right."

Mona shooed Lucy back out the door a couple of hours later. Lucy went home and gratefully collapsed. She was able to get a few hours of sleep out of sheer exhaustion, but the excitement wouldn't let her stay out for long. She got up, ate a little lunch, grabbed her poster and a small bag, and headed for her car.

She left so early that she didn't hit any of the commuter traffic. Before she knew it, she was sailing across the George Washington Bridge, watching carefully for the exit that would send her into the Bronx and toward the stadium. She arrived so ridiculously early for the game that she had time to kill, so she wandered through the small, locally owned stores that lined the streets outside. She noticed she wasn't the only fan already there; countless Yankee—and even a few Oriole—jerseys were on the backs of almost everyone she passed. Most of the stores were only selling Yankees souvenirs, but because of the media attention on this game—and specifically on Thomas— she found that a few clever businesses had pushed Orioles gear out front as well. When she spotted a Layton jersey, she bought it and slid it on. True, there were probably tons of fans out there with his jersey, but she couldn't help feeling a little closer to him, hugged by the shirt bearing his name.

She queued up in the security line early and was one of the first fans through the gates. In her manic research the night before, she'd learned about Monument Park and the small museum, both housed inside the stadium and open to fans who arrived early. She followed the signs to Monument Park first, browsing the plaques honoring former Yankee legends as well as their retired numbers. Standing in Monument Park made her level with the field. She lingered a while, hoping that maybe Thomas would walk out. But she only saw Yankee players warming up, so she eventually left, looking for the museum. She had to wait in line a while, and she saw why when she finally was allowed inside: The museum was tiny. Lucy knew almost nothing about the history of baseball, but she recognized some of the names on the autographed balls, like Babe Ruth and Lou Gehrig. She saw championship trophies and rings, relics from older versions of the stadium, and a tribute to a team captain who'd died in a plane crash during one season.

This is Thomas's world, she thought, trying to look at everything through a player's eyes. *What must this history mean to him?*

With her sign rolled up and tucked under her arm, she headed to her seat in the second tier overlooking right field. She stopped to get something to eat and drink on the way. Once the game began and Thomas was out there, she wouldn't want to tear her eyes away. She decided on a hot dog and a pretzel, the whole traditional experience. She didn't buy any beer though, opting instead for water. Her nerves were already jangling.

She found her seat and got her first really good look at the stadium—from the decorative slats that created a white-picket effect circling the top of the stadium to the enchanting view of the elevated subway train that periodically rolled by. She admitted to herself that she was charmed by the atmosphere, the sights, the sounds, the history. She popped pieces of her soft pretzel into her mouth while soaking up the experience. She watched groups of fans filing in, searching for their seats, smiling when families came with kids wearing baseball gloves, no doubt hoping to catch home runs or errant foul balls. Her life had been all about getting to a destination without really savoring the trip for years. It felt liberating in that moment to simply sit, observe, and enjoy the relaxing atmosphere.

Once the activities like the first pitch and the National Anthem came and went, however, those feelings of happiness fled and she was left with a sense of bubbling, nervous excitement. Yes, she was thrilled about the possibility of catching Thomas's attention today, but she was nervous, too. Nervous *for* him. In all her frantic research the night before, she'd watched videos of his original injury, which was devastating to see in spite of the knowledge that he eventually recovered. And she'd seen some interviews he'd done concerning today's game. He hadn't admitted to being nervous, but she knew it was certainly a big deal to him. It had to be.

The Oriole players were announced first, and she cheered when Thomas's name was called. The Yankees took the field, and the Orioles went up to bat. The lineup showed that Thomas would be fourth, and she watched nervously as the first batter made an out, then the second batter did the same. The third batter was Dante, and she cheered again when he made it safely to first base.

Tommy appeared. Lucy noticed that flashes were sparkling madly through the crowd—it seemed as though everyone in the stadium wanted to capture this moment. Her stomach ached with nervous energy, and she regretted eating the hot dog while realizing she hadn't pulled out her sign yet. This was the big moment of the game for Thomas, and now was the perfect time to support him. She quickly unrolled the poster as Thomas took a few practice swings. Then she glanced again at the words she'd worked so hard to assemble the night before. It would've been impossible to say everything on a tiny poster, and she certainly didn't want to write anything *too* personal; for all she knew, he might be married now. So, she finally settled on something he'd recognize but wouldn't embarrass him. Something short, but with enough information for him to understand. She'd written, and then filled in with fat block letters, the words—*Hey, Layton, 67: Look, we're out of the park! Lucy.*

She wanted to hold the sign up high over her head,

but she figured the Yankee fans were already being generous letting her cheer so wildly for Thomas and Dante in the first place. She doubted they'd also let her block their views. So, she held it up in front of her, as high as she dared, and nervously watched as the first ball sailed right past Thomas for a strike.

First throw down, she thought, her teeth clenched nervously as she watched, praying he'd be okay, and that this moment wouldn't whittle away the confidence he certainly must have worked so hard to rebuild. She gripped her poster even harder, holding it up a little higher than she'd dared before. She noticed then that Thomas seemed a little distracted, almost like he was looking around the crowd.

He probably noticed all those flashes going off, she thought, even as a part of her wished he was searching the crowd for *her*. She knew she was too far away for him to see the sign from home plate, but she wished for it anyway. Just another item on her growing list of things she hoped would happen here tonight.

More pitches came, and the crowd roared for the strikes and groused about the balls. The energy was electric; Lucy wondered how Thomas could focus in such a situation. What a joke that she always believed her own ability to focus was so off-the-charts. He must have been chuckling inside, thinking about the kind of laser-focus he himself must possess to deal with situations like this.

Thomas hit the ball finally but was thrown out. His first matchup with Zach Hiller since he got hurt was past him now. She was sorry he hadn't blasted a home run out of here to prove how strong and resilient he was. But she was so proud of him, nevertheless. He'd faced down an extraordinarily stressful moment with strength and dignity. She smiled as she saw him tip his hat toward the pitcher, and Zach Hiller nodded back at him. She stood and cheered wildly right along with the crowd, then held her poster up even higher, bursting with pride and happiness in that moment.

"Hey, look, it's you up there," said the man next to her, pointing to the huge screen in the outfield.

He was right! The cameras had caught her holding her sign, no doubt a small kindness to the player who'd gotten hurt on their field all those years ago. This, she knew, was her chance for Thomas to notice her, so she held the sign higher than ever, smiling at her good fortune. This was it! He would see it, and then he would see *her!* Maybe he'd send security to come get her, she thought, her mind spinning with possibilities.

She held the sign up for most of the game, and even tried to call his name when he was out in right field. But he never looked up, and security did not come find her. The rest of the game played out, inning after inning, but there was no indication that Thomas had noticed her.

Maybe he's waiting for the end of the game, she thought, so she stayed in her seat while the other fans filed out. Soon the seats were all emptied out, however, and there was still no sign of him. So, she rolled her sign back up and walked to the stairs, disappointment starting to fill her up inside.

He probably has to shower and do interviews, she rationalized. So, she wasted some time in a long line for the women's bathroom. When she emerged, though, there was still no indication she had reason to do anything other than simply leave.

Well, that's that, she thought. There was a restaurant in the stadium on the outside, and she stood pondering the line after she'd walked through the main gate, wondering if she should delay leaving by sitting down and ordering some food. But in the end, she didn't know what that would accomplish. The players wouldn't likely come and dine with the fans—especially players from the opposing team.

She trudged slowly around the outside perimeter, trying to figure out where she was in relation to the parking garage. It was time, she decided, to admit defeat, find her car, and head home before it got too late. There were still plenty of fans swarming around, which made her feel safe enough. But she knew she needed to be moving along. Thoughts about how wonderful it had been to see Thomas in this new setting floated through her mind. She was still so happy for him. And proud of him.

She noticed a bench sitting empty in the middle of the pedestrian plaza, and a small, delighted laugh tumbled out of her. What better way to end her day? She went over to it and sat, allowing herself to think about their time together and the evening she'd just experienced. She couldn't deny the disappointment that her sweeping romantic gesture hadn't worked. She'd been so hopeful, especially when she and her poster were captured on the big screen. But in the end, it hadn't made any difference. He hadn't seen her. Or, perhaps even worse, he *had* seen her but simply didn't care. Maybe her gesture was, in the end, much too little and much too late.

Well, this is it, she thought, slowly exhaling. A part of her would always love him, she knew without a doubt. But clearly the universe was screaming at her to let him go.

It was time to move on.

Chapter 43

TOMMY HAD GIVEN so much of himself to the media in the days leading up to the game, so he didn't feel too bad about dodging the reporters and heading for the showers afterward. When a member of the Yankee staff came and told him Zach Hiller had gotten his request to meet and was ready to talk now, he forgot all about showering and told the staffer to lead the way as he grabbed his bag.

When he walked into the room on the Yankee side of the stadium, he was surprised to find Hiller waiting, still in his Yankee pinstripes, with his arm around a beautiful blonde, whose arm was wrapped around him, too.

"Tommy, hey man," Zach said, reaching out to shake hands. "I figured the press was going to want to have their way with me for hours tonight, so I asked them if they'd mind waiting a while. This is my wife, Emma, by the way. Emmy, meet Tommy Layton."

"I'm so happy to meet you!" Emma said, a wide smile on her face. "And, of course, so happy that you're all healed up and back in the game."

"Great to meet both of you," Tommy said, "and thanks for taking this time tonight. I just wanted to tell you I'm so happy you're back. When I heard you'd left the game…I don't know. I just had so much guilt about it. Like my hard head and slow reactions that night had destroyed your career. I just wanted to tell you, I guess, that I'm sorry."

Zach's head jerked back in surprise, and Emma's mouth opened. Tommy chuckled at their dueling levels of shock.

"Wow, Tommy, that is *not* what I thought this conversation was going to be about," Zach told him as he looked him over thoughtfully. "I figured you were looking for the face-to-face apology you never quite got since you were still so out of it when I talked to your family that night in the hospital."

"Nah, Zach, I never thought it was on purpose," Tommy said. "Not even for a minute. It was a full count. No one goes head-hunting in that situation. Besides, you've never been known for that kind of thing anyway."

"No, I would never throw at a guy's head on purpose," Zach replied. "*Never.* But I *was* going after you in another way. I was trying to push the rookie back off the plate and teach him a lesson. But the only lesson that got taught that night is the one that *I* learned. I needed to get knocked down a few pegs and get over myself. I'd never even considered the idea that failure might be an option before that night. But then I saw you fall, and I realized that my cockiness could have killed you. That's why I left the game; I lost the confidence I needed to pitch after the shock of that moment. Took me a really long time to work through it—and finding the love of my life in this gorgeous woman here—to get me back to being myself again. So you gave me an apology, but I'm giving it right back to you. I'm sorry for what happened, and I'm really sorry you got hurt and missed the rest of that season."

"No hard feelings man," Tommy said, smiling now. "Especially after you let me get a double off you tonight in the fifth."

Zach laughed, then, clapping him on the shoulder. "Consider it my gift to you."

"Hey, do you mind giving me your number?" Tommy asked. "I'd love to buy you guys a drink someday."

"We'd love that!" Emma said as Zach gave it to him, and Tommy tapped it into his phone.

"Where'd you disappear to, if you don't mind my asking?" Tommy said then as he slid the phone back in his pocket. "And how'd you meet Emma?"

"I was hiding in Dublin, licking my wounds," Zach replied.

"I showed up on vacation one summer, and we just…clicked," Emma added. "Even though I was actually engaged to someone else at the time, and Zach was going through everything—well, you know what he was going through—and he was in exile, it just seemed like none of that was ever going to keep us apart, no matter what."

Lucy leapt into Tommy's mind just then. He wished that had been their story, too—that they'd been able to stay together no matter what the challenges.

"That's great, you guys," Tommy said, forcing a smile to his face. "You have something romantic to tell the grandkids someday."

"Yeah, we really do…oh, wait! Speaking of romantic, that reminds me!" Emma said, clapping her hands together excitedly. "I meant to ask you, what did that sign mean?"

"Sign?" Tommy asked. "You mean from one of the coaches?"

Zach was looking at her like he didn't know what she meant, either.

"No! The fan's sign in the crowd," Emma went on after not seeing any flickers of understanding from either of them. "They showed a fan on the big screen during the game. She was in the stands holding up a sign for you. It was kind of a mysterious message, though. Y'know, not a typical 'go team!' type of thing, or even an obsessed 'marry me and let me have your babies' stalker thing, either."

A burning excitement slowly worked its way through Tommy now, flooding his chest. *Could it be...?*

"What was the message?" Tommy asked, trying not to sound as demanding as he felt in that moment. "I didn't see it."

"Wait, they put up a sign for an Oriole player on the Yankee Stadium screen?" Zach asked dubiously at the same time.

"Yeah, I don't know why, except that maybe it was because of the big moment. You know, a nod to Tommy after what had happened to him in this stadium," Emma said to Zach before turning back to Tommy. "I don't remember exactly, but it said something like, 'Hey Layton we're out of the park. From Lucy'."

Excitement thundered through Tommy now. "Lucy?" he repeated. "You're positive it said '*Lucy*'?"

Emma nodded. "Yeah. Who is she?"

"She's...well, she's my Emma," Tommy told them, the words tumbling out awkwardly. "But then some stupid things happened, and we lost track of each other. Z, what do I do? How can I find her?"

"They clear the fans out pretty quickly, so I don't know, man. She's surely outside the stadium by now. Maybe security can help? I'll see if I can put the word out."

"Thank you, thank you both so much!" Tommy said. "If we weren't even before, we definitely are now...."

Before he left, Emma gave him a quick hug and a whispered, "Good luck!" Then he was jogging away toward the closest exit.

*   *   *

He called Dante as he ran.

"T, where are you?" Dante asked the moment he answered. The background noise of the locker room made him a little hard to understand. "We're loading up soon."

"Lucy was here!" Tommy said as he reached the main gate and slipped out of the stadium. "She had a sign in the stands! I'm looking for her now!"

"Wow, okay, what do you need me to do?" Dante asked. "Need me to help look?"

"Talk to Coach. Tell him I'll catch up to the team, okay?"

"You got it, my man," Dante agreed. "Now go find your lady."

Tommy ended the call and continued his hurried pace, scanning the few lingering groups of fans milling around. He wished he wasn't weighed down by his bag as he kept hunting for her familiar face. By the time he reached Babe Ruth Plaza, he was getting discouraged. Had he lost his chance to find her? *Seriously, are we ever going to catch a break?*

He stopped and looked around, scanning the small crowd that remained on this beautiful spring night. Just as he was about to admit defeat, though, his eyes landed on a bench in the distance. A woman was sitting there by herself—a woman wearing his jersey.

She also had a rolled poster under her arm.

Relief and excitement and nerves all thrummed through Tommy now as he stood staring at her. He was almost rooted to the spot where he stood, afraid to move forward and worried the vision would prove to be nothing more than a mirage.

Eyes never leaving her, he finally took a deep breath, shook off these thoughts, and slowly started to move again.

Chapter 44

"WHAT IS IT with you and benches?" a voice asked suddenly, cutting through her solemn reverie. She'd been thinking just then how much she wished she could say a proper goodbye to Thomas. Hearing what sounded like his voice in that moment seemed too good to be true. Like a dream…or perhaps a trick her mind was playing on her.

"Is it like an accessory that you carry with you, or…"

No, that's definitely his voice….

She turned around then, and one of her hands flew up—causing the poster to drop—before she realized it and covered her mouth, which was hanging open now. It was like her brain was having trouble catching up to what was happening, and she suddenly forgot what she was supposed to do with the rest of her body.

"Thomas!" she said with all the emotion that was working its way through her, her brain finally catching up to the moment. "You're here! You're really…I had hoped, but I didn't…oh, wow, I'm sorry! I'm having trouble finding words right now."

"Okay, then how about I start?" he asked, a twinkle of humor in his eyes as he studied her.

"O..kay…," she slowly said, her gaze locked with his. It felt like the same emotions bursting inside of her were reflected on his face, too. But, well, she still didn't know for certain. She wondered if this moment meant the same to him. That uncertainty was holding her back from fully expressing her own feelings.

"I'm so sorry, Lucy," he began. "Sorry for the way I treated you the last time we were together. I was shocked and jealous and just…gutted, I guess. And I had a splitting headache on top of all of that, so I couldn't even really hear or process what you were trying to say to me. I thought I had just discovered that what we'd found together wasn't real, and I couldn't take it. I'm not trying to give you a justification here. I honestly don't even understand myself why I was so quick to jump to those conclusions. The way I acted, and the things I said, were inexcusable. Please believe that I am so very sorry, and I've been praying that one day I would have a chance to tell you that."

"It's okay, Thomas," Lucy said softly. As the shock of seeing him gradually wore off, she found that she was suddenly able to organize her thoughts into words again. "Really, I understand, and I forgave you a long time ago. I swear to you that Mona and Tania shoved me out of the house that night. And everything I ever told you about my mom and my situation…it was all the truth."

"I know that, too," he replied, "but I didn't for a long time, because I wouldn't let Dante explain it to me. I guess I just *wanted* to be mad. And on top of everything else, I was in trouble with the team for getting injured again, so…."

"What?" Lucy asked, cutting him off, alarmed now. "You were injured again?"

"Yeah, it happened that same night, actually. I told you I had a headache, but then...well, the doctors think the alcohol plus the stress of what was happening with us caused my blood pressure to spike, and I'd also pushed myself too hard that day exercising. I somehow managed to walk out of the club, pass out on the sidewalk, and give myself another concussion."

"Oh no!" Lucy said, her eyes wide. "Wait…I remember that! Tania told me that a drunk person passed out, and she wanted to wait to leave until the ambulance was gone."

"Yeah, that was me," Thomas said, nodding. "I woke up the next morning completely confused. I thought for a minute I was still there from the first concussion and that I had imagined you."

So, he had been hurt, lying on the sidewalk unconscious, and I'd been just a few feet away and totally unaware of it?

Tears began forming in her eyes as she worked to weave Thomas's version of that night into her own. "All that time we lost," she said. "Years we wasted. And over what?"

"I know, and I have felt so guilty about it for so long, beating myself up with all the 'if I'd only' scenarios. Like if I'd only shut up and listened to you, or if I'd only arranged to have my folks stay with your mom for a night out the way Mona did. If…well, if only I hadn't thrown what we had away, where might we be right now?" Thomas brushed through his hair now in that still-familiar gesture.

"Nope, that's the thing, Thomas," she said, shaking her head. "I carry all the blame here, or at least the majority of it. And I've spent the years we've been apart beating *myself* up about refusing to exchange contact information with you. You offered again and again, and if I'd only listened, none of this would have happened. I had all kinds of problems, and I used those as my excuse to keep you at arm's length. I've thought a lot about why I did that, and while I didn't make up any of the things I told you, I think it all comes down to the fact that I really wanted to be miserable rather than do what it was going to take to move past my troubles. If I had let myself jump into a real relationship with you, then I would have needed to move forward with everything else I was dealing with and, well, I guess the status quo, even though I was miserable, was where I wanted to stay. I was carrying a lot of guilt about my dad's death, and how I'd messed up by being so involved in my classes and studies that I didn't even realize my mom was slipping away. I missed precious time with both of them. And then they were both gone in the blink of an eye. It didn't seem right to jump into something with you. I think…I think I didn't believe I deserved that kind of happiness."

"You *did* deserve to be happy then, and you still do," Thomas said. "And for the record, you couldn't have prevented what happened to either of your parents. You do know that now, right?"

"Yeah, although it took a lot of time and space," Lucy admitted. "But, well, I got there eventually. Unfortunately, it took losing you to realize how completely I'd blown it. I'd made a total mess of my life, and I had no one to blame but myself."

"But I messed up, too. I guess I don't know if we'll ever agree on who carried the most blame in ripping what we had apart. But I think the real question is where does that leave us now?" Thomas's face was lined with a look of apprehension, like he wasn't sure he wanted to hear her answers. "Lucy, what were you hoping for when you came here tonight?"

"My answer depends on *your* answer to a question I have for you," she replied, feeling uncertain of herself suddenly. "So you first."

"Really? Okay, what question is that?"

"Are you married? Do you have kids? Are you dating someone?" Lucy asked, rattling the questions off in a nervous, rushed string.

"That was more than one question," Thomas said, a smile slowly lighting his face as he started moving toward her.

"Thomas, don't tease me. Don't take another step unless the answer to all of those questions is 'no'."

He drew close then, until they were right in front of each other. She looked up at his face, seeing him closely for the first time in years. His hair was a little longer, and he looked a bit tanner. There were also a few lines in his face she didn't remember.

"No, I couldn't move on," Thomas replied finally. "I couldn't let you go. I confess, though, that I never tried very hard. And how about you, angel? You still free?"

"I haven't been free since the moment I met you," she said, smiling happily into his handsome face. "I've been yours since the day you attacked that tree like a crazy person."

Thomas laughed. "I may have been crazy, but I think that's the day I started falling in love with you."

He leaned down then, until their lips were a whisper apart.

"And this time I'm not letting you go."

Chapter 45

LUCY GASPED as he gently brushed her lips with his, their incredible chemistry coursing even at that small, feather-light touch.

She was feeling more in that moment than she'd felt since…well, since the last time he'd held her, she guessed. Being here with him was like coming home. At that one thought, she threw her arms around him then, intensifying the kiss and welcomed his response as he then met her lips with the same hungry energy. After several long moments, though, he must have remembered where they were because suddenly he was pulling back. He looked at her, smiled, and then leaned forward until their foreheads touched.

"Are we finally on the same page, angel?" he asked. "Are we about to get things right this time?"

"It sure seems like we are," she said, letting him pull her into another hug. The emotions and the happiness were overwhelming. She couldn't believe that they'd been given this precious gift of a do-over. Finally, it was their time.

"Want to sit with me on the bench?" she asked, her voice muffled against his chest until she pulled her head back to look up at him again. "You know, for old times' sake?"

"Of course," he said with another laugh, "we have to." He sat then and patted the spot next to him. She tucked herself by his side, leaning her head against him as he wrapped his arm around her.

They were quiet for a time, and she knew in that peaceful moment that she had never been happier.

"Still don't know your name," Thomas said then, his words causing Lucy to bark out an embarrassing half-laugh, half-snort. "What? I don't. And if you think you're leaving my sight tonight without giving me your phone number, then *you're* the crazy one."

Lucy pulled back then, a goofy smile on her face as she thought about the absurdity of it all.

"It's so great to finally meet you," she said, extending her hand to shake his. "My name is Lucy Marie Valente. I recently passed the bar and was hired by Cohen and Cozart, a law firm. I'm going to be dealing primarily with immigration law."

"You're a lawyer?" Thomas asked, clearly surprised, as he reached for her hand, holding it between his gently, rather than completing her offered handshake. "Huh, I never would have guessed that, although I suppose it fits with the stories you told me about how serious and studious you've always been."

"Yeah, but when you met me, I was working as a waitress at the Fork It Diner. Well, I guess I still am, until this new job starts," she said. "I was working there the day you came in with your sister...Jessica?"

"Jenna."

"Oh, okay. When I was trying to put the clues together—you know, assemble the concrete facts I knew about you so I could find a way to track you down—I briefly considered calling every Jessica in northern New Jersey. I guess that wouldn't have gotten me very far."

"No, probably not," he said as he gently tugged her back into his side, his arm wrapping snugly around her again. "So how *did* you find me, Lucy Marie Valente?"

"Well, we were out celebrating that I finally passed the bar exam," she began. "I had put off taking it for so long when I was dealing with everything with my mom. So, the buildup to my finally taking it and passing it was huge. Anyway, I was asking Pat, Mona, and Tania for ideas about how to find you, and then Tania looked up, and there you were on the television. She recognized you from that day you came to the diner. Wow, that party was just yesterday, actually. That's crazy. Just forty-eight hours ago, I still had no idea what your full name was or that you were a professional baseball player. Well, anyway, it was Pat's idea for me to make a sign to get your attention. But it worked because you saw me on the screen!"

"No, I didn't, actually," he said. "I had no clue you were here."

"What? Then how…?"

"Emma Hiller, Zach Hiller's wife," Thomas told her. "She saw the sign and asked me about it. I heard the name 'Lucy,' and I started running for the exit."

"And here I was," Lucy said.

"And here you were," Thomas agreed. "I should have known to look on the bench, though. Should have been my first stop."

"Yeah, duh," Lucy said with a laugh. "I guess we've officially come full circle."

"We have, but we probably shouldn't just sit here on the bench all night. It's getting cold, for one thing." Thomas stood and held out his hand. "Where's your car?"

She smiled and let him pull her to her feet. "It's in the parking garage. Oh, and wait—here's my poster!" She grabbed it from the ground where it had dropped and unrolled it.

"Perfect," he said, reading it with a smile and then watching as she rolled it up again. Then they laced their hands together and started toward her car. "So, you mentioned your mom. How's she doing?" Thomas asked as he leaned over and pressed a kiss on the side of her head.

"She died a while back," Lucy said. "She was in an assisted living facility by then, and she slipped away peacefully in her sleep there. It's been almost two years now, I think. After she died, I suddenly had all the time in the world I needed to reclaim my life, right? But I was just so sad. Sad that she'd died, sad that I'd lost you, and sad that I was all alone in the world. Well, except I'm not really. My friends at the diner are my family now."

"I'm so sorry, angel," Thomas said, squeezing her hand gently. "I'm sorry I wasn't there for you when she passed away, and I'm sorry I wasn't there when you were grieving and dealing with all of that. I should have been by your side."

"It's okay," Lucy replied. "You're here now."

"You used to say that your mom being sick was only part of the issue. What was the rest of the story?"

"Well, I couldn't pay off my student debt because of my mom's healthcare bills. And because of all of that, I couldn't study for the bar exam and take care of my mom at the same time. So, I got extensions on the loans, got that job in the diner, and said goodbye to my law career for a long time. It doesn't seem like the same big deal now, when I say it out loud, that it felt like back then. But there were days when it all seemed insurmountable. Like I'd never be anywhere other than lost in that soul-crushing blackhole of misery."

"How'd it get resolved?" Thomas asked. "How'd you fight through it? I mean, you *are* through the bad times now, yes?"

"Yes, I finally am. You know, I guess that night in the club changed everything," Lucy said. "I went home and cried on Mona's shoulder about everything that happened with you. She's absolutely been my rock all along. Then, from the next day forward, she started coming to my mom's house each afternoon and letting me go to her house to study for a few hours. It was just a start, but she got me moving finally."

"Is that why you stopped going to the bench?" Thomas asked. "After I finally let Dante tell me your side of things, I found a day off in the team schedule when I could come back and try to find you, but you didn't show up. Once the season was over, I tried again, but...well, you know the rest."

"I kept going back for a long time," she said, "but eventually it became too hard. It was taking too much out of me to get my hopes dashed like that, day after day. Plus, I figured I should be using the time to study. So, I went back to the bench one last time and said goodbye. I didn't go back again for a really long time. But when I did, I saw your message on the plaque. It gave me hope that maybe, just maybe, you'd forgiven me. And that if I was able to find you again one day, maybe we'd finally be together again."

They reached her car then. She unlocked the doors and dropped her bag and poster into the backseat, then let Thomas toss in his bag, too. After that she was back in his arms.

"Let's get in the car," he suggested, "but first...we really need to exchange numbers before, I don't know...a meteorite lands between us and we have to search for each other in the crater for another decade or something."

She laughed as she opened the door again, pulled her phone out of her bag, unlocked the screen, and handed it to him. After they got in the car, she watched him pull up her contacts list and enter his name and number. Then he called his own phone.

"There," he said, handing it back. She smiled when she saw him typing out her name as a new contact and saving it as *Angel*. "We're not going through any of *that* again."

"Nope," Lucy agreed. "Honestly, Thomas, if it were up to me, we'd never be apart again."

He leaned over to kiss her again, but he paused right before their lips touched.

"Okay, then let's make it *be* all up to you...," he whispered before closing the space between them again.

Chapter 46

TYPICALLY, wives and girlfriends weren't allowed to stay with the team at the hotel during away games. And sometimes the team left immediately for the airport after the last game of a series so they could get to the next city on their schedule, traveling at night so they'd arrive and be able to catch a little sleep at the next hotel before the first game of the series.

But the situation was a little different this time. The Orioles had the next day off for travel—they were about to embark on an extended road trip along the West Coast for a twelve-game stretch. So, although it was a little unusual, the team was still in New York at the hotel when Tommy and Lucy left the parking garage.

Tommy couldn't decide what to do. What he wanted was exactly what they'd just agreed on—to never be apart again, and to start that by taking her back to his room. Team rules were pretty clearly against that idea, though, and that could get him into a lot of trouble. He was really torn. He wasn't ready to say goodbye again just yet. Plus, it likely wasn't safe for her to drive all the way home so late, especially since her emotions and focus were likely all over the place. So, after a few minutes of indecision, Tommy called Jack while Lucy drove them toward the hotel.

"Layton, where are you?" Jack said immediately upon picking up the call. "Jackson said you had a personal matter come up—you okay?"

"Yeah, Coach, better than okay, actually," Tommy said, stealing a quick glance at Lucy's face. She looked over and met his gaze with a sunny smile, love and happiness shining in her eyes. "Do you remember I told you that the night I hit my head on the sidewalk at the club that I'd had a pretty messy breakup with my girlfriend?"

"I guess so," Jack said, sounding unimpressed. "She's been history for years. Wait, you telling me you're off getting back together with some woman who messed you up that badly instead of being with your team? Gotta be honest here, I'm not liking where this conversation is headed, Tom."

"I know it sounds crazy, and it's a ridiculously long and complicated story. Even if I told you all of it, though, I still don't know if you'd believe me. But the short version is that she's the love of my life, Coach. We had some really huge problems and misunderstandings and missed opportunities keeping us apart for a long time. And then we lost contact with each other. But tonight a miracle happened—she tracked me down. I know this sounds like I'm talking about a movie script instead of real life, but I swear to you fate finally stepped in to fix the mess we'd made and handed me the best present I ever could have hoped to receive."

"Layton, is there a point somewhere in th—wait, does this have something to do with that fan sign out in the crowd?" Jack asked. "Some of the boys picked up on it. Think your new team nickname might be *Romeo*."

Tommy barked out a laugh, shaking his head. "You know, after the day I've had, I'll happily take the name and the jokes."

Lucy shot him a quizzical look before flipping her blinker to turn onto an exit ramp.

"You trying to ask for time off here, son?" Jack asked. "Now's not exactly ideal, with our utility player out with that groin pull."

"No, Coach, I'm not asking for any time off," Tommy replied. He wished he *did* have time off coming up, but the rigorous baseball season was just getting started. It wouldn't be until the All-Star break in July before anyone would get a real break, and then only if they weren't named to the All-Star team, which Tommy likely would be. "Just wanted special permission for her to stay at the hotel tonight. We've been talking so long that now I'm worried about her driving home alone this late at night. With this long stretch on the road coming up…well, I was just hoping the rules could be bent just this once."

There were a few moments of silence on the line before Jack replied with a gruff yes. "But never again, Tommy Boy. You need your focus on the field, you got me?"

"I got you," Tommy agreed easily.

"I want yours to be the first face I see tomorrow on that bus," Jack continued. "And you're sitting next to me on the flight. We'll have plenty of time for you to share this long story with me. It better be a good one."

"It is, Coach," Tommy said. "And thanks. I appreciate this more than you'll ever know."

"Be on that bus, Layton," Jack repeated as he ended the call.

*   *   *

"So we're okay for tonight?" Lucy asked.

"Yeah, just tonight," he said, then remembered he hadn't texted Dante. He typed out the message rapidly:

I found her D. We're back together.

Tommy watched the blinking dots, indicating Dante was typing a response. Tommy smiled when it arrived seconds later. Nice going Romeo. Happy for you brother.

It's going to be a while before I live this down, he thought with an internal chuckle.

"I can't believe we have to say goodbye again so soon," Lucy said quietly as she pulled into the hotel lot and killed the engine. "We can't ever seem to get our timing right."

"Let's get your car registered with the front desk, and we'll talk," Tommy told her, getting out and grabbing both his bag and her small purse from the back seat. They walked inside with their hands linked together.

Once they were in the room, he locked the door and dropped his bag on the dresser. Then Lucy walked into his arms. They stood in a tight embrace as his thoughts and feelings swirled around his head.

How would *this work?* he wondered. Was Lucy going to want to deal with a complicated long-distance romance? She was, after all, the woman who once told him she couldn't focus on two big things at the same time. Would she be able to start her new career and maintain their relationship? The life of an attorney, especially one starting out and trying to prove herself, seemed like something that required more than just the standard nine-to-five lifestyle. And his job was as irregular and unpredictable as it got. Had they gone through all the pain of their separation, then the exhilarating joy of finding each other again, only to find themselves in a no-win situation?

"What are you thinking about so hard?" Lucy asked, looking up at him now.

Tommy walked over to the bed and sat down, pulling Lucy forward so that she was standing between his legs. "Are we going to be able to make this work?" he asked, wrapping his arms around her waist.

"What do you mean?" Lucy replied, sounding a little alarmed now.

"This. Us. A relationship. I know you're just starting up your new career, the career that you fought for so hard and so long. You're the self-proclaimed queen of laser focus. You'll be jumping into that new job with both feet, I know you will."

"Yes, of course, but what does that have to do with us?"

"I'm on the road all the time," Tommy said. "And our home games are in Baltimore. Are we going to survive if we can't see each other for long stretches of time? Will you be able to divide your focus? I guess the more I think about the logistics, the more I wonder if we're not just setting ourselves up for more heartbreak."

"Thomas, everything you just said is fair and reasonable," Lucy replied, looking as though she was gathering her thoughts and choosing her words carefully. "You're right that when I focus in on something, I sometimes let the whole world fall away. That's true."

"I guess what I'm saying is that I don't want to be the thing in your life that falls away," Tommy told her. "Not this time."

"I know I've given you every reason in the world to believe I can't do things differently. But what you're not understanding is that *you* are where I'm going to be aiming that laser focus of mine. You and what we have between us—that's my main priority. I meant what I said earlier: Now that I've found you, I'm not letting you go. I won't make those same mistakes again. Our time apart taught me a lot of tough lessons, and one is that I can't let my life fall apart while I'm pursuing outside things like degrees and careers. Those things aren't what will ultimately make me happy. I made that mistake with my parents; I focused so hard on law school that I didn't see what was going on with them, and I missed so much time with them as a result, time that I will never get back. You are so precious to me, Thomas. I did a lot of thinking while we were apart, and I considered how I'd do things differently if fate gave me a do-over. I mean, yes, I've only known you're a baseball player for about a day, and I'm not really familiar with your world. I can't tell you precisely how we'll figure this out. But I know I'm never allowing what happened before to happen again. Mona told me to learn to spot happiness when I see it, grab onto it, and never let it go. She's a smart lady. I'm taking her advice."

Tommy nodded. "Okay...good." He was starting to believe that what they wanted to build together might actually have a strong enough foundation to last. "If we're each going to focus on the other, then we can find a way to make it work."

"Exactly. And I think maybe I should start by talking to my new law firm and finding out if I can do some of the work remotely from Baltimore. If the answer is no, then I'm quitting before I even start there. I wasn't kidding when I said I never want to be apart from you again. I mean it. I'll move to Baltimore and find a law firm there, if that's what works for us. Or I'll drive back and forth so I'm there when you've got home games, if that's what we decide. The only thing I need to be happy is sitting right in front of me, Thomas. I'm not losing sight of that ever again."

"I want all those things, too, angel," Thomas said. "I hope we can find a way to make all of our dreams come true. I know your career is important to you, so we need to figure out a way to let you keep it going. You know my job isn't flexible, though. It comes with a lifestyle and schedule that's pretty tough on families and relationships. It's not going to be easy."

"Like I said, I know I don't know all the specifics of your world and precisely how it's all going to work...." Lucy leaned forward and playfully pushed him onto the bed, then landed on top of him. "But you and me? This time it's forever."

Tommy laughed and smiled at her, thoroughly enjoying the feeling of her in his arms. "I think I'm going to enjoy being the object of your legendary laser focus, angel," he said.

She leaned down to kiss him, and all the worries he'd had about their ability to make the relationship work faded away. He met her lips with his own in a kiss that started playfully then ignited into so much more.

Epilogue

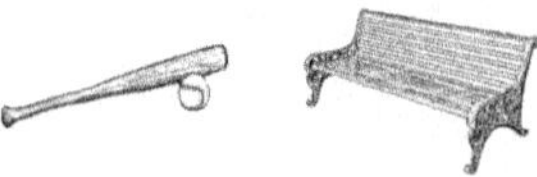

"Zach? Emma? This is my wife, Lucy," Thomas said with his arm around her waist.

Emma beamed radiantly at her. "Lucy, we are so happy to meet you! Can I hug you? I feel like we're practically family already!"

"I agree!" Lucy said, accepting her embrace and squeezing back. "It probably makes no sense, but I know exactly what you mean. I'm so glad you guys could make it today."

"Wouldn't have missed it," Zach said then, leaning in for a quick hug and kiss on her cheek.

"Thomas told me about the role you guys played in helping us reunite that day at the stadium," Lucy went on. "When he found me outside the ballpark that night, I was thinking that I needed to finally admit the whole evening had been a wasted effort. Basically a flashing neon sign from fate telling me it was time to let him go. If he hadn't walked up right at that minute, I would have gotten into my car and driven away for good. So, truly, from the bottom of my heart, thank you both so much!"

"That was all Emma," Zach said with an affectionate glance down at his wife. "I can't take any credit here. As usual, she's the one running things."

"I'm so glad I did see you on the big screen and think to ask Tommy about it," Emma continued. "It was the least we could do to thank him. He's the only reason Zach and I were able to find each other, after all."

"Are you standing there giving me credit for being too slow to move out of the way of one of this guy's pitches?" Thomas asked, his teasing tone at odds with the incredulous look on his face. "Really?"

"Emma's right," Zach said, nodding. "If the 'Curveball Incident'—that's what I've always called it, by the way—never happened, I wouldn't have flipped out and gone to Dublin to lick my wounds. And I definitely wouldn't have been standing there behind the bar serving beer to tourists the day this gorgeous lady wandered in with her guidebook and lit my world on fire."

"Yeah, I guess you're right, Z. That pitch sent me down a similar path," Tommy said thoughtfully. "I was furious that I was off the team and missing so much time, and that fury drove me to throw an epic fit in the park one day. Somehow this angel, even after witnessing that, was there to help me learn to enjoy that time off and see it as the gift it really was. None of us would be standing here today if things hadn't happened the way they did."

"Still hate that I was responsible for injuring you, man," Zach said, looking rueful. "But I'll accept it as a big present from above, I guess. It clearly was supposed to happen just the way it did, for all of us."

Lucy smiled as Thomas and Zach exchanged a shoulder-tapping, back-thumping bro hug, and she thanked Emma and Zach again for coming. Then she and Thomas continued making their way to the next table at their wedding reception. The room was full of people from all parts of their lives, including the diner, the law firm, and, of course, Tommy's team.

Feelings of happiness, relief, and joy fought for supremacy inside her as she spoke to their other guests. After the whirlwind year they'd had, she felt like they'd crossed a finish line of sorts today when they exchanged vows in a simple ceremony at their bench in the park. The ceremony itself had been attended only by family and the wedding officiant. Dante served as his best man, and of course his parents and Jenna had been there. On Lucy's side, Tania was her maid of honor. Mona and Pat, inasmuch as they were capable of appearing happy in public, gladly accepted the roles of parents to the bride. Pat even managed to look suspiciously teary-eyed as he walked her down the path toward Thomas, who'd been waiting for her at the bench. She could see the same love and adoration she felt for him mirrored in his handsome face. Pat had leaned in and given her a kiss on the side of her head, then Lucy had to fight back tears of her own as Thomas reached out and gently grasped her hands in his.

"You're the most beautiful thing I've ever seen," Thomas whispered as they turned toward the officiant. Then, during the vows he'd written just for the occasion, he said, "When I got injured and sidelined from my career, I was mad at the world for ripping me away from baseball, which had always been my life's focus, my sense of purpose, and my heart. But then one day, right here at this bench, I saw you, my beautiful angel, and nothing has been the same since. Your happiness is now my life's focus. Being with you and building our lives together is my true purpose. You, my sweet Lucy, are my heart. I love you today, and I will love you for the rest of our lives together and into eternity."

Tears slid down Lucy's face as she listened. Then it had been her turn—

"Thomas, when we met that day right here, I was at one of the lowest points in my life. My father had recently passed away, my mother was slipping away, and I was drowning in debt and grief. I could see that you were special almost immediately, but it took me a lot of years, a lot of pain, and a lot of tough lessons to realize that none of what I'd gone through—and nothing that life might send my way in the future—was bigger or more important than what we had found in each other. With you right by my side, there's nothing I can't face or overcome. Thomas, I love you. I adore you. And I vow to you today in front of our family and friends that I'll never lose sight of that again. You will always be my main focus. You and me? We're forever...."

*   *   *

"What are you thinking about so hard, angel?" Thomas whispered, shaking her back to the present and their reception as he led her onto the dance floor and wrapped his arms around her.

"What I'm always thinking about," she replied as they began gently swaying together. "How much I love you. I can't stop thinking about how dangerously close we came to losing all of this. It terrifies me to think that we so easily might never have found each other again or felt the happiness that I'm feeling right now, in this moment."

"Don't torture yourself with those kinds of thoughts," Thomas told her. "The truth is, I don't think I ever would have stopped looking for you in every crowd. Eventually we would have ended up right here, together, no matter how long it took."

Lucy was surprised at how comforting she found these words even though there really was no way to prove he was right. "Do you honestly believe we would have found each other, no matter what?"

"I swear to you, angel, I would have looked for you forever," Thomas said. Then a teasing smile spread across his face. "I mean, really, how many benches *are* there in New Jersey?"

She smiled back and leaned her head against him, letting the happiness and contentment flow through her. He was right: They would have found each other eventually.

Lucy soon looked back up into Thomas's face as memories flashed through her mind again of the many moments they'd shared that, when woven together, created their love story. She'd originally sat down on that park bench looking for peace; instead, she'd found forever.

Thank You!

Thank you for reading Tommy and Lucy's story! I would appreciate it so much if you took a moment to rate or review it on your favorite site.

Can't wait for more? Be sure to read *Curveball: A Love Story* to find out more about Zach and Emma's story and what happened when he broke his contract and vanished from baseball!

And if you subscribe to my newsletter (go to annetrowbridgebooks.com) you'll receive a free *Curveball* novella!

Here's a sneak peek of Anne's upcoming contemporary romance, *The Honeymoon: A Second-Chance Romance*—

Prologue

"OLIVIA, I'M WORRIED about you, girl," Donna said as she leaned back to sip her wine, her brown eyes narrowed in Olivia's direction over the top of the glass. "I don't even understand what's going on with you, and you won't tell me anything. You're not yourself, you're not eating, you're being super emotional and mysterious, and, oh yeah, no one's seen your husband since your wedding day."

Donna's words floated through her mind as Olivia dragged her fork through her salad, searching among the leaves of lettuce as though they held all the answers if she only dug through them fervently enough. What words could she even assemble that could begin to ease her friend's worries? She could fill an ocean with her problems right now. Which one specifically would Donna want to hear about first? But, honestly, none of that mattered anyway, because the truth was that she just couldn't bring herself to confide in anyone right now—she didn't even want to try. If her tears started, they might never stop...

"Hello? Olivia? Are you in there?" Donna persisted, setting her wine glass back down before leaning back, crossing her arms, and narrowing her gaze even further. "Did you even hear me? I was worried before, but now? I'm working my way up the ladder to atomic-level freak out."

"No, Don, really, I'm okay," Olivia said with a sigh as she abandoned her fork on her plate and sat back, finally drawing her eyes up to meet her friend's steely, assessing gaze. "I just have to get through this year. That's it. I'm simply slogging through, one day and then next. If I can make it to my anniversary…well, things are going to get better. You'll see."

"Your anniversary? Months and months away? That anniversary?" Donna asked, not looking relieved or pacified one bit by Olivia's attempt at an explanation. "That makes absolutely no sense."

Olivia knew she was being maddeningly vague, but how could she ever truly explain what had happened anyway? No one could possibly begin to comprehend—or even to believe—what she'd been through since her ill-fated wedding day. Even if she wanted to find the words, there just weren't any that could accurately summarize it all.

"Why?" Donna said, cutting through her inner turmoil again. "Why would your anniversary be so very magical when your wedding day was such a complete horror show?"

"Oh, come on, now. You say that like it's a bad thing. You know how much I love horror shows," Olivia said, her weak attempt to make Donna smile falling flat. "It's like a dream that I got to star in one of my very own."

"Okay, you're making sad attempts at humor," Donna said, her head nodding as though she were making an exciting breakthrough. "So, tell me, did you murder your husband on your honeymoon? Was that how your horror movie ended? Because I know I said this before, but no one's seen John since you two flew off to Paris. Where'd you hide the body?"

"As far as I know, he's alive and well," Olivia mumbled, trying to ignore the lurch of fluttering nerves and worries that the mention of John's name elicited inside her.

"As far as you know? As far as you know?" Donna parroted, looking flabbergasted now. "You don't know where he is either?"

"No," Olivia confessed, the misery in her voice matching the pain in her heart. "But that's going to change. Like I said, I just have to make it to my anniversary, and then everything will be better."

"Okay, I'll bite," Donna said with a sigh. "What's going to happen on your anniversary?"

"I'm going back to Paris," Olivia said, a hint of a smile on her face now as she watched the confusion play across her best friend's face.

"Would you just spit this story out already?" Donna asked, looking even more frustrated with her now. "Why are you going back to Paris on your anniversary?"

Olivia took a deep breath as the smile on her face slowly turned up its intensity. With a fast exhale of air, the words tumbled out of her mouth then, almost as though she couldn't hold them back if she tried. "I have to go to Paris. It holds the key to everything," Olivia said fervently. "I'm heading back, and I'm going on my honeymoon."

Acknowledgments

I WROTE *Out of the Park* more than a decade after *Curveball.* Zach and Emma's story had always felt whole and final to me, but when I was working to publish it, suddenly the idea came rushing to me for this book. Zach was devastated by that wild pitch, but someone else's life got derailed too. The question "what happens when a top athlete suddenly gets yanked out of the game, forced to stay away from his team, and made to sit around and recover?" launched the idea for Tommy's story. I love the thought that two lives were changed forever in a split second, so adding this book and making them a series makes the story feel more complete now.

There are so many people to thank, and I am certain to miss someone. So, and you know who you are, thank you for the help, encouragement, and support. It means the world to me!

Thank you, also, to my friend Wil Mara for helping me launch this story out into the world. Thank you to my mom Sarah Trowbridge; my siblings Marisa Trowbridge, Amy Smith, and Matthew Trowbridge; and my sister-in-law Brittany Trowbridge for all their help and encouragement. And for always spreading the word about my books! Thank you also to my extended family, especially Hilda Garcia and Maritza Mariera for your words of support and love regarding my writing. I appreciate it so much! Much love and thanks to Maria Stepien, my loving mother-in-law, who has been in my corner for 25 years!

I acknowledged a list of friends in *Curveball*, and I'd like to add some more names to that list, including Alexis Heydt and my teacher tribe, including Jennifer Cassini, Paul Tomasheski, Danielle Trokan, Samantha Emery-Allen, and Vanessa Samuels. They've all encouraged me and helped me in so many ways, and I could never thank them enough.

Thank you to my kids, Madelyn and Alexander: Madelyn, for being so smart and independent and hilarious, and Alex for being so smart and silly and always so very kind. Finally, thank you to my husband, who believes in me and supports me always. (He's a huge Lucille Ball fan, and I named the character Lucy as a nod to him.) I love you!

About the Author

ANNE TROWBRIDGE loves writing romances that hit major emotional beats in swoony, angsty stories in which the couples really earn their HEAs. Expect banter, angst, and deeply emotional connections that resonate!

She lives in New Jersey with her husband, two kids, and two dogs. When she's not reading or writing, she's teaching language arts to seventh graders, which really should involve medals for bravery. She grew up all over the Midwest and somehow still loves to travel and see new places.

Join her and learn more about upcoming books at:

https://www.annetrowbridgebooks.com/

www.ingramcontent.com/pod-product-compliance
Lightning Source LLC
Chambersburg PA
CBHW070622300726

48975CB00006B/1894